ELDRID REYNOLDS

Whispering Dust

HEATHEN EDITIONS

THEIR BOOKS. OUR WAY.

Published in the good ole United States of America
by Heathen Editions, an imprint of
Heathen Creative
P.O. Box 588
Point Pleasant, WV 25550-0588

Heathen Editions are available at quantity discounts.
For information and more tomfoolery, check us out online:

heatheneditions.com

@heatheneditions
#heathenedition

First published 1913
Heathen Edition published August 31, 2023

Book and cover design by Sheridan Cleland
Set in 10pt Miller Text
Chapters in Sand Dunes

ISBN: 978-1-948316-37-8

FIRST HEATHEN EDITION

"***Whispering Dust*** by Eldrid Reynolds is a book of indescribable charm, which is all the more enjoyable because of its elusiveness."
—*The Boston Globe*

"A clever book, pulsing with life and emotion . . . laid amid the color, mystery and terror of Egypt."
—*The Observer*

"A distinctly out-of-the-way novel."   —*The Publishers' Weekly*

"The charm is not felt at first — but it grows steadily as one progresses with this tale of the young woman who goes to Egypt — to the desert — to seek space and to find herself . . . The book speaks to all lonely women — to all who long to give and know not to whom to give — who long to seek — and know not how to seek . . . this book is of such compelling power that one will long for Egypt — to go there, to live there, to experience that call of the desert that this woman felt."
—Mabel Margaret Hoopes, *The Book News Monthly*

"There can be no half measures in any reader's attitude toward this book: it will either leave you cold, speaking to you in an unknown tongue, or else you will hail it with delight, as one of those rare and delicious discoveries, to be lingered over and reverted to, again and again, with ever new and infinite appreciation."
—Frederic Taber Cooper (from his Introduction)

"***Whispering Dust*** is a novel which has caused somewhat of a controversy among the reviewers." —*The Birmingham Age-Herald*

"Miss Eldrid Reynolds has the true art of the novelist . . . In the present story she has chosen to interpret a very difficult phase of emotion, and one that will not be immediately appreciated by every class of reader . . . Yet, in spite of a certain vagueness of touch, she succeeds to a remarkable degree in interpreting the undefined yearnings of a woman's heart . . . This is a very clever, rather subtle, and highly imaginative story. Women with a temperament will adore it; while those men, who profess themselves unable to understand women, will perhaps learn something more from its pages of the inscrutable enigma of femininity."   —*The Daily Telegraph*

And here I am on the threshold. . .

Contents

Heathenry: Thoughts on the Text

While researching another Heathen Edition, we happened upon the title of this book — *Whispering Dust* — and were immediately intrigued. Enough so that we sought out the book and, after reading the first few chapters, found ourselves delightfully charmed by its humor and poeticism. *Who was Eldrid Reynolds, exactly, and why aren't more people aware of this book?* we asked ourselves — and that's when we realized this novel was destined to join the Heathen family.

Dora Eldrid Reynolds was the daughter of artist, poet, and author Amy Dora Reynolds (1860–1957) who wrote 42 novels and one book of verse using the nom de plume Mrs. Fred Reynolds. Therefore, it's safe to assume that Eldrid, as she was known, surely knew a thing or two about the craft of writing when she set out to pen novels of her own, and, we might add, at a fairly young age, starting with her now insanely difficult to locate first novel *Red of the Rock*, published in 1911 when she was just 21 years old.

Her second and, sadly, final novel — the one you now hold in your hands — was published in November 1913[1] when she was only 24.

History doesn't tell us much about Eldrid, but we do know that she was born sometime between July–September 1889 in Headingly, Leeds, Yorkshire, and an article that was syndicated in several newspapers during the first year of *Whispering Dust*'s release gives us probably the only biographical sketch currently available today:

BOTH VERSATILE AND STRONG

Young English Author Especially Gifted With Talent
Along Many Lines Other Than Writing

Eldrid Reynolds, the young English woman who is the author of the novel *Whispering Dust*, belongs to an old Yorskshire family, and numbers among her ancestors Elizabeth Fry, the prison reformer,[2] the poet Bloomfield,[3] and James Ward[4] and George Morland,[5] both noted as painters. Miss Reynolds spent her childhood on the wide, heather-covered Yorkshire moors and the

[1] Books Received. (1913, November 15). *The Saturday Review*. (p. 625).
[2] Elizabeth Fry (1780–1845), known as the "Angel of Prisons," was an English prison reformer, social reformer, philanthropist, and Quaker instrumental in the 1823 Gaols Act which mandated sex-segregation of prisons to protect female inmates from sexual exploitation.
[3] Robert Bloomfield (1766–1823) was a working-class shoemaker who achieved brief fame as a poet.
[4] James Ward (1769–1859) was an English painter and engraver.
[5] George Morland (1763–1804) was an English painter.

wild Cornish coast. The passion for space, freedom, and the immensities which she voices in *Whispering Dust* is doubtless the result of her early environment.

The book itself is the result of a winter on the Mediterranean and in Egypt, but the heroine, who after thirty years of cramping duties as "a curate's daughter and a curate's niece" longs to accomplish something, can by no means be identified with the author. Miss Reynolds has accomplished a great deal in less than thirty years. She created stories before she could read; wrote, acted, and produced plays for home and school before she reached her teens; published her first novel, *Red of the Rock*, at twenty. She has a decided talent for drawing and singing and her favorite recreations show that she can be by no means a dreamer. Among them are riding, sailing, fishing, dancing, winter sports, caravaning, amateur theatricals, photography, painting, drawing, and singing.

Additionally, our research led us to some interesting information concerning her and her mother: They had settled together in Bordighera, Italy, near Nice on the Italian Riveria, but had miscalculated the seriousness of hostilities in the lead up to World War II and were taken into custody by Italian authorities on June 10, 1940, when Italy declared war on England.

Relocated approximately 30 miles east of Naples, to the province of Avellino, they were interned and placed under house arrest in the mountain village Mercogliano, where they remained until Avellino was liberated by the advancing United States Fifth Army in September 1943. It would take another 18

ends next p.

months before they could leave Italy, finally making it back to England on April 24, 1945.

Eldrid never married and died on the Isle of Wight on September 28, 1958, a little over a year after her mother's passing.

For reasons unknown, she never published another novel after *Whispering Dust*, which is surely a shame. Perhaps, she may have been deterred by the critical response to this novel, as it seems most critics at the time of its release tried to hang a "romance" label on it when it's quite obvious viewed through the lens of today that Miss Reynolds' nearly romance-less prose is far more in-line with, and was slightly ahead of, the modernist literature movement that exploded after World War I.

It's certainly not "modern" to the extent of the writings of, say, Virginia Woolf, but absolutely leans in that direction as evidenced by the heroine Naomi's ambling and elliptical inner monologues addressed to "You" as she progresses through Egypt in search of what she can only inadequately express as "Space" with a capital S.

And to cement the fact that this is *not* a romance, she peppers her prose with blatant clues such as, ". . . romance and I have had nothing to do with one another" and "romance when it came was this foolish mockery" and "is it only habit that keeps Romance going in the world?" A contemplation on romance — *maybe* — but certainly not a romance outright.

As for the text, we have updated several hyphened words to reflect their modern usage: to-day is now today, to-night has become tonight, and so on.

We have also combined and condensed the book's original 28 footnotes with our own since most of the originals were translations or explanations of Arabic words or phrases, which we have sometimes expanded on, and because a few of the originals were duplicated. In addition to those originals, we have added over 180 footnotes of our own for a grand total of 212, which we believe will prove useful as most of the story takes place in Egypt and delves into a fair bit of Egyptology.

We've also added some period-specific images to help better establish how two of the story's locations appeared at the time of this book's original publication in 1913.

Finally, we are very much in agreement with a notion found in Frederic Taber Cooper's introduction: "There can be no half measures in any reader's attitude toward this book: it will either leave you cold, speaking to you in an unknown tongue, or else you will hail it with delight, as one of those rare and delicious discoveries, to be lingered over and reverted to, again and again, with ever new and infinite appreciation."

We are most assuredly of the latter because we've found that this book has lingered with us long after finishing it.

Additionally, Mr. Cooper is exactly right when he states: "Do not be impatient with its subtle vagueness, do not be in too great haste to pluck out the heart of its mystery. . . ."

Eldrid herself even pinpoints, we believe, why one should avoid haste while reading this book when she says: "We move slowly. *'El agela minin esh Shaitan,'* the Arabs say."

A phrase that translates as: Haste is from the devil.

A phrase certainly worthy of rumination. . . .

With that, we leave you.

Allah salimah.

Introduction

Of all the thoughts which crowd forward, clamoring for utterance, under the stimulus of this strange, compelling volume, the one that is paramount and that in a measure encompasses and comprehends all the others, is that of the charm of its elusiveness. Do not be impatient with its subtle vagueness, do not be in too great haste to pluck out the heart of its mystery; be content to enjoy it, like the emanations of a rare flower, and to accept the fact that something of the fragrance of this mystery will linger, even to the end. There are certain prosaic souls who, having adventured into the opening pages of such a book as this, are like inexpert swimmers who suddenly find themselves out of their depth, and exhaust themselves with futile efforts to gain a footing or grasp something tangible. And, of course, the fluent and impalpable substance of the story yields and slips away, giving no sustenance. But if you surrender yourself to the current of the narrative, asking not too particularly whither you are being borne, you soon become conscious of its underlying strength and definite trend.

To be more specific: What the prosaic, unimaginative reader

confronts at the outset is this — here is a story, written from time to time, by a woman who, at the age of thirty-three, feels immeasurably old, because she fancies that she is different from other women, that she is capable of "doing things," and yet in all her drab, monotonous life has never had an opportunity to do anything. She has vague, intangible longings, vaulting ambitions for some big accomplishment, which she can express only inadequately by saying that she "wants to find Space." She is on her way to Egypt, where even the impalpable dust whispers of the immensities of space and time; yet it is not her desire for self-expression, her longing to find space, that has brought her to the land of the oasis and the desert, but rather her hope to stave off the Shadow — a shadow which, on days of pain and weakness, seems to draw frightfully near. There is another personality whose presence is felt behind every page, yet whom we never glimpse clearly — a man who is referred to as "You." The whole narrative is written to "You," and there are days when "You" becomes very near and real, and she writes, "I can see just how You feel about it; if You were here. You would say — but what nonsense, when You aren't really, You never were. You are only an idea, an absurd idea of my own. I never invented You until I got Nonsense at Marseilles, in the Church of Notre Dame de la Garde." Yet, little by little, this absurd, unreasonable Idea, this "You" who never really "would have been," if she had not invented him in the church on the hill with its offerings of "little, sad, dim ships," takes a more and more definite form, and we see him, big, strong and fair, a silent man with expressive eyes, who sits and smokes his pipe, and loves the scent of heather and the feel of soft, warm rain. This idea which she has invented, and plays with, is simply the idea that this man might mean something to her, if she were just an ordinary woman, and not "different" — not a woman who is a bit "mysterious" and who wants to "find Space." And this idea of the big, silent man goes through the book, sometimes helpfully near, sometimes so far withdrawn that she gropes impotently and ceases to believe in him; yet always, in a crisis, his nearness saves her from irreparable mistakes.

Such, in brief, are the surface difficulties and obscurities which leave the unimaginative person floundering quite helplessly — for to your unimaginative person, the literal identification of "You" is of prime importance, overshadowing all the really big things which the author has succeeded in saying so potently, just between the lines. For we have always with us the type of person to whom the dot is the essential part of the i, and who never will be happy until he knows whether Donatello[1] had pointed ears. To such readers the story will remain to the end a sealed book.

Interpretation is always somewhat rash. Yet some of the author's meaning seems so clear, in spite of her indirectness of method, as to make it well nigh impossible to mistake her. What she has to say is addressed more specifically to women; yet much of her philosophy might well apply to humanity at large, independently of sex or age. There is, she preaches, no greater misfortune for man or woman than "to have no nonsense about them." To find Nonsense, with a capital N, is the first step toward finding the significance of life. To the self-sufficient, ambitious, rather hard young woman of today, the young woman who is convinced that she is "different," that she must express herself, that she has in her a capacity for achievement that requires nothing less than infinite space, she says quietly:

---

[1] Donatello, born Donato di Niccolò di Betto Bardi (1386–1466), was an Italian sculptor of the Renaissance period.

ends next p.

Find Nonsense; it is worth more than all your hard, cold, sterile self-sufficiency; find Imagination, and play with it fancifully, for it will imbue you with that glamour of mystery that bids defiance to encroaching years; find Love, for it is better than ambition and fame and wealth — "it is more blessed to give than to receive."

It is not within the province of this introduction to touch upon the specific details of the plot, or to analyze individually the little group of central figures who have speaking parts. Miss Kershaw, the woman with "no nonsense about her," the Flapette, the Prawn, the Clergyman, and the Author; — or to touch upon the really wonderful background of magic color and scent and strange, weird sounds, the whole unmistakable atmosphere of Egypt. I have never seen the thing done in quite the way this writer does it; she makes it seem real and near and tangible by little familiar touches: "There is a turquoise sky with great shining English clouds. Somehow I hadn't pictured clouds in Egypt; I had always been led to imagine 'brazen skies.'" And always she gives us the sense of the all-pervasive, ever-present dust, with its "warm, sad sort of smell," — "I told you I was going to love the dust. Already dust seems to mean Egypt and Egypt dust. And after all, dust is rather wonderful, isn't it? We ourselves are supposed to be just dust — at least, I am. You are not even dust. I shall never be able to think of Egypt without thinking of dust, gilded dust and dust from the desert with its strange, sad smell."

No, the thing cannot be done: the subtle, elusive, haunting charm of this strange, enticing little volume cannot be communicated at secondhand; the best that can be done is to pass on something of the contagion of one's own enthusiasm. There can be no half measures in any reader's attitude toward this book:

it will either leave you cold, speaking to you in an unknown tongue, or else you will hail it with delight, as one of those rare and delicious discoveries, to be lingered over and reverted to, again and again, with ever new and infinite appreciation. But if you want, either for your own enlightenment or that of others, to find the essential substance of the book already summed up for you, turn to page 282: "I thought to find Space and found God; I thought to find myself and found You." Faith and love: two immensities, which it is not granted to every woman to find at one and the same time. I almost made the mistake, a moment ago, of speaking of *Whispering Dust* as "a sad little book," and the mistake would have been a most natural one, for an essence of sadness seems to emanate from the characters, the setting, the whole atmosphere, the inaudible whispers of the desert dust. And yet, paradoxically, it is a joyous book, a book shot through with the glory of golden sunshine and the glamour of romance — all through the magic power of laughter, born of Nonsense.

Frederic Taber Cooper.[2]

---

[2] Frederic Taber Cooper Ph.D. (1864–1937) was an American author best known as the editor of *The New York Commercial Advertiser* (1898-1904), *The Forum* (1907-1909), and, briefly, the *New York Globe*.

MARSEILLE — *Notre-Dame de la Garde*

You first Began — first merged from my brain — at Marseilles in the sad, vague dusk of Notre Dame de la Garde.[1] Why You should not have Been before, I cannot say; why You did not Begin at Gibraltar, or when first I sighted foreign land — Portugal, I suppose it was; I remember how I was moved. But You Began at Marseilles. You didn't come suddenly like an inspiration; I can't pretend that the thing was wonderful, though sometimes it has seemed so since. No, I created You, an Idea — created You with difficulty. I am not young, and romance and I have had nothing to do with one another. I am a curate's orphan and a curate's niece.[2] Over thirty years I lived among grime and turnip fields; I had not even been a dreamer — turnips are not conducive to dreaming. Thirty years of it. The faculty for dreaming seemed left out, or wiped out, in me.

With infinite labor I created You, the Idea; You did not come

[1] Notre-Dame de la Garde, translated literally as "Our Lady of the Guard" (seen at left circa 1910, and not to be confused with the Notre-Dame in Paris), and known locally as *la Bonne Mère* ("the Good Mother"), is a Catholic basilica in Marseille, France, and is the city's best-known symbol.

[2] A curate is a member of the clergy engaged as assistant to a vicar, rector, or parish priest.

suddenly. But it seems wonderful to me now. Why did You Begin in the old, vast Church on the hill? It is extraordinary even now, though it was only a day or two ago, to think You could ever have been an Idea, nothing more; You are so real to me already. I cannot understand why You did not come sooner — only, I have never had many ideas. But were You just an Idea? It is so hard to think so. Only, of course, I know You were and are; You owed your existence to my brain in the old Church of Notre Dame de la Garde.

It happened rather curiously.

Traveling quite alone, I did not think I should go ashore at Marseilles; I had not been ashore at Gibraltar. But the most unexpected person offered to take me — a brusque, hard-featured Yorkshire woman with whom I had not exchanged a dozen words. Miss Kershaw simply said, "Of course you're going ashore," and I knew that of course I was. I like her, I don't know why. She isn't at all likeable really. She had quite a little crowd under her wing; a very young girl who is, I think, her niece, and amongst others a very young youth who sits at my table and looks desperately homesick or lovesick (I think perhaps it is the niece). Sometimes I feel dreadfully afraid he is going to confide in me. People always have confided in me, and I don't want them to confide in me. Can You understand how I feel? What is it that makes them choose me? I used not to mind, but since I left England I've begun to mind.

Perhaps I resent it unreasonably because I have never had anything to confide in anybody myself — until now. And You are a ridiculous, an utterly ridiculous secret. I've got You to confide in now, and I can confide in You all about yourself!

Archie Snell hasn't confided in me yet, but I think I see it in his eye, see it coming; and I know so well it is the very young girl — and I shall feel so old and You will be less real for a little while. You always are when things remind me I'm not young — because I haven't really left ten years behind me in the Church on the hill; as a matter of fact, I left nothing but my umbrella.

You see what nonsense I am writing. Me and nonsense! Doesn't it seem incongruous to You? But of course You have only known the new me; You have only known me for two days! And yet I feel You have known me always and have just been waiting for me to know You. That's absurd; yes, I know, but You can't think how delicious it is to be absurd after being sensible so long. I think, do You know, I am rather glad You have only known me — since Marseilles.

Marseilles was wonderful.

Remember, I have never been out of England before, scarcely ever left the grimy turnip fields.

It is hardly possible for You to realize what I felt on setting foot in France, I suppose.

It made my breath come in jerks, but the tears pricked the back of my eyes and the masts were indistinct — I felt so old. I never imagined, when the unbelievable happened and I was able to go abroad, I never imagined I should feel old. But I did. It wasn't just that I didn't feel young; I felt old — and suddenly alone I don't know if I had ever thought about it before, certainly I had never imagined I could feel such loneliness when I attained my desire. But I felt old and alone. Perhaps that was how I first thought of You; only, it must have been subconsciously, because, as I say, You, the idea, came to me in Notre Dame de la Garde. I haven't felt old once since then — unless things have reminded me. I am so afraid Archie Snell is going to remind me. I don't think I shall go up on deck tonight. I saw it coming all through dinner; I watched the stages; he came to

ch. ends p. 9

a decision by dessert — the nuts helped him. He is a harmless youth, rather like a prawn that has been out of water sometime; he is rather out of water on board ship — but I think I shall hate him if he confides in me.

I used to take it for granted, but everything is different after Notre Dame de la Garde. I suppose it is unreasonable to expect anyone to know that. I suppose I look just the same. Do I? What does that odd smile of yours mean? Do you know, I think You're going to be positively aggravating sometimes! And You're only a thing of my imagination. I wish You'd remember that. . . . Of course You know I don't wish it, and it was nice of You to give the go-by to the obvious retort.

Marseilles reminded me forcibly of a cinematograph.[3] I did not like to mention this, as it didn't seem the sort of thing one ought to feel — or at any rate to say. And yet that is what I felt. It doesn't matter telling You, because You won't laugh, or if You do, in that funny way You have, with your eyes, I don't think I shall mind. I wonder how I know You'd smile like that? I seem to know such a lot about You already — and yet You are constantly surprising me, and all the time You owe your mere existence to my brain.

It was just like a cinematograph. All the gendarmes[4] standing about with baggy trousers and ridiculous cloaks, waiting, I felt sure, for an amazing Frenchman to pop through some unexpected door or window. I can confess here that I have only twice seen a cinematograph — at a parish tea.

Why don't You laugh? I don't seem to know You a bit yet. I thought it would amuse You.

---

[3] A motion picture film camera, which also serves as a film projector and printer. It was invented in the 1890s in Lyon, France, by Auguste and Louis Lumière.

[4] Armed police officers in France and other French-speaking countries.

Marseilles is a most fascinating place; yes, squalid, I suppose, but fascinating.

Miss Kershaw, when we left the Quai,[5] rounded us off like an old sheep-dog and hustled us into a stuffy little tram that pitched and rolled worse than the ship in the Bay; a tram full of grubby people of all nations, exciting people, but a bit on the "gruesomely sweet side," as the flapper said. The flapper's expressions are distinctly original.[6]

The streets are cobbled, and I thought the noise deafening, and wondered whether it was because I wasn't young. The flapper said, "Doesn't all the noise give you a funny, delicious feeling inside, like swinging? We used to call it tummy-lingers when we were kids!" I knew what she meant — on the way back from Notre Dame de la Garde.

The carts drawn by strings of mules with high-peaked collars fascinated me, and the old, old houses that made even me feel younger; the strange little back streets crowded with all nationalities. The French boys were so absurdly French, wearing socks and long overalls; horrid small people, quite as horrid as their prototype in England. How funny that You should ever have been a boy! — but I am forgetting. You started life after You had passed that stage. You never were a boy. And yet — somehow I can imagine what You were like.

It seemed so strange to see French notices and French signs everywhere and to hear French spoken on every side. It was all so utterly different from anything I had ever seen before. I have seen pitifully little — done pitifully little. I've *done* nothing.

[5] The Quai d'Orsay is a Paris street that parallels the southern bank of the Seine River.

[6] Flapper originally meant teenage girl, but evolved in the 1920s to mean a young woman who flaunted her unconventionality.

It was bewildering as a dream to see all manner of strange people in costumes of strange countries sitting at little tables outside the dirty, delightful cafés, drinking and gesticulating. If France were wonderful, Egypt—— But my heart felt like a stone. Only my mind was feasting upon color and novelty, not my heart; only some cold, detached part of me. It had come too late.

Suddenly Egypt seemed drear,[7] almost menacing. All the magic had gone out of it. I was going to Egypt — but I was going alone.

I don't think I have ever been self-sufficing; I just haven't thought about it, I suppose. I had not realized what it would mean.

I must have shivered.

Miss Kershaw told me I was cold. She never asks questions, always makes statements.

I wanted to tell her I wasn't cold, that it had all come too late, but of course I didn't say anything of the kind. One never does; besides, Miss Kershaw reads people as easily as she reads French signs. I was aware she knew all about me — till we came out from the old Church on the hill.

There was so little to know before, You see. No one knows all about me now. I am quite a mysterious person.

I felt so desolate I shivered in the hot sunshine. My brain was absorbing it all, thinking it more wonderful than I could have dreamed among my dreary turnip fields; but the rest of me — all the part I haven't recognized as me till now, the part which matters — was standing shivering, facing the fact that it had come too late. I was desolately incomplete, and the incomplete

---

[7] Literary form of dreary.

feeling grew like ice-cold water rising slowly inch by inch. I knew bitterness for the first time. I was called Naomi, but the name had never possessed any significance.

My brain received the impression of much color, in the crowds, in the awnings, in the massed flowers and paper-kiosks; the rest of me felt that it was all gray, the tired sort of gray an east wind would be if winds had color. I've had such absurd thoughts since You began.

Is it Your influence? I don't think so. Besides, You've no business to have any influence. You are merely an Idea, the only Idea I shall ever have, perhaps. You do smile at odd things; I never know what will amuse You — or what will hurt You. Sometimes You smile just like that when anything hurts. I was going to say I know all about You, but I don't. That's so funny. You are the most unexpected person I ever—— But I've never met You. You just Began in Notre Dame de la Garde; better still. You *are* here and now on board the "——————."

But then I did not know that You were going to be. I had not the slightest premonition of what would happen in the Church on the hill when the lift began to jerk upward.

It seems so strange I should not have known, that I should not have felt what was coming.

I am talking now as though You happened, whereas You didn't happen at all; I created the idea consciously, with difficulty. That's the difference. In some lives people happen. No one ever happened in mine; I couldn't expect You to happen. As soon as I stood in the darkness within the Church — the Church that looks like a dream-thing amidst a haze of sunlight from the harbor — You, the Idea, began to take form, just as those little, heartbreaking ships gradually take form, hung from the roof, when your eyes become accustomed to the sad, listening gloom.

ch. ends next p.

I think the others must have gone out to buy souvenirs from the queer shops that cling to the Church like children to the skirts of some still-faced nun. I know I was quite alone when it happened.

Three long tapers were burning palely before a shrine, the Church was full of silence, of dusk and incense — and whispering sounds, prayer-echoes perhaps.

The strings of little phantom ships in the gloom were like presences; I felt rather than saw them.

And then You Began, and I laughed.

In the dim, wonderful old Church I laughed out loud, and the echo of my laughter got mixed up with all those whispering prayer-echoes that make the place so mysterious and dim — till I didn't know which was which.

I was not frightened, hearing my own laughter, and I don't think it surprised the Virgin where the candles were burning palely. I suppose no human emotion can surprise her much. I stood looking at the little ships, and laughed.

When I came out the sunshine blinded me, and when I could see I saw with the whole of me, not just with my brain. Don't You know what it is like to see with the whole of you? I had never done it before. One can't look at turnips like that. At least, I don't know; since You Began I can almost imagine it. I never had such ridiculous thoughts till You Began.

I was acutely conscious of the icy wind and the generous sunshine, conscious of being alive. Do You know what I mean? I'd somehow always taken it for granted before. I was conscious of all sorts of little, curious things; the sounds that came up from the city lying in its haze of smoke made my ears tingle — like the piercing note of a mosquito! Most of all I was conscious of You.

I looked at Miss Kershaw gazing down at the whitish lime-stone hills and soft tiled roofs — Miss Kershaw with her harsh face and queer, amused eyes. I looked at the very young youth, who was looking at nothing in particular. Then I looked at the flapper, who was merely looking bored; and at the rest, who were merely looking bewildered — and I wondered if any of them realized there was a difference, that they no longer knew all about me.

They couldn't know that anything had happened — but did they realize I had become a little bit mysterious? I don't think they did. No one seems to have noticed. I rather think I'm glad.

It is so absurd and nice and — satisfying to have the knowledge all to myself.

No one appeared to notice anything.

The flapper remarked that the wind had made my hair untidy; I laughed again then, I don't know why — rather uncertain laughter that sounded odd to me.

"I wish I could put a little brass in the Church — the little round brasses that say '*Merci*,'" I said. I was still laughing.

They all looked blank and rather startled. None of them had the least suspicion what I meant.

And it would have spoiled it rather if they had — wouldn't it?

2

I told You I knew it was coming, and it has. At least, it was just as bad — the effect was the same; I almost lost sight of You and my new self.

I am not making things a bit clearer. You will screw up your eyes in a minute in that horrid, exasperating way.

I am talking of Archie Snell, You know.

I loved coming on board last night, though a ship in port is supposed to be a hateful thing. It seemed to have some new significance. Are You really responsible for all this? I don't see how You can be; I am afraid You will grow to imagine yourself too important.

Marseilles is wonderful at night because it is a place of ships and countless lights; their reflections so mysterious in the dark, still water (I've begun to love mysterious things, do You know?); the plash[1] of waves; the sudden shriek of a siren trembling into silence; water and sky full of star-brightness.

I have never been in a world of ships before; I think ships

[1] Literary form of splash.

will always have a sort of special meaning since I saw the little, sad, dim ships of Notre Dame de la Garde.

At night ships are so mysterious. There isn't much that is not mysterious when you come to think of it — or have I begun to see mystery where there is none? You are responsible, You absurd person, though there isn't a scrap of mystery about You — in more ways than one, for You are just an Idea, and You've only been that a couple of days. You see how old and sane and uncomfortable I am feeling tonight — all because of Archie.

There were great liners slipping out into the unknown, brilliantly lit and vast. I peered from my port and could see the lights of a grimy tramp steamer rippling in long, limpid reflections. I could hear the glug and gurgle of water, the hiss from an exhaust; I could feel ships all round me in the night. I have never felt anything inanimate before. I have felt cold and heat and dullness, but not Things. Ships are going to be Things always after this.

I managed to "wander" Archie (this is the flapper's phrase) all yesterday, which was not difficult, as in the Gulf of Lions we were heading into a stiff gale and the ship began to move.

The groaning and creaking and queer sudden sounds, the way she shivered right through when a heavy sea struck her, excited me. I liked it.

Toward evening she grew steadier, and Archie appeared.

I was sitting in that strange little time before it is really dark, the deck brilliantly lit; and beyond blueness, the wonderful blueness of twilight at sea.

I let the soft blue lap round me like water, drowning thought.

I wanted only to be conscious of that; it was so sheerly beautiful, and I have felt so little that has been beautiful. I think I had got right outside my body.

ch. ends p. 16

Have You ever done that? You feel You're not there. That sounds absurd, but all the nicest ideas are absurd, don't You think? You are the most absurd of all.

I felt I wasn't there, and then Archie sat down in a chair which did not belong to him and scraped it backward and nearer me.

I pretended not to see him — as though I could put off the inevitable.

I knew it was coming. I had known all along. He was going to confide in me, and I was going to feel old and sane and perfectly horrible again — and I was going to hate him.

I had begun already.

He said it was not a bad sort of night, and scraped the chair.

I said it wasn't. I resented his referring to the night at all — it was my night till he had come pushing into it. Such a blue, still, near sort of night.

I didn't help the boy out at all; I just tucked my rug round me and waited.

I was aware of a chill breeze and the throb of the engines, my body, all sorts of things I had forgotten. And it was the boy's fault. I was hating him desperately.

He breathed loudly for some time and rolled a handkerchief between his palms. It was horrid, and I knew it so well — the prelude. I wanted to implore him to be done with preliminaries. I thought if he didn't stop breathing in that hideous way I should scream or something.

He said, whispering horribly loudly (people always do that when they confide things)——

"I expect what I want to tell you will surprise you rather . . . "

I felt so tired, tired out suddenly, all over. As though it could surprise me; as though I hadn't listened to it all dozens of times!

"I don't think so," I managed to say. I felt so tired it was an effort even to say that.

He scraped the chair across the deck and my nerves simultaneously. He appeared to pay no attention to my remark. They never did; I didn't expect it. It was all as it always was, terribly.

Archie had got hold of the fringe on my rug and was plaiting[2] it elaborately. They always did that, too.

Confession may be good for the soul, but not for the confessor. My soul was as black as a coal-coolie[3] just then.

"It's — I didn't realize it till Marseilles," he began. I supposed not. Those who looked on always realized it first.

I felt sure now that it was the flapper. For a minute I was almost sorry for him. And then he took another of those loud, stuffy breaths, and I hated him again.

"Why," I exclaimed, unable to contain myself any longer — "Why should it be me? Why should it always be me?" I suppose I was crying out against fate as much as against Archie.

He said an odd thing then:

"I don't quite know why, unless——" He seemed to see suddenly what a blue, wonderful night it was; he seemed to have got mixed up with it as I had been.

"I don't know really — unless it's because you're so jolly mysterious!"

I had been hating him.

I think I must have laughed, because I felt so utterly unlike laughter.

I said, "I've been hating you so all the evening."

A deck steward passed. The sound of his steps died and

[2] Folding.

[3] A "coolie" is now an offensive term for unskilled Asian workers, usually of Chinese or Indian descent.

ch. ends p. 16

seemed to leave a blank in the night that was gradually filled by the ticking of Archie's wrist watch. I could hear it quite distinctly.

He didn't say anything more; instead of breathing loudly, he seemed not to be breathing at all.

My thoughts were busy with the fact that he, he of all people, had found something mysterious in me — since Marseilles.

And then he said "Why?" rather quietly. He seemed not to know what a long time the wrist watch had been ticking.

For a minute I wondered to what he referred. Then:

"Because you've made me," I began; but I should have felt older still: so I only said, "You've made me tired, I think."

It was a stupid thing to say, especially in the vague, helpless way I must have said it.

"I'm sorry," the boy answered, and there followed the pause you make when your lips are dry. "I don't think — I understand you."

I couldn't help it; I felt quite warm and alive again.

Everybody has always understood me before. You've no idea what a snug, nice feeling it is, not to be understood. I had supposed it tragic.

"Of course you don't understand me," I said. "Didn't you just tell me I was mysterious?"

"You're jolly mysterious, somehow."

I laughed.

"Mysteriously jolly, you mean. Since Marseilles. I know."

I could see three stars swimming in the blue between two of the ship's boats; they seemed to throb to the persistent throbbing engines of which I had become aware as one becomes aware of a clock — or as I had of the wrist watch.

I must have sighed.

The boy asked me why, but not with any eagerness, with a slight shiver as though he were cold.

"Because," I said, horribly deliberate; I was bitter — "Because I'm feeling old — again."

I was. I had known his confidence would have that effect, would remind me. I had hated him for it. But now this that he had sprung upon me, this laughable, preposterous, pitiful thing — the other could not have made me feel quite so old and tired.

I knew when I told him I felt old he had begun to see it himself.

A woman ought not to tell a man she's old, I think. I wonder if I ought to have told You? Only somehow You are different. We all say that, I suppose. And perhaps You're only different because You're merely an Idea and not a man at all.

I knew how ridiculous this was — and I knew how soon it would be the flapper. Yet it seemed so pitiful. Not from Archie's point of view: I am afraid I have been thinking a lot of mine; but then, You see, I haven't had any point of view to speak of all these years — and at least my point of view matters to You. It's got to matter. If I make it matter, it does matter. I believe You don't half like being reminded so often You are only an Idea — but it is myself I am really reminding, because I begin to be afraid. Tonight I am feeling old and dried up; You know that east-wind feeling.

Nothing, nobody had ever happened in my life, as I told You. Surely it is worse than suffering, this nothingness?

Sometimes now — since Marseilles — I almost want to suffer rather than nothing should ever happen. Can a man understand that? I wonder.

Nothing had ever happened in my life, You see, and now romance when it came was this foolish mockery; a boy with a

ch. ends next p.

face like a prawn thought he loved me, told me I was mysterious. I had been given something I had desired vaguely through drab years — given it, and yet robbed of it. I was conscious of a vast, relentless power somewhere in the dark that leered and mouthed at me. . . .

Eight bells. It is midnight. What wild stuff I have been writing! I realize it with the sanity that morning imposes, morning being a few seconds old.

Miss Kershaw came on deck soon after that, and I knew the boy was glad. I had told him I was old, and he recognized it; I wasn't mysterious anymore. It was all so ridiculous, miserably. I don't suppose it could have happened anywhere but at sea on a blue, still night. And I'm sorry it did. I suppose life is like this?

I said when Miss Kershaw sat down heavily in the chair Archie had left:

"I don't think I believe in Romance, do you know?"

I had never ventured upon the abstract with Miss Kershaw.

She rubbed her chin, and I expected it would make a rasping sound; her voice rasps rather. She didn't reply.

"I used to think I believed in it — for myself, I mean. I suppose most women do. . . . And you?"

I had a feeling she was trying not to see the blueness beyond the lighted deck.

"And you?"

"My hair always grew too far back on my head for Romance!" she answered.

I suppose life is like that?

The nights have begun to take on some indefinable mystic quality since Marseilles. Is it the East that I feel already?

I love the Mediterranean best at evening; by day it is too persistently, unchangingly blue; at night it is mysterious. Last night the sunset — I'll try to tell You, but it is so hopeless. The sea was darkest blue (it is so blue that even on a black, moonless night I believe you would *feel* the blue was there; you can't get away from it; you are conscious of it all the time — or I am).

The whole sky swam with color, not dazzling, but infinitely soft and melting. I could not tell if it were faint pink or palest green or primrose; and yet it was all three; the colors throbbed.

I begin to feel already the nearness of the East. I can't help spelling it with a capital. The thought that I am on my way to Egypt is too big a thing to realize. I feel now as though all my life, with only turnip fields to look at and blanket clubs to fill my mind, I have had this hunger for the East; it has been there, somewhere.

In a few days I shall be in Egypt. It doesn't mean anything yet — only words. How could it?

It doesn't mean half as much to me as You do, I think I'm glad Egypt is so very, very old. Don't look like that. It hurts. You ought not to have read any meaning into it. It is dangerous to read meanings into things, especially things women say. Besides, You are not a bit a subtle sort of person — so don't dare to pretend again that You are.

I said I would welcome suffering rather than nothing at all, didn't I? But suffering doesn't come like that. It comes in the most unexpected ways, to the most unexpected people.

I have described some of the passengers, but I don't think I have pictured for You a little couple who somehow interested me from the first. They are quite a common and commonplace little couple — but rather sweet, if you understand? They are absolutely insignificant, mousy little things, undersized, and underfed until recently, I should say.

I am sure he originated in a linen-draper's; he always contrives to take up his knife and fork as though they were scissors. Their name is Jones — or Smith. It doesn't much matter which. How they come to be traveling first saloon[1] on a P. & O.[2] and going to Cairo, I cannot imagine; I cannot place them. I have talked a good deal to Mr. Smith, and Mrs. Smith has talked a good deal to me.

She told me they have left a baby at home. It would be the

[1] A large social lounge on a passenger ship.
[2] The Peninsular and Oriental Steam Navigation Company, founded in 1837, has the oldest heritage of any cruise line in the world.

sort with a plaid frock and a hydrocephalous head,[3] I know. I have heard several people say the Smiths are quite impossible.

Mr. Smith worries olives off a fork, and pares his nails on deck, and Mrs. Smith is just like one of those cheap dolls that are sewn into cardboard boxes — I always expect to hear stitches ripping when she gets up from her chair. They are refreshing in their childish interest and pleasure. Evidently they have never been abroad before; I daresay it is equally evident that I have not; only, I try to conceal the fact. They don't. I wonder how this chance came to them?

Have they come into money as I have, like the first chapter of a newspaper feuilleton?[4] At any rate for them the chance has not come too late. For me — I don't know. Sometimes I think it has. Sometimes You are less real and I have to grope for You.

I overheard the Smiths discussing the "wireless" with bated breath and squandered aspirates.[5] They were sitting together under one rug. She was keeping her place in *Home Chat*[6] with a work-hardened finger and occasionally looking up to gaze at passing feet. On-board ship people always do look at your feet; you soon lose the weak-kneed feeling it gives you. But Mrs. Smith wasn't really seeing the passing feet. They seemed absolutely to suffice one another, these two rather impossible little people. I saw her small, anaemic face light up suddenly, and she crumpled *Home Chat* in both hands.

"'Erb," she whispered (I had put him down as Perc') — "'Erb, if we could 'ave one, you and me — a wireless messige, 'Erb!

[3] Enlargement of the head due to fluid accumulation in the brain.

[4] The section of a European newspaper devoted to serialized fiction, light literature, or reviews and criticism.

[5] When speaking, the sounds followed by a puff or exhalation of breath.

[6] Home Chat was a British weekly women's magazine, founded by Alfred Harmsworth (1865–1922) and published by Amalgamated Press from 1895 to 1959.

Suppose we could get one thousan's" — her geography was vague — "thousan's of miles from anywhere? My word, wouldn't it just be . . . ?"

She was leaning toward him, her mouth wide, showing imperfect teeth; her eyes wide, showing her transparent little soul. 'Erb sucked in the scanty, straw-colored mustache, and his weak face grew long. "There's no one as could poss'bly send us a messige," he said. "You're ridic'lous, Annie."

She pulled an "invisible" hairpin out of her fringe net and pushed it back again slowly. "No, 'course there isn't. You take anyone up so quick, 'Erb. I only meant it would be a bit of all right to get a messige out 'ere from 'ome, 'erb." Her eyes had gone dull, and she was turning the crumpled pages of *Home Chat* very rapidly.

The deck steward came with soup and confidential remarks.

Her teeth clattered against the cup.

"You're ridic'lous, you are, Annie," Mr. Smith repeated, gulping soup. "Do you know what these messiges cost? You don't, eh? Nor me. But I can guess." He blew out his cheeks and laid a finger against his nose; his voice had died to an awestruck whisper.

He was feeling for her hand under the rug. I think he was ashamed to own that he shared her desire. I wished I had the power to gratify it on the spot.

Later we were playing bucket quoits[7] when the deck steward with the confidential manner tapped Mr. Smith on the shoulder as he leaned forward, hot and intent, with his tongue thrust out.

Mr. Smith turned to his wife.

---

[7] A game in which players toss rings of metal, rope, or rubber at an upright peg or stake in the hope of encircling or landing as near as possible to it.

"Annie" he said excitedly, "it's a wireless messige — a wireless for you and me...."

She ran to him in her awkward, quick way, and clasped his arm. I knew her eyes must be shining, and I knew something else long before they did.

"'Erb," she said when she could speak, rapturously; and then, "Oh, you rotter, you've been and gone and 'ad it sent yourself! Now, 'aven't you?"

For a minute I think he longed to have achieved the impossible.

He laughed. Then he read, and the smile on his pallid little face remained as though he had forgotten about it, whilst his features twitched.

"A wireless for you and me, Annie..." he said stupidly, with the frozen smile on his face.

I was afraid he was going to laugh: I felt I couldn't stand it if he did.

But he just stood there saying, "A wireless for you and me...."

After a long time she gave a cry that made an officer leaning on the rail take up his pipe out of his mouth and two old ladies look up from a game of Patience.[8]

The cry was shrill yet stifled, the sound one makes in dreams — but there were words somewhere in it.

"Not baby ... not Alfred Charles ..."

It was the husband who broke into a storm of noisy weeping.

They had had their message.

At half-past ten we are supposed to pass Stromboli.[9] Somehow I don't feel any interest in it now. I can't forget about the

[8] Another name for Solitaire.
[9] An island in the Tyrrhenian Sea, off the north coast of Sicily, containing Mount Stromboli, one of the four active volcanoes in Italy.

ch. ends p. 24

poor little baby with the big head and the plaid frock. The fact of the plaid frock — which isn't a fact at all — seems to make it the more tragic.

Everyone crowded forward beyond the range of electric lights, hoping to see the volcano.

It was nearly eleven when we sighted Stromboli, a vast, formless mass above the dark sea; our funnels belching black clouds which swamped the stars. I had thought it would be erupting, that at least there would be a glare, but there was not even smoke.

All the same it was wonderfully impressive; we passed close, and Stromboli rises so sheer out of the sea, looming gigantic, black.

There is something awful about a mountain rising suddenly from the sea. It looked so remote, not threatening, nor terrible.

And yet for me it was symbolic of some dark, shadow-thing waiting for me just a little ahead, always just a little ahead.

What is it? I was frightened, and You seemed as remote as Stromboli.

After I had turned in I leaned at my port to gaze at the dark mass. It fascinated me — but the shadow-thing has made me fearful.

I don't think it has any connection with the Smiths and the Marconigram.[10] It has suddenly risen out of the darkness of

[10] A message or telegram sent by radiotelegraphy, named after its Italian inventor Guglielmo Marconi (1874–1937).

the future — just a little ahead. It eludes me. I don't know what it is, and that makes me fear it more.

One of the Scotch officers — and they are nearly all Scots-men — walks up and down every evening on the bridge-deck playing the pipes. Their shrill wail is rather lovely above the waves' rush as you look over a vast, jewel-dark expanse; stream-ing white foam with the glitter of phosphorescence beneath a yellow moon.

He was playing tonight when a cold, shapeless thought came up to me out of the sea and laid hold of me where I stood leaning on the rail amidst voices and laughter.

The flapper leaned beside me; I almost thought she would see it — I saw it coming myself. I had been watching it for a long time whilst I listened to the shivery, shrill pipes above.

It laid hold of me, but it was still a shapeless thing. It has grown, and I know what it is.

I am afraid I may never return.

I have been sitting on my bunk ever since, facing the thing and wondering why it chills me. Why should it matter if I never return?

England is merely the place where I wasted thirty blank years. If there were anyone to whom I were going back — but there has never been anyone in my life; at the best people have crossed it. Perhaps it is my fault; I daresay it is.

Why should it matter, then?

ch. ends next p.

Yet somehow, just the possibility of never returning oppressed me with a kind of terror. I was in a panic.

I have got You. There aren't any people, real people, in my life — never have been. England is nothing to me. I don't feel any desire to go back. It is not a desire to go back — it is an unreasoning, blind terror that I shall not go back. I can't explain it any better; it goes beyond me.

The thought came up damp and cold out of the sea, and now it obsesses me; I feel vaguely it has some connection with the shadow that has been there ever since I saw Stromboli rise black and sudden from the muffling night.

It is late, but I think I shall go on deck again before turning in; my head throbs, and the cabin is confined and close. I feel that frantic desire for space I have known in dreams. And my life has not been spacious: my life has always lacked space. I want it. Don't You see that that is what I want? I can't endure this heat much longer. . . .

I have been wondering all day how to break it to You.

Now I know, I don't mind in the same way. The only thing I mind is the fact that I may, possibly, never return to England.

There, I suppose I have told You. I wish You wouldn't look like that. I wish You'd say something. I didn't mean to tell You so crudely. But You never cared for beating about the bush. (How do I know?) How do I know anything about You? Perhaps I don't. I never thought You'd take it in this still, waiting, white sort of way. You have grown beyond my understanding. You frighten me. And You're only an Idea . . . only an Idea.

I'm groping for You — You're going, and I want You most just now. I need You.

I think, You know, it is as well You are nothing more. I don't mind for myself. If only You wouldn't look like that — if only You could say something. But all the time I am glad You cannot.

I wrote feverishly last night. Today I have seen the ship's doctor — and now I know what the Shadow is, the Shadow that has been waiting always a little ahead. I've overtaken it.

The doctor is gray and elderly and northern — Yorkshire,

I think. I have never been drawn to Yorkshire people before, but somehow I like Miss Kershaw in spite of myself. And I liked the doctor.

When I asked a question he answered it with slow deliberation; otherwise he did not speak much.

There was only one question I wanted to ask: was there, did he think, the possibility that I might not return? I must know. He saw that I must know. He told me quite simply there was the possibility. Egypt was the best place for me; it was not the lungs, it was the heart; I must take care — but I was not to alarm myself, because my nerves——

I knew he would add something like that.

I think I must have looked toward the port, because he rose and opened it, letting in a rush of sound and damp salt air.

But that was all.

I supposed it was rather tragic; in books such things seem so — but it wasn't. It all seemed very commonplace, almost tiresome.

I sat quite composedly whilst the doctor spoke in his matter-of-fact, slow way. I did not mind very much, I found — save that I might never return. But the thought of You swamped other things; how I should tell You?

And then I remembered that really there wasn't any You, and I laughed a little out loud.

The doctor asked me why; I think he suspected hysteria. I told him I laughed because there was no one whom I need tell.

He said, "I see," very gravely and quietly.

It was strange; when he said that, it reminded me of You. But You aren't Yorkshire. I don't know what You are; I've never really thought about it.

I liked the old doctor, in spite of the fact that he gave me to understand I was in a nervous state, was panicking about myself.

You are so real to me — it is difficult to remember. And just now I don't want to remember. I need You.

But I am glad You are not real. It is far better You should not be. . . .

You must try to make me forget the terror of not returning.

I can't understand what it means if it is not connected with You — and yet how can it be, possibly?

I don't know what it is; I cannot account for it; I am filled with an insidious, cold dread. But for that I do not mind — much. I could consult a specialist, of course, only I knew of the Shadow before ever the doctor told me there was this possibility. Why should I trouble to question it? I don't mind. I shall see Egypt; I shall share Egypt with You.

Tomorrow we reach Port Said.[1] You must help me to forget. It is so hard to remember that You *aren't*. I can't help it; I need You. Almost I could wish You had really happened. And yet all the time I'm glad, glad there isn't any You.

Women are like that, I suppose.

Before breakfast I could see land dimly. Northern Africa. There was a fresh, almost a keen breeze blowing, and the morning was gray; not at all the sort of morning I had imagined.

The ship was rolling, so that packing was not easy work.

[1] A city that lies in northeast Egypt along the coast of the Mediterranean Sea, north of the Suez Canal.

ch. ends p. 31

Miss Kershaw came through a crowd of lascars[2] and baggage-stewards to my cabin, and found me on my knees fighting with a new and obstinate trunk, which was making dashes across the floor when it was not closing with my head inside.

"Alexandria's in sight," Miss Kershaw stated, fastening back the door and clinging to it.

I abandoned my trunk and hurried along the corridor and out on deck into the gray morning.

I thought I should see white houses gleaming: even on a gray day I supposed Eastern houses must gleam; it was expected of them; in books they spend their time doing it. But all I saw were a few tall chimneys, gray and dim on the gray horizon.

Miss Kershaw said, "Well?" with her eyes; she seldom permits herself a verbal question.

I hesitated.

"It — it's not quite what I expected," I said, wondering if Egypt were going to prove a gigantic disappointment; I felt it must be on a vast scale — if it were disappointing it would be overwhelmingly.

Miss Kershaw pulled her hat down onto her head with both hands (she never wears hatpins). She didn't say anything.

With rather a sick, blank feeling, I said, "But it's the unexpected that always happens."

Miss Kershaw bashed in the top of her hat. "No," she stated. "It's the expected that always happens — to the pessimist. I've always cultivated a kind of radiant pessimism myself."

The sun has suddenly burned through the gray, and is searingly hot. The dazzle on the water is almost blinding. All

[2] Sailors from India or Southeast Asia.

the baggage and most of the passengers are crowded forward, silhouetted against the dazzle. I have begun to wonder where they are going and why. . . . I feel sorry I have known so few of them. But I daresay they felt no overpowering desire to know me. And I think somehow the sea has been enough — just to be at sea with such a sense of space; I have craved for space. . . .

The Smiths are leaning on the rail, with white little faces. They are going to book their passage back at once, I believe; though what good can they do now to the poor baby with the plaid frock and the big head?

Mrs. Smith is wearing a green veil, the crude green of a butterfly net. I fancy she told 'Erb the sun was dangerous, but this is her last opportunity before she goes into mourning — and I can picture her looking longingly at that green veil every day during the voyage.

Port Said!

The town seems to rise suddenly out of the sea, a long line of buildings and chimneys, looking black, and not white as I expected. We are approaching the entrance to the Canal, and tugs are fussing out to meet us.

Already we are gliding within the far-stretching stone embankments, and I can see flat-roofed houses and palms, and in a glare of white painful sunshine the great statue of De Lesseps.[3] Huge coal-lighters are coming alongside (though we are not yet in port), swarming with black, grimy Arabs; things that don't look human. It seems a terrible, soul-destroying way to gain a livelihood; it is difficult to realize they are men.

[3] Ferdinand de Lesseps (1805–1894) was the developer of the Suez Canal, and from 1899 to 1956 a monumental statue of his likeness by French sculptor Emmanuel Frémiet (1824–1910) stood at its entrance. The statue now resides at the Suez Canal International Museum in Ismailia, Egypt.

ch. ends next p.

There are ships everywhere, and a few little, bright-colored Arab boats, and natives fishing from the stone embankment.

I must be writing rather incoherently. I don't think even You can know quite what this means to me, realizing this desire. And here I am on the threshold — I don't know why, a little frightened.

That cold dread which came up to me out of the sea before I *knew*, creeps behind every now and then, reminding me I may never go back. . . .

Then in a panic I wish wildly that You really Were. Just for a little while. Not for long. When I am quite sane, and thirty-three and ten months, I know it is much better it should not be; and when I'm — most a woman, perhaps — I'm glad that it cannot be.

Launches are dashing out with friends of passengers. There is a smart police launch with flashing brass and a crew of Soudanese in white uniform and red *tarbush*.[4] I can see little dazzling specks everywhere since looking at the glitter of the sun on the water. Amongst these dazzling specks I see Archie Snell joining his friends in the police launch and taking a lengthy farewell of the flapper, who is halfway down the swinging gangway. The Prawn's friends are smiling skeptically, but the Prawn is very much in earnest. I think he will turn up again later on.

The flapper is looking delicious in an eclipsing hat and yards of superfluous veiling. Quite a lot of people are thinking so; the chief engineer and the third officer are evidently saying so.

I wonder how Miss Kershaw will ever get ashore. The flapper is in her charge, and the flapper will have so many goodbyes

---

[4] Also known as a fez or tarboosh; a typically red brimless felt hat in the shape of a flat-topped cone and ornamented with a black silk tassel that hangs from the crown.

to get through — unless she takes it into her cool little head to dispense with goodbyes: "After all, they're rather rot, aren't they? Seeing the last of anybody is always rot anyhow, especially when they've been decent to you." A good many people have been dangerously decent.

Miss Kershaw has just come and shaken me. The blots resulted. She says the tender will be alongside "directly." She uses "directly," meaning "soon"; Yorkshire people do. Which reminds me I must go and hunt up the old doctor, or I shall not see him again. I like him. And he knows about the Shadow; it seems to make him more intimate than the others, who don't know. He's cool and grave and silent about things — like You, I sometimes think. You silent? You couldn't well be anything else, seeing You don't even exist! It is funny the doctor and Miss Kershaw are both Yorkshire, and I've never been drawn to Yorkshire people before. I shall be sorry to say goodbye to them, somehow.

I am at Suez with Miss Kershaw and the flapper (or Flapette, as she is called; her name is Constance, which of course is impossible).

You can't be more surprised than I am. As You know, I ought to be at Cairo, according to my own plans.

But Miss Kershaw wouldn't hear of our parting. She just said it was nonsense, and when the Flapette actually joined in I began to think it was nonsense. Miss Kershaw said in her rather defiant way that Suez was as well worth seeing as Cairo. "People can't think what on earth I stay there for," she added. "That's the very reason I go."

So I am at Suez, and I have so much to tell You I don't know where to begin; I think it will take me a week to write it all.

I feel so bewildered that my head whirls when I try to put events down as they occurred; I say events, because for me the smallest thing in this country is an event. You see.

We arrived in port too late to catch the noon train, so, as Miss Kershaw had friends in Port Said, she took me to tea.

We drove in an *arrabiyeh*;[1] it was no good: I couldn't believe I was really in Egypt.

Everything was so strange and new, the house as strange as the rest of it; the rooms immensely high and airy, with great tall windows opening on to wooden balconies, warped and bleached by the fierce sun.

From the front balcony I saw a Roman Catholic funeral pass, a little child's coffin in a monstrous white-and-gold hearse, a gorgeous priest and boy acolytes walking before and *arrabiyehs* behind. The whole procession stopped whilst the *arbaghis*[2] wrangled violently. The dispute was still in progress when we left the balcony.

After tea Miss Kershaw took us to a nursery-ground, where trees are grown for the streets; but how different from the dreary expanse of dusty glasshouses and seedmen's hoardings one associates with the name!

The Belgian gardener presented us all impressively with roses, warm and golden.

The nursery-ground was more than that: it was a garden, a fascinating garden with Arabs in white skull-caps and soft-colored tunics, watering plants in the dusk under a pergola[3] with palms and hanging pots, the Arab figures silhouetted against the melting glow beyond.

I saw Eastern houses gleaming then, flat-roofed and many-colored; dazzling mosques growing dim beneath a wonderful orange sky. I did not hear the cry of the *muezzin*,[4]

---

[1] An Egyptian taxi in the form of a horse-drawn carriage.

[2] Cabbies; the drivers of the *arrabiyeh*.

[3] A framework of horizontal trellis supported on columns or posts on which climbing plants are trained to grow.

[4] The Muslim official of a mosque who summons the faithful to prayer five times a day from a minaret (a tall slender tower with one or more balconies).

ch. ends p. 39

which somehow has always appealed to my imagination. I think, do You know, I have had one all these years and not realized the fact.

We walked back in the weird, glowing dusk, over deserted wastes of hard, caked mud, where the salt shone in white patches and where little Arab boys were playing games.

We sat on the balcony overlooking the garden; the balcony was lit up, and we looked through black velvety palms and trees, sighing and mysterious, that gave glimpses of the dusky-glowing sky beyond. I smelt the thrilling, warm smell of an Eastern night; I gave myself up to it. I had no power to withstand and no desire. It was drawing something from me. I gave myself up to it, and was startled when Miss Kershaw told me we must leave for the station.

Time had ceased to be for a little while. I had forgotten the Shadow; as on that blue night at sea, I had got outside my body. I just wasn't there — and You were very real to me. I hated Miss Kershaw because when she spoke I was there again and You weren't — at least, I had remembered, and had to grope for You.

It was extraordinary to see at the station advertisements of Colman's mustard[5] and Van Houten's cocoa[6] and the platforms thronged with black and brown faces and strange costumes.

There were fat, prosperous *Effendis*[7] in the universal

[5] Colman's is an English manufacturer and one of the oldest existing food brands, famous for a limited range of products, almost all being varieties of mustard.
[6] Coenraad Johannes van Houten (1801–1887) was a Dutch chemist and chocolate maker.
[7] Men of high education or social standing in eastern Mediterranean or Arab countries.

tarbush who stared; there were men wrapped in the muffling *burnoos*[8] who showed no curiosity.

I thought I should fear the natives; but I did not, even when they brushed close past.

A sense of bitter disappointment overtook me when I realized it was so dark I could see nothing of the desert, nothing but a stretch of blackness, and near, along the line, mysterious shrubs and palms and desert scrub that looked gray and ghostly.

But I could smell the desert! I sat by the open window drawing in the strange smell of it, that I have heard about and dreamed about. And it caught hold of me, more than anything I had *seen*, I think. It was a warm, dusty, sad sort of smell I can't describe — if I could, it would be less compelling. I don't know what it is, this that takes hold of you; but it was wonderful, coming in from the desert lying weird and silent somewhere beyond the darkness. I kept leaning out to draw great breaths of it. I could feel the desert's nearness.

We had more than an hour to wait at Ismailia.[9] We walked up and down the platform amongst crowds of natives: black, huddled figures of women; Bedouins[10] with the desert in their strange, sad faces, even in their walk; I felt the desert again when they passed. A Bedouin came and gazed curiously into the train, his face shaded under the white hood held by twisted camel hair silver-gilt; a dark face with black beard and piercing eyes that yet suggested infinite melancholy.

---

[8] Also known as burnoose or burnous; long, loose hooded cloaks woven of wool in one piece, worn by Arabs and Moors.

[9] A city in northeastern Egypt, situated on the west bank of the Suez Canal, and located approximately halfway between Port Said to the north and Suez to the south.

[10] Members of any of the nomadic tribes of the Arabian, Syrian, Nubian, or Sahara Deserts.

ch. ends p. 39

It was a very warm, dark night. The warm blackness was muffling, but not oppressive.

Bats flitted about the station in the white glare of electric light, which made the darkness more profound.

Above and through hoarse Arab voices came the persistent shrill sound of crickets that I think will always be bound up for me with Egyptian nights.

I am conscious of the crickets as I was conscious of the intense blue of the Mediterranean. They are always there. They are as much a part of an Egyptian night as the warm, strange scents which make you a little breathless.

There were giant Sudanese coastguards in khaki; Bedouins lay huddled asleep close to the platform edge like bundles of rags — rags that a little breeze stirred and fluttered.

After Ismailia we had to veil our faces. The dust and sand blew in clouds like smoke, gritting between our teeth, filling our eyes, nearly choking us. Everything in the carriage was coated with fine, yellow dust.

It excited me. I rather liked it.

Do You know, I think I am going to love the dust more than anything else; the dust and the smell of it — I don't know why.

The Flapette refused to eat gritty sandwiches and went to sleep, leaning forward uncomfortably to admit of her hat, and muffling herself in chiffon.[11] She didn't think she was going to like Egypt, she said before she went to sleep; it was too much like being inside a vacuum cleaner.

I watched Miss Kershaw, who, imagining herself unobserved, was snuffing up the dusty warm air like an old dog, as though she were glad to be back in Egypt.

---

[11] A fine, sheer fabric typically made of silk, cotton, or nylon.

"I believe you are glad," I said suddenly, thinking rather meanly to take her at a disadvantage, to surprise her into some revelation of herself.

She drew a sharp breath that sucked in her veil, and then said, "Glad? One has to cultivate that condition after about thirty-five." (I have not long in which to be glad!)

She was smiling whimsically.

"I was always a 'nice, sensible girl,'" she said, laying stress upon the words that placed them in inverted commas; "and nice sensible girls are not——"

"Are not glad," I said; "and their skirts always sag at the back."

Miss Kershaw's funny eyes were screwed up and twinkled; her mouth was stretched and rather hard.

"I hope you're not nice and sensible," she stated. It wasn't a question. She must have known — and, anyhow, my skirts don't sag at the back.

"I'm the least sensible person in the world!" I answered, with an odd, glad sound in my voice which I didn't put there, and thinking of You. You most absurd of all Thoughts.

"You must be happy," she stated. She couldn't make it sound a question through habit, but her eyes made it one. Of course she knew I wasn't; women always know. What have I written? I didn't mean to write it. I didn't even know. Only I'm not. I ought to be perhaps, but I'm not; I can't pretend to You. And it isn't the Shadow either; I've got quite used to that. Besides, I never really minded when I had come up with it — before I knew what it was, I feared it. My life has broadened out at last; but I suddenly felt — oh, how can I explain? — I suddenly felt all the wideness, the spaciousness for which I chafed, had disappeared, and just a narrow black way opened, with no

ch. ends next p.

going back! No going back. That's what the Shadow stands
for — and no going forward.

For an instant I felt this spaciousness I craved a mere delusion; it was a sort of illuminating flash; I can't recapture it.

And it all passed whilst Miss Kershaw took off her "nice,
sensible" hat and shook the dust from it

I found myself saying, "Of course I am happy!" I felt quite
fierce. But Miss Kershaw knew, and I knew she knew I shouldn't
say that if I were happy.

Women do know such things, even women like Miss Kershaw, who seem to have got hold of the wrong body. I don't
suppose You would have divined it. You aren't subtle, remember.

Sometimes You surprise me, though; most of all by the
things You say through leaving them unsaid.

So in the rattling, dusty train Miss Kershaw and I came a
little nearer knowing one another.

The Flapette slept, looking white and soulful as she never
does awake. The awakening was a disillusion; she crossly
demanded the gritty sandwiches she had rejected. All the same,
I wish I could look soulful under any circumstances. I am quite
sure I don't.

When at last I crept into bed under a mosquito-net, I could
not sleep for weariness and strangeness; weird cries outside,
stray cats and the cocks that in Egypt crow day and night.

My body was dreadfully weary — You know that heavy feeling like a log sunk in deep water? — but "the top of my head
was awake," as the Flapette puts it.

All I had seen kept getting mixed up with my old blank life
among turnip fields, and with You and with the Shadow that
is Always There. Yet all the time I was wide awake, staring

through the dim whiteness of the mosquito-net, listening to innumerable strange sounds of an Egyptian night.

And I wanted to sleep.

In dreams I forget You're only an Idea, that there isn't any You.

Somehow when Miss Kershaw told me I wasn't happy — for it amounted to that — somehow You became less real. I groped for You and couldn't find You. So I wanted sleep, because asleep, better than forgetting — one need not remember.

I awoke to the blinding white glare of sunshine falling in bars through the half-closed jalousies;[1] the white glare, and the harsh cries of street-sellers. The man who sells Arab bread has an anguished cry which ends in a long-drawn moan. I don't think I shall get used to it; it breaks through sleep with startling suddenness.

Another street-seller groans dismally, dropping on the last note to a queer, uncanny whisper.

There is a turquoise sky with great shining English clouds. Somehow I hadn't pictured clouds in Egypt; I had always been led to imagine "brazen skies" — a description that used to make me sorry, long before I had a remote prospect of ever seeing Egypt, sorry because in my mind I connected it with brass-band contests.

I am glad there are clouds.

The hotel is very high and white and new. There is a garden in the middle. (Haven't I explained this is a hotel?) I mean the

[1] Shutters made of adjustable angled, horizontal slats for regulating the passage of air and light.

garden is in the form of a courtyard. It is curiously unlike an English garden — not that I know much about them; ours at home consisted of tile-edging and zinc labels.

There are tiers of plants in pots as one sees them in a greenhouse.

I hate greenhouses. They give me a gasping feeling. I can't bear to be shut in or confined in any way; it's a sort of "claustrophobia." I suppose that is why I am longing for my first glimpse of the desert. I suppose that is why I have come so far seeking wideness — space.

In this sweet Eastern courtyard are palms and corals in big faded green tubs, and a little stone well (it may be cement, but stone sounds nicer and older), on top of which is some feathery, drooping plant.

Spreading over almost all the court are branches of a great goldmore tree with soft, delicate foliage and long seed-pods. The wonderful scarlet blossoms are over.

There are fan palms, the sort that look so tired always in bay-windows, and vivid poinsettia, whose live crimson throbs if you look long at it. There is a smell of musk and rosemary.

The Flapette and I saw a Praying Mantis and a great brown locust on the climbing geranium, that with bougainvillea[2] makes a mass of passionate color over the balcony and against the sky.

The Flapette said she thought John Baptist was a beast if he really ate locusts. The Flapette is not to be suppressed; evidently the top of her head hadn't kept her awake.

---

[2] Any woody shrubs or ornamental vines of the genus Bougainvillea of Central and South America, having small flowers surrounded by large vibrant and variously colored bracts (leaflike structures often positioned beneath a flower).

A frangipani tree[3] has a few exquisite waxen blooms whose sweetness is almost piercing.

There are roses and chrysanthemums and a picturesque villain of a gardener with gold-and-white *mandil*,[4] black waistcoat, blue *galabieh*,[5] and baggy trousers bunched round the waist, whilst he paddles to and fro watering the flowers.

The Flapette thinks it a rotten garden, because there is no grass and most of the plants are in pots; philistine that she is, she calls it the "area." She contrives to be charming when she is most hateful.

There is a banana tree in the garden (I wonder which way up bananas grow?). There is mimosa — not the lodging-house mantel sort; there are flowering bushes of which I don't know the names, and red pepper and Cape gooseberries, which I dislike because so often I have had to "make them do" for church decoration.

I hoped there would be tobacco plants, but perhaps it is not the right time of year. There aren't any. I had so thought there would be; I feel like a woman looking for some specially sweet, dim white thing in the life that is not there, and never will be for her.

I don't know why I have these odd thoughts about insignificant things. But nothing is insignificant now — ever since I felt those little ships like presences in the Church on the hill, things have had an extraordinary significance. And the strange part is, I don't know what all this significance signifies. . . .

I've wandered. But You must make allowances. It was the

---

[3] Of the genus Plumeria; deciduous shrubs or small trees that produce clusters of fragrant flowers.
[4] Turban.
[5] A djellaba; a typically woolen and loose-fitting, ankle-length hooded robe worn by Arabs.

scent of the tobacco flower. You know what tobacco is; I've seen what a long way You've got sometimes when that old meerschaum[6] has gone out (how do I know so much about You — and so little?)

I like Your meerschaum thoughts. Somehow they are so absolutely Your own thoughts, no one else could think them — except me! I suppose I think them. Sometimes it is hard — I write "hard" because I don't mean "difficult," but "hurtful" too — so hard to believe You aren't and weren't and never will be. I don't see why You should look like that when You are merely an Idea, an absurd Idea of my own. It is very unreasonable.

Opposite the hotel is a waste[7] sandy space, and beyond this again three palm trees that are going to mean rather a lot to me, I don't know why; a strip of yellow sand and turquoise sea. No, not turquoise — more intense; dreamy mountains, rose and yet violet, a color you cannot believe in till you see it.

To right and left are flat-roofed houses, each with its shutters and hanging balconies, crooked and sun-blistered. The houses are yellow and white and salmon and blue, shades that have faded and at evening seem to reflect the sunset colors — at least, I feel sure they do. My imagination is running riot; You see it has been such a poor, pallid, starved sort of thing till now. And now I feel as though I were drinking color; I've not only been starved, I've been thirsty all these years.

Some of the houses are a mellow rich cream that is strangely lovely against the deep blue sky. "Deep" is the right word. To look up into it is like looking down into deep water. The sheer depth of color is a delight.

---

[6] A pipe with a bowl made from meerschaum (a soft white, yellowish, or pink clay-like material consisting of hydrated magnesium silicate, found predominately in Turkey).

[7] Unused or uncultivated.

ch. ends p. 47

Still farther away is an Arab village, low cream and brown ruined-looking buildings and a long line of gray-green palms; beyond these a strip of desert in a brownish-violet haze.

At the back of the hotel is a yard which I love even more than the garden; it is utterly Eastern and delicious. Imagine a delicious backyard in England! Across this yard are the servants' quarters, flat cream-washed buildings.

Here the brown cows are brought everyday to be milked, a *soffragi*[8] standing by to see that the milk is not adulterated; the milkman carrying round with him a stuffed calf, a relic presumably of some ancient superstition. There is a little enclosure with aloes under a flat trellis, which supports a gnarled old vine, and there is a big palm, gray and dusty, whose stiff branches I hear scraping stealthily at night.

One of my windows looks out over a vista of hanging balconies and green jalousies, white flat roofs and palms.

Another window looks on to the crumbling wall of a tall house with a little balcony, where an Arab girl crouches all day, peering through the woodwork.

As I write I look up the street to an enclosure full of goats, which are always wandering; sweet things with Dachshund ears and queer Roman noses. They are black and brown, white and dust-color. I love already a brown one with white spots, who has a passion for straying.

Fowls and lean cats and pariah dogs (don't pariahs sound nice and Eastern?) are always prowling the sunbaked streets, and Arab babies, scarcely bigger than the fowls, stagger in trailing robes.

Down this street — already I call it mine — pass water-carts

---

[8] An Arabic laborer or worker.

drawn by mules, an Arab in blue *galabieh* and white turban perched high up; women muffled in the black *hubarah*[9] and *yashmak*,[10] many of them wearing striped stockings and European high-heeled shoes, and over the stockings big brass and silver anklets.

Often they carry flat baskets of dates on their heads; ripe dates are a luscious red, with green leaves hanging down all round. There come men selling native bread on a flat board, or fruit piled in gorgeous heaps, riotous heaps of color on a barrow. Everywhere such color. Arabs in long robes, European coat, white tennis boots, and *tarbush*; Greek priests; monks in brown habits with shaven heads and huge umbrellas; Bedouins with their graceful walk — Bedouins always seem to "go softly," like Agag, wasn't it?[11] — Bedouins in their dust-colored dusty rags; blind beggars feeling their way with a long staff; Arabs selling lemonade and liquorice water in jars slung round the waist in a wicker stand; donkey-carts with black, glistening goatskins, which I try not to connect with those live, most lovable goats; donkeys hidden beneath great masses of green sugarcane, sweeping the ground on either side.

There goes an Arab in orange turban, blue *galabieh*, and orange shoes, riding a white donkey jingling masses of coins and bells. There go some dignified old men with white beards and slow gait. Their glorious robes are of shimmering satin, maize and violet, steel-blue, green, and brilliant orange.

Think of the color! Think what it must be for me after those

---

[9] A large shawl which envelops the whole person. Upper-class women typically wear black, while unmarried women frequently wear white.

[10] Also yashmac or yasmak; a type of veil worn by women to cover their faces in public.

[11] In the Bible (1 Samuel 15), Agag is the Amalekite king who was spared King Saul's extermination campaign.

ch. ends next p.

colorless years — they were worse than drab, they were colorless. I have wanted color so, color in my life.

Perhaps it would not have been such a meager, meaningless thing had there been more color in it. But what goes to make up color in lives? . . . Isn't color glorious? I feel I want to bathe in it and the wonderful dusty sunshine.

You must imagine all this I have just tried to describe seen through a haze of sunshine, blinding, blistering sunshine, and golden dust! I told You I was going to love the dust. Already dust seems to mean Egypt and Egypt dust. And, after all, dust is rather wonderful, isn't it? We ourselves are supposed to be just dust — at least I am. You are not even dust. I shall never be able to think of Egypt without thinking of dust, gilded dust and dust from the desert, with its strange, sad smell.

All this I have described has passed within a space of perhaps twenty minutes down my wonderful little street. Are You surprised I feel bewildered by such wealth of shifting color?

Though I have not ventured yet beyond the courtyard, it has all begun — begun? it began when I smelt the dust last night — to fascinate me. No, that is not the word. To grip me. Almost I feel as though it wanted to absorb me, take away my individuality. I don't know why I struggle against this feeling; I suppose it is ridiculous. And all this has happened within the last twenty-four hours!

The Flapette has just rushed in to drag me to see a native funeral pass. I shall have to get used to funerals. They pass all day. It was very weird: crowds of Arabs shuffling along to a more or less European band making distinctly cheerful music; the Arabs all chanting from the Koran and carrying the coffin covered with crude pink cotton and sprigs of greenery; stuck at the head — rather pathetic, somehow — the dead man's red *tarbush*.

Behind came a crowd of women waving black scarfs. They looked as though they were dusting the coffin, the Flapette said. They wailed in the Biblical manner, shrill and shivery. It gave me a queer feeling in the spinal column, like the bagpipes.

It was such a mixture of the weird, the humorous, and the pathetic; I suppose pathos ought to have predominated, but I am afraid humor predominated as far as I was concerned. Only the red *tarbush* gave me a pang somehow.

That was such a human note. It made me remember a man had died. . . .

This is the end of my first day at Suez, and, do You know, I've come near to a big conclusion about Egypt. I don't quite know what it is yet! So You will have to wait.

I have been into the town with Miss Kershaw and the Flapette.

The strange charm of it; the jostling Arabs, the hoarse voices, the stalls piled high with gourds and gleaming fruit; the smell of it and the color! I longed to penetrate some of the dim side-streets which lead to that dream-place, the native bazaar.

We strolled afterward down the dock road where you can see the Red Sea, looking most palely blue, and the wonderful Attica hills away beyond shining stretches of wet sand. I did not think the mountains would seem so near; I don't even know whether I expected mountains at all. I somehow like to feel mountains near, though I have never known any before.

I don't know why mountains satisfy and at the same time give you a sort of ache for something you've never had and probably never will have. The sea is like that, too.

Miss Kershaw said the night was not effective. It wasn't a

night of brilliant color, but the mountains were dusky purple and the sky full of purple cloud-masses through which golden light streamed, touching the tide-left pools.

Any kind of night here would be wonderful. There is something about an Egyptian night — just because it is so elusive and dreamlike it is wonderful, I think. You have to feel an Egyptian night to know what I mean. To say you would have to see one is not a bit the same thing. Perhaps that is really the difference: an English night you just see; you feel an Egyptian night.

I've come to my big conclusion — or rather it has come to me.

I don't think I often come to conclusions; do You? Or not about big Things. Most Things seem to have no end but go on and on, so there isn't any conclusion to be drawn. The biggest Things always are going on.

The Conclusion, or perhaps Conviction, came to me, then, and I had to accept it.

Miss Kershaw and I have been for a walk by the Sweet Water Canal (the name quenches thirst) without the Flapette. She had insisted on "prowling round" in the hottest part of the day, whilst I meekly took my siesta, pitying Miss Kershaw.

And mosquito bites and three new freckles had spoiled the Flapette's temper.

So Miss Kershaw and I went alone, and I was glad. I always suspect I am jealous of the Flapette's youth because I feel so much older when she is there; and I think it is hateful to be jealous in just that way.

ch. ends next p.

We reached the Canal by a sandy road bordered by palm trees, soft gray tamarisk,[1] and great dusty clumps of prickly pear, which when the sun is low all seem massed together, dim in a glittering haze of dust. How I love the dust! Down the road come Arabs riding white donkeys or driving goats; shy Bedouins, their faces muffled like their tread, walking with rhythmic slow grace, and seldom speaking; tall, splendid Coastguards odorous of garlic; Arab children whose garments only half conceal their supple beauty; grave monks; tired women in the universal black *hubarah*; all passing with shuffling feet through the thick dust and the low sunshine that gleams in sad, restless eyes or touches, dazzling, some silver ornament.

Between the gray, rustling palms, between the sighing reeds and vivid *berseem*[2] fields, the long procession of strange people comes.

The Sweet Water Canal winds toward the desert — this in itself is alluring — with tall reeds on either side, and natives in every color imaginable, and many I had never imagined, washing at its margin.

I saw a man put down his praying-mat and bow himself — a strangely impressive figure.

Each side of the Canal are fields and little gardens, not gardens as we know them, not even enclosed — gardens where roses still bloom and white turbans glimmer in the dusk beneath vine-covered trellises.

I saw a buffalo — a *gamŏos*,[3] I mean — wallowing at the water's edge, such a quiet gray thing with mild eyes. And I saw

---

[1] Also known as salt cedar; any of numerous shrubs or small trees of the genus Tamarix with slender branches bearing tiny scale-like leaves and feathery clusters of pink or whitish flowers.

[2] Also known as Egyptian clover; flowering clover native to Egypt and Syria.

[3] Water buffalo.

camels for the first time, excepting the dismal sort you see in menageries, that somehow look as though the moth had got at them. These were Coastguard camels, beautiful creatures with rugs and a hole left for the hump!

It was as we walked back the Conviction came to me.

As we walked back the sky was throbbing color; a gold that was dusky yet glowed, mingled with purest rose which seemed to glow through the violet mountains till they looked translucent. The light streamed through them!

And against the wonderful sky soft palm trees stood, infinitely mysterious. Palm trees are strangely beautiful at night. I can't convey even a little the wonder of it.

A great deathlike sudden silence came swiftly from the desert engulfing day — the desert that far away seemed a blue, dim expanse, so vast it was almost terrible.

The silence flowed round us till it filled the waiting night like water filling to the brim an earthen *goolah*.[4] It filled and ran over in little, whispering sounds almost too small to hear. The crickets' piercing note grew audible.

It was just then I knew — that Egypt is a country to be happy in. . . .

I didn't mean You to understand. I don't think I understood quite myself till You looked like that.

But it is, isn't it?

---

[4] Water pot.

Two things have happened. To begin with, the Prawn has happened. Already; yes. I did not think it would be so soon. He arrived at the hotel more nearly resembling a lobster than a prawn, but cool enough to pretend he had turned up by chance. The Flapette was cool enough to make no pretense of believing him.

I think she is glad.

She had been growing "nourished" for some time past. The Flapette is staving off that condition for the time being, and the Prawn is naturally ubiquitous. As a consequence of his descent upon us. Miss Kershaw and I are thrown more together — age gravitating to age, or something unpleasant of the sort! But anyhow I do feel drawn to her, especially since this that I am going to tell You.

We had walked down to Port Tewfik.[1] At Port Tewfik is

[1] Originally named Port Tewfik (or Tawfiq) after then ruler Khedive Tewfik (1852–1892), the port was built in 1867 by the Suez Canal Company, being their third after Port Said and Ismailia. Today it is known as Suez Port and is located at the northern tip of the Gulf of Suez on the Red Sea at the southern entrance of the canal.

a long, straight avenue of *lebbek* trees[2] or Nile acacias,[3] through which you catch glimpses of the Canal with beautiful lateen sails and far away a line of sandy hills which at evening take a soft, exquisite rose — a color that seems unreal, a color you never thought could exist.

And the water is pale and glittering with long, oily reflections of boats, dreamy greens and reds and blues.

It happened just when the trees seem to shroud themselves in a warm, sweet dusk whilst water and sky still glow, and a dusty wind full of strange sad scents rises, rustling the dry leaves of palms.

Again the conviction seized me. Egypt is a country to be happy in. . . .

Otherwise you must find how pitiless it is. For there is something pitiless about Egypt, just as the desert is pitiless, and the sun. All the time I struggle against that feeling of being absorbed, losing my individuality. I can't explain what I mean.

We sat down in the scented dusk beneath the *lebbek* trees, and I leaned forward with my chin in my hands. I had passed the borderland between thinking and Thoughts; my thoughts were all mixed up with the pale glitter of the water.

"There's a lot in hands, you know," Miss Kershaw stated, suddenly and harshly. I didn't know she had been looking at mine. I have rather nice hands. I have always felt a certain satisfaction that I am "finished off" nicely in little ways, whatever else I lack.

I dragged my thoughts slowly from the wonderful glitter beyond the *lebbek* trees.

"Do you mean my hands?" I said.

---

[2] Albizia lebbeck; a large deciduous tree that bears fragrant white flowers and long seed pods.

[3] A frequently thorny tree or shrub that bears spikes or clusters of yellow or white flowers.

I looked at them with sudden interest and sudden shamefacedness.

"I'm afraid they've never done anything worth doing," I remarked; "I'm afraid they're not a bit capable hands." Instinctively I had glanced at hers.

"Capable hands!" she repeated, with a queer sound beneath her rasping tone. She paused, and I read bitterness into the pause, as though she had spoken. I was frightened at the emotion which she hid. When the pause had lasted so long I felt a kind of mental goose-flesh, she said:

"I had capable hands. It's enough to — well, to damn a woman's hands to look capable. . . ."

Her tone was quite expressionless, but I felt emotion tearing its way through.

"And what's the good," she went on harshly, "of capable hands — if they're not capable of securing happiness?"

I seized on a thought that was still part of the pale glitter.

"But if they're capable of giving it?" I said.

She turned and looked at me; then looked again at my hands.

"Giving. . . . You're always talking of giving, aren't you?"

I was rather breathless suddenly.

"Because I've been allowed to give so little. And I could have given so much . . . I think sometimes."

All at once I knew it. I wanted to Give. And I mayn't; it is all thrust back on me; it just isn't needed. If You had really Been — no, it is such a big thought I can't see all of it at once.

Yet perhaps I've given more because You haven't Been; it sounds like a paradox. It almost frightens me to know how much I might have given.

"How many women's lives are summed up by that?" I don't

know if I said it aloud, but I suppose I did, because Miss Ker-shaw answered, "Good Lord, thousands. . . ."

It was extraordinary and rather terrible to hear Miss Ker-shaw speaking like this. I suppose the dusk made her able to speak. Darkness enables you to pretend you are alone, or at any rate gives you a fictitious courage, like having your face blacked for theatricals.

You say so many things at night that you simply couldn't say in the morning when you'd just said your prayers and brushed your teeth. I mean I do; but I should not have dreamed Miss Kershaw would.

It was somehow quite a shock. But there's a woman shut up inside that odd exterior. I saw the eyes of her last night — just like any other ordinary, tragic woman.

I said:

"I've never given — anything."

I felt so desolate I wanted the assurance of human sympathy, and Miss Kershaw seemed human suddenly.

"Perhaps it has been your own fault," she stated, so harshly I was startled. I didn't know if it had.

"It often is," she said, without an atom of feeling; the shut-up woman was taking cover behind her native millstone-grit.

"It was in my case," she added.

Somehow I had never imagined this. Somehow I had never imagined her different from what she now appeared.

Had I shown the faintest sign of curiosity or sympathetic interest she would not have said another word.

Intuition, perhaps instinct, told me that. So I said nothing.

"You've a sense of humor," she stated. "Perhaps you will see the humor of it. I can put it in a nutshell. I was a girl with 'no nonsense about me.' There was no nonsense about — him either. Because of it we got on well. We were good pals. We knew what we were doing; there was nothing left to the imagination — we should have scorned imagination. It was all — well, cut and dried, if you like. There was no nonsense about us."

She paused, and the sound that wasn't quite a laugh made me wince.

"We prided ourselves upon it. Doesn't look as though this nutshell held elements of tragedy, does it, eh? . . . But that's why — nothing happened in my life. Don't you think it amusing? I thought you had a sense of humor. I laugh at it yet."

She did, but it was laughter that froze.

I didn't say anything; there was nothing I could say. I knew a girl with more nonsense than most must have come along; I read it in the eyes of the tragic woman crouching behind the grim stone wall.

"I hope there's plenty of nonsense about you," Miss Kershaw said almost savagely. "For goodness' sake acquire it if you don't possess it."

My mind was filled right up with You and Notre Dame de la Garde and the little ships.

"I have acquired it," I answered.

"Some are born nonsensical — and they inherit the earth; some attain nonsense, and some have to be content with nonsense thrust upon them!" she remarked with a queer jumble of misquotations and a laugh more like herself — at least, I mean less like Herself.

"How did you get Nonsense?" she suddenly demanded, as she might have asked how I got religion or measles.

"I don't know," I said; "I think it — got me."

"Then for heaven's sake stick to it."

"There isn't anything as satisfying as nonsense," I said, feeling I had hit upon a new truth, possibly because it is so old.

"As to that," Miss Kershaw returned, unexpectedly, "platitude though it may be, there isn't anything as satisfying as giving — for a woman."

"But most of us can't give, or mayn't give."

"No, most of us mayn't give," she agreed.

And I want to give. I need to give. . . .

I seemed to know such a lot more about Things when we left the *lebbek* avenue.

That is the second happening; I have met Miss Kershaw tonight for the first time, and it has frightened me.

Life is so much more tragic and laughable than I had thought.

I can't shake off the memory of Miss Kershaw saying "I had capable hands. . . . There was no nonsense about us." . . .

Do You like capable hands, I wonder? I wish I knew.

There must be quite a lot of Nonsense about me, I think.

The others have been into the desert, and I refused to go. They went in a motor, and I couldn't bear my first glimpse of the desert to be like that. Things never happen as one imagined, I know — but I felt I couldn't do it. An old clergyman, one of the few people in the hotel (it puzzles me what he or any of them are doing here) made up a party to go over the new oil refinery, which is a monstrous blot on the desert. He is the fat sort of person one would expect to take an interest in oil refineries.

The Flapette said when they all left the car they were pushed by natives on a trolley for about half a mile. I should have hated that, hearing their sobbing breath as they toiled in the sand. It is a good thing I haven't to deal with natives, I suppose; I endow them with all my own sensations. Miss Kershaw told me today I had got nerves and ought to be ashamed of myself. I must confess I didn't know I had the things, though the doctor hinted at it. Perhaps I "got" them when I got Nonsense! I am afraid I derive a certain satisfaction in the knowledge that a "nice, sensible" person wouldn't have them, anyway.

Besides the clergyman there are only three other people

here at present, all rather unsatisfactory from the Flapette's point of view.

There is a sallow woman in the thirties and green spectacles. Horrid thought! I'm in the thirties myself, and it is only a chance I'm not in green spectacles.

If I had been, would You still — should I have been just as much to You? I don't think if I had worn green spectacles I'd have had the face to invent You — yes, invent; I make myself write it now and then.

There are two maiden ladies who disagree about closed shutters and get feverish when the *mish-mish*[1] doesn't go round; they bring a *minsha*[2] to every meal. They wear silver discs with Moslem prayers round their necks — and are aggressive supporters of a Nonconformist mission!

It is rather tragic, growing like that. I suppose one might easily.

The worst thing about these well-meaning people is their depressing, desperate cheerfulness.

I wonder if these old ladies started out seeking Space, as I am seeking it, and found — Space was just a delusion.

The parson is stout, rather like a well-stuffed leather armr-chair; he moves smoothly on oiled castors.

He has a shining outlook, which blinds you rather at first, and a shining morning face.

This drew from Miss Kershaw the caustic remark, "A shining face may point to sanctity; more often it merely points to yellow soap."

There is something about the Rev. Arthur Clarges I don't like. Perhaps it is the shine; somehow I suspect the shine comes off when he is alone. His glossy surface dazzles.

---

[1] Stewed apricots.
[2] Fly-whisk.

ch. ends p. 65

He turns on his smile in a switching sort of way like a lighthouse; you find yourself waiting for the next flash. Your eyes haven't time to adjust themselves to the dazzle before it is turned on again.

One night I heard women wailing over a death in the old part of the town; the sound came across the water. It is the most weird and utterly desolate sound I ever heard; there is in it a stretching out of empty arms toward emptiness, the wail of all women who have ever been, and suffered. Yet I suppose they are just hired wailers.[3]

> "Is all that we see or seem
> But a dream within a dream?"[4]

You are. . . .

The Rev. Arthur has conducted us through the native bazaars. I have heard the *muezzin* on a minaret calling the Faithful to prayer; I think it is far more impressive than a church bell clanging, though, or because, I am a curate's orphan and a curate's niece.

I told Miss Kershaw I didn't like Rev. Arthur. "He is the fat sort of clergyman," I explained, "who constantly says 'I believe you' with no conviction——"

She grunted, "And 'I Believe' with less!"

But I was grateful to him for piloting us round the bazaars. Such color; such dusky interiors — fruit stalls piled high with sumptuous color beneath dim lanterns, where shadowy

[3] Professional or paid mourners, also called moirologists and mutes, are compensated to lament or deliver a eulogy and help comfort and entertain grieving families. The occupation originates from Egyptian, Chinese, Mediterranean, and Near Eastern cultures, and is still practiced in China and other Asian countries.

[4] The final two lines of each stanza of the poem "A Dream Within a Dream," by Edgar Allan Poe (1808–1849).

forms sit cross-legged within; Arabs squatting at the roadside grinding; Arabs offering for sale dull green beans in bowls; or, crouched on the curb, fat and immovable, smoking the bubbling *sheesha*.[5]

There are knots of dignified old men always with the word *feloos*[6] upon their lips; Arabs roasting *doura*[7] over charcoal fires, squatting on the barrow amongst the corncobs, keeping the charcoal in a glow with a little fan. Always mouthing *"maslum"*[8] and *"maskin"*[9] as you pass, beggars clutch with maimed and withered hands, turning terrible sightless eyes black with loathsome flies that buzz and crawl.

Twisting narrow streets are brimful of color and of movement, crammed with strange faces and strange costumes. Yellowish, curly Barbary sheep, tied up and lying in doorways like dogs; dusty fowls and dusty goats; cats creeping round the *zerhalahs*.[10]

The presence of the *Nasrani*[11] is not resented, though few penetrate into these odorous, dusky streets. An old man I noticed preaching a Holy War, from a long strip of parchment like an author's proofs. He paid no heed as we passed.

The Arabs are curious and often eager to be photographed, always for a *baksheesh*.[12]

Bedouins stalk through the crowd, obviously not of it, dignified and aloof in their dusty, black-striped garments. There are shops where the brilliant *mandil* or head-scarf is hung in

---

[5] Water pipe.
[6] Money.
[7] Indian corn.
[8] Afflicted.
[9] Poor.
[10] Ash bins.
[11] Christian.
[12] A small sum of money given as a tip or charity.

ch. ends p. 55

dazzling assortment; shops with strings of wooden rosaries, orange and brown and scarlet; potter's shops with pale earthen *zeers* [13] and *goolahs*; shops warmly glinting with old, dented brassware.

I mean to take some photographs for — what am I saying?

Anyhow, they could not give You the riot of color, the warm duskiness, the nauseating, compelling smells and sounds. The air is heavy with incense, with garlic and the oily reek of *fessikh*. [14]

The hoarse cries of "*Ya meenuk*" [15] and "*She maluk*" [16] are not so frequent in these streets; *arrabiyehs* do not often penetrate.

The bazaar is one of the bewildering confused places you find in dreams, almost as impossibly delicious.

I rarely sleep till late. The natives talking and singing — a monotonous harping upon one note — below my window sound almost in the room, their voices are so loud and harsh; they frightened me at first. They pass at all hours of the night. Sometimes I hear the *darabooka* [17] like heart-throbs in the stillness; sometimes drunken Italians go by, singing and playing mandolins.

We have been for a fishing picnic on the Gulf. It was

[13] Large vessels of porous clay used as filters.
[14] Small fish, salted, and partly sun-cured and swathed in rancid oil.
[15] "To your right."
[16] "To your left."
[17] Tom-tom.

organized by the Rev. Arthur. He has taken it upon himself to organize things. He is that sort.

I wish the Flapette wasn't dazzled by that searchlight of his, but he won't make a fool of the Flapette; in her eyes he is quite an old, "stuffy" person, doubtless. She was brought up against a happening today which may put her on her guard. The Prawn is stuck fast in the meshes of the net; he proposed to the Flapette today.

Breakfast on the launch was a little depressing. The meal was too early or too late for everybody.

One or two of the party became unnaturally quiet over ham-and-eggs, and no one but the Rev. Arthur appreciated the buttered toast. I noticed he let butter run down his chin. I hated all of it; I wanted to be out there on the water quite alone; well, with You, then. When I say alone it means with You.

After the boys had removed unappreciated eggs we dropped anchor and baited our lines.

The Rev. Arthur seemed to take a horrid pleasure in baiting hooks; he fingered the bait lingeringly, always with his persistent smile. He and I shared a line because the Prawn had forestalled him with the Flapette.

The Rev. Arthur's hands are fat and white and freckled.

We caught unwholesome, freakish-looking fish, Biblical fish, the sort you ought by rights to cook over a neat Moses-in-the-wilderness fire of sticks.

The sun blistered, but it was dreamlike out there on the water, calm as a lake, a color You couldn't imagine; I couldn't till I saw it. The water has a crystal purity, suffused with color, liquid chrysophase.[18] The wonderful rose-deep mountains spilled rose into that sea-color.

---

[18] A milky or grayish microcrystalline translucent variety of quartz.

ch. ends next p.

I tried to shut out the Rev. Arthur, smiling as he unhooked monstrous, fishy things. I tried to shut out the woman with the spectacles and jaundiced outlook; the maiden ladies with their platitudes and crochet. I tried to shut out the Flapette and Archie Snell with their simulated boredom and enthusiasm; even Miss Kershaw, the only one intent upon her fishing — and she kept as it were a weather eye for the Flapette.

I tried to shut them all out and be sumptuously selfish for a little while, with the green-cool water and rose mountains and devouring sun.

You see what I am like. I don't intend You to get a wrong impression of me. I want You to be unreasonable, sometimes, and like me because I'm myself.

You sometimes are unreasonable for all that cool, judicial air. We both are sometimes, splendidly.

I knew something had happened when the Flapette left her place in the bows. She came and inquired after my luck with exaggerated interest and a trembling lip. She told me afterward her cheeks felt as though they had been starched. I can't help thinking she was at the same time a little triumphant as well as scared and indignant. She looked pale, almost spirituelle;[19] but I could hear her uneven breathing as she leaned over me and slipped a small, clammy hand into mine. It was so unlike the Flapette that I knew at once what had happened, and the Rev. Arthur knew. He turned his searchlight upon her, and I saw her blink.

I hated his slow, dazzling smile and horrid insight.

I pressed her hand tentatively, watching the many native boats, brilliant greens and reds, that drifted over the dreamy

---

[19] Marked by refinement, grace, or delicacy of mind.

sea, their reflections brilliant as jewels, their crews bronze Arabs in soft blue *galdbiehs*, with white or yellow turbans.

I was still trying to shut the Flapette out, to keep her out.

She gave my hand a squeeze. There was tremulous appeal in that squeeze. I should think the Flapette had never stooped before to appeal — to another woman. I was touched. And then I realized what it meant. She would confide in me. I should have to listen sympathetically to yet another confidence. Bitterness welled. Then a lurking sense of humor got the best of it. There was something so ironical concerning this second confession; the Flapette confiding about the Prawn, who had already confided in me — about myself.

I was tempted to tell the Flapette all, only I suspected it was not my sense of the ridiculous which prompted me. She would, I knew, assume an air of superiority, almost mystery, and all the time it would be on the tip of my tongue to tell her I had refused the stupid boy. It was a sore temptation.

After some time I looked up. The Flapette was laughing rather shrilly with the maiden ladies. I knew by some expression of her face she was aware of the searchlight turned upon her.

The Flapette isn't a child. And yet what a child she is! Younger than I ever was or ever could have been, I sometimes think. I was done out of my childhood; I have never really been young.

The Prawn was rather piteous, crumpled up, and very pink as though he had been shelled and potted. No doubt it is desperately real to him; his partiality for me was desperately real — at the time.

The Flapette came to my room and brushed her hair in silence for at least three minutes.

I suppose she expected me to make the plunge. Not only am I the official receiver of confidences, but invariably I am expected to pave the way.

I wasn't going to; I was rather hating her because I wanted so much to tell her about that ridiculous night at sea, and I had determined I wouldn't.

The hand holding the brush moved more and more slowly, but still she said nothing and still I gave her no help. I almost enjoyed making the opening difficult. You see what I am like——

The brush stopped suddenly, and I heard a strand of hair snap with a brittle sound in the waiting silence.

"Look here," she began characteristically, hoping I should break in, but I didn't.

"Look here," she said again; "I suppose you knew something was — going forward today?"

"I saw you and the Prawn going forward," I replied, venturing a weak pun with the idea of keeping the conversation on a plane that would emphasize her childishness.

"I'm not a child!" she retorted.

The brush became animated.

"And, look here, I don't see why you shouldn't say Archie Snell." The Prawn was evidently upon a different standing now he had proposed.

"It can't be very exhilarating to be proposed to by a prawn," I said meditatively, playing with my desire to divulge the truth. I forgot that I had given her, thrust upon her, an opening.

"I knew you twigged all about it." She clutched at the opening, and the silver brush paused. "But I did think you'd be decent, and not go out of your way to make fun of him." The Prawn had attained quite an enviable position by being refused.

"I'm sorry," I said, inadequate.

She accepted this with a wave of the brush.

She began, "After all, a man can't do you a greater honor——"

I seemed to have read that somewhere, many times.

I watched a mosquito making persistent efforts to insinuate itself through the mesh of the net.

"Yes," I said, more than ever inadequate. I have always believed myself adequate as a confidante, if in no other role.

"I say, you're not exactly sympathetic." The Flapette was aggrieved.

"I sympathize more than you know," I said, handling again the desire to impart the truth.

"I don't mean like that!" she cried indignantly, and caught the brush and her knuckles against the chair back.

"You talk as though Archie were——"

"A prawn. Well, wasn't he — not long since?"

ch. ends p. 72

She flushed quickly and charmingly. She does everything quickly and charmingly. When I flush I feel it is cruelly slow.

"Well," I said, wishing to get it over before I betrayed myself. "He proposed and——"

"I refused him, of course."

"And——?" I questioned. I must have been exasperating.

She looked at me with pity. I could have borne it had she looked fierce.

"You don't understand, of course," she remarked quite gently; then, petulant, as the child who has been deprived of the desired scene, "I might have known you wouldn't. How should you?"

After a short silence the Flapette did a most surprising thing. With a swish of satin kimono she was half kneeling beside me.

The woman I suppose lurks even in her was brought up against something she could not fathom, but only just missed fathoming. She had begun to wonder. I warmed to her; she was suddenly soft and shining, questioning and wholly bewildered. Even while my heart warmed I felt a sudden bitter sense of the unfairness of things, seeing her soft and shining like this.

"Tell me all about it," I said, and felt rather noble actually to beg her confidence when I knew she had been dying to force it upon me.

She sat back on her heels, prepared to enjoy herself. She wasn't shining and soft any longer: that had passed already; she was very young and rather hard and absolutely self-satisfied again.

"Guess how he put it," she said.

"Is that quite playing the game? Even a prawn——" I dreaded the protracted account of what he had said and how he said it.

She ignored my remark.

"He had just hauled in a particularly gruesome grues,"[1] she explained; "and suddenly his ears went red — they're the sort with down on them — and I knew something was going to happen. I didn't quite know what. And I wasn't sure if I wanted to know or if I wanted to cut it; but I suppose I wanted most to know, because I stayed."

"And then?" I prompted.

"Then he said I'd got him on land all right and begged me not to chuck him back!"

The Flapette gurgled nervously. "It was so silly," she said. And then, half wistful, half petulant, "It was so different from what I — from what——"

Was she going to say "imagined"? Had the Flapette, then, imagined? . . .

She didn't finish the sentence. I took it up.

"It usually is," I remarked sagaciously, off my guard.

"What do you mean?" she flashed quickly; her dark brows were incredulous.

"I mean I believe it usually is," I amended without conviction, inviting questions. Her incredulous brows made me, and perhaps the fact that they are dark and her hair is fair.

"You don't sidetrack me," she said, but still incredulous. "Have you ever had a proposal?" she asked crudely. You can't afford to be crude unless you are fluffy. The Flapette combines the two most successfully. She has a genius for that sort of thing. The way she manages her nose is wonderful; she has a big nose, but imposes upon everyone the idea that it is small!

I couldn't deny I had had a proposal. I owned the fact.

---

[1] In this context, likely a reference to a suborder of Gruiformes consisting of cranes and crane-like birds.

ch. ends p. 72

"I suppose a long time ago," she said, with unnecessary conviction.

"Not so very long," I replied, discreetly vague. I was beginning almost to enjoy the situation; I have developed quite a useful working sense of humor.

The Flapette thought upon this for a time.

"I suppose you refused him?"

"Yes."

The Flapette was not to be put off with monosyllables.

"How did he do it?" she asked curiously. I longed to say, "Better than he did it the second time." I was small enough to be glad my proposal was less ridiculous than hers; I know it was small of me. I would like to be big. You are big; everything about You is somehow big.

I said, "He did it in much the same way they all do it outside books, I suppose."

"Yes, I suppose it's only in books——"

The Flapette had never left so many sentences unfinished.

"But what did he say?" she asked.

"He said I was mysterious."

I had almost as much satisfaction in saying it as though I had told her he proposed first to me; more, for she wouldn't associate the absurd Prawn with a sentence like that. It was rather surprising of him, when you come to think of it. I couldn't help seeing the humorous aspect. How little that sentence conveyed the actual happening!

The Flapette was impressed, and something besides, I didn't quite know what. She unscrewed the top of a scent-bottle, took out the stopper, and put it in again. Glass squeaked against glass.

She was staring into the mirror, but I don't think she was

looking at herself. After a long time, "That must have been — rather nice," she said slowly, half ashamed and very thoughtful.

I smiled crookedly.

We were both silent again, and outside in the night a *daraboka* throbbed, monotonous, incessant. The night was full of sounds as all Egyptian nights are full. I became conscious of them. I think, listening to those compelling sounds, I had forgotten the Flapette, when she said suddenly:

"You know, there *is* mystery about you."

I was so astonished I sat quite still and stared at her.

She was looking at my reflection in the mirror and then back at me as though she suspected it was some trick of the glass.

"I don't know what it is," she said in a groping way. "You're the last person I should have thought could be mysterious. Only somehow you are. It never struck me before. . . . I didn't think you were when I first met you, I'm sure."

"I don't suppose you did," I murmured, with my eyes fixed on little phantom ships and incense rising between me and her. "I wasn't," I added.

But she did not seem to hear. She was holding one slim foot and gazing into the glass.

"I've heard there's mystery about the East," she said. "I haven't felt it. Have you?" She turned swiftly toward me, seeming to hang on my answer.

Somehow a cloud of golden dust full of strange voices, dust and the smell of it, rose between us where the incense had been and the little ships.

"Yes," I said.

"I wonder if you've got——" She searched for a phrase in her vocabulary of pithy slang, threw them aside, and went on:

"I wonder if you've got to have it in yourself to feel it."

ch. ends next p.

The sentence was involved, but I knew what she meant. I was wondering, too.

"You know, there is mystery about you," she repeated, as though by repetition she might discover wherein the mystery lay.

"Now there's none about me. If I wore — hair 'additions,' say — perhaps I shouldn't be quite so obvious. That's what I am," she declared with tragic emphasis, "absolutely obvious!"

There was a new passionate note that yet was childlike still.

"I'd like to be mysterious," she said.

"All women are mysterious," I told her. I don't know how I knew it. I feel as though You had said so — but it is the last thing You would be likely to say.

The Flapette was impatient. "Yes, but I'm not a woman!"

She had forgotten the dignity the proposal had conferred.

"Just what are you, I wonder?"

"A beastly sort of betwixt and between! I sometimes wish I'd been a man," she added somberly. "It's so — uncomfortable being a woman."

"I thought you said you were not a woman?"

"Well, I mean it's going to be rottenly uncomfortable being a woman. You know it is." She pointed her forefinger at me accusingly.

"It is rather," I admitted.

"I would like to be mysterious——"

I looked at her curiously. Her face was shadowed with unaccustomed thought and something more, something which puzzled me.

"Flapette," I said, "do you want to give?"

"To give? What's that to do with it? Give what?"

That told me. She didn't understand.

The Flapette and I have met with an adventure — and incidentally with an author.

We only went out intending to walk to the Arab cemetery, but you can never tell what a day will bring forth.

The Arab cemetery is a weird place; nothing could be more unlike an English cemetery — numberless crumbling buildings with shuttered windows and a few white-washed graves. Here the women come every Friday to visit their dead; I see them, squatting on donkey-carts, cross-legged, crowded together in their sombre *hubarahs*.

The Arab cemetery is a very still, dusty place. It seems given over to dust and silence. Yet there is about it no sense of desolation; the brooding stillness is not desolate.

There seemed a dry whispering within the shuttered windows, a reedy whispering as though the dead whispered. Even the Flapette felt it. She said it was an uncomfortable sort of place and made her think of stories about mummies.

"Why can't they bury them away and have done with it?" she asked, shivering a little. "It's — it's kind of indecent."

"To thrust death on the living?" That dry whispering as of very ancient things caught me in its dusty mesh.

"Life's good, isn't it?" I said irrelevantly. The Flapette thought it was uncomfortable of me to talk like that. Life was naturally all right, but you didn't say so. The abstract alarmed her, though at the same time it held for her, I think, a certain fascination which she would never have admitted.

"Look here," she protested; "can't we keep clear of life and death and all that sort of thing? If you were the Rev. Arthur, it'd be different."

"Do you think the Rev. Arthur would talk to you about life and death?"

"No," she said, smiling a little, and added with disarming frankness, "he wouldn't. He'd talk about me."

"Do men always talk to you about yourself?"

"Yes — except when I let them talk about themselves, so they shan't get tired. They really like that best, you know." She nodded sagely.

"Do you like the Rev. Arthur?"

She screwed up her eyes.

"I do and I don't. He's the sort of man who speaks to you as though you were a child — and looks at you as though you were a doll."

"That searchlight of his blinds one to his own defects?"

"Yes; it reminds me of a bazaar I once went to; I spent every penny I had, and my only excuse was that the band played so loudly!"

"You didn't quite know what you were doing? The Rev. Arthur's searchlight has the same effect?"

The Flapette laughed in a non-committal way. She had forgotten all about dust and dead things; there was no room for discomfort on her horizon; she was completely happy and self-satisfied again.

She threw back her veil with a characteristic, quick gesture as we came in sight of a Bedouin encampment.

"Look!" she said. "Isn't that topping?"[1]

The encampment was amazingly dirty and fascinating: little tents made of skins and tattered rags; dogs and cats and hens running over the tents; a group of camels; still blue smoke pillars; muffled, still figures — merged, all of it, in the glow of a golden evening.

Then, turning, there burst upon us a great herd of dust-brown goats crossing a wooden bridge, driven by two Bedouins in dingy white, the goats stirring a white cloud of dust which the low sun turned to moated gold. Behind were palm trees lit so brilliantly, their green against the dim blue mountains seemed the green of flames. You were somehow very real just then. I never know when You will seem near and when I shall have to grope for You, perhaps not find You at all. You are such an unexpected sort of person.

You took your pipe out of your mouth and looked and were silent. But I thought I never need feel alone — when I was startled by a hand clutching at my skirt and a voice like a person in delirium, incessant, monotonous, demanding *baksheesh*. A brown face was turned to mine, a face swathed in rags about which the flies buzzed blackly, and lips that moved in rapid Arabic.

I could distinguish the inevitable *"maskin." "Maskin O Sitt"* and, over and over without a pause, *"baksheesh, baksheesh."*

The Flapette, with a look of horrified repugnance, was beset

---

[1] A dated British word meaning: excellent, very good, or pleasing.

ch. ends p. 83

by the other boy. The true Bedouin, the desert man, is, I have heard, above begging; he despises begging.

Neither the Flapette nor I had money. We tried the few words of Arabic we knew, "*Ru—Ru—La—la—la!*" without success, and made inexpressive flapping gestures such as you feel impelled to make when addressing deaf persons or foreigners. The boys clawed at us and went on with their monotonous reiteration, grinning but importunate.[2]

The Flapette looked round rather wildly. She didn't like it.

I tried "*Imshi*"[3] still without result.

Suddenly a peculiar, drawling voice said "*Imshi*" very quietly, just behind me, and in a moment the two Bedouin boys, clutching their fluttering rags, padded after the goats, which had scattered and were browsing in a *berseem* field.

I looked round, gasping a little, and saw — the Author. I didn't know he was an author then, of course; I've only learned that since — at least, it didn't take long to find out. The Author does not keep his identity in the dark.

I murmured vague thanks and tried not to show surprise at his sudden appearance.

"You needn't thank me," he said. "I watched for quite a long time."

I thought he might have come to the rescue earlier, and I could see the Flapette got nearly as far as saying so; but there was something about him that stopped her.

The man was very broad and square in the shoulders, but for the rest singularly slim and angular in an odd way; he reminded me irresistibly of ancient Egyptian bas-reliefs.[4] His

---

[2] Persistent.

[3] "Go away! Be off!"

[4] A method of molding, carving, or stamping in which the design stands out from the surface but no part is completely detached from it.

movements, too, were slow yet jerky, somehow unfinished: the sort of movements that would belong to those painted figures had they life.

His eyes were long and narrow beneath heavy lids, but their color was unexpected, a contradiction to one's first impression of the man.

They were a queer red-brown, a smoldering red. They were speaking eyes; I had an absurd thought about them: that they would drawl as his voice drawled.

His face was curiously pale, and there were odd lines in it just where you would least expect them. His lips were red, too red, and rather full.

There was something inscrutable about him, the inscrutability of a mask. He did not smile, and yet behind the mask you felt he was smiling slowly and ironically just as he spoke. There was something exasperating about the man.

Hanging straight and lank, oddly lifeless over his brow, was a long red lock. He kept putting it aside with a slow, awkward gesture that yet seemed studied.

Instead of a topi[5] he wore a dull gold *mandil*; otherwise he was dressed like a European.

Who and what he was, and from whence, I could not imagine, but he interested and piqued my curiosity; I guessed the Flapette was aching to know more about him. He guessed it too, which was intolerable.

I thought I would let him speak first. I knew intuitively he would speak; he was really anxious to impart his identity.

"You wondered where I sprang from," he said, dwelling on the words as though the sound were pleasing to him.

---

[5] A lightweight hat worn in tropical countries.

ch. ends p. 83

The Flapette flushed quickly.

"I can't say we did," she replied, driven to rudeness. "We were only wondering how to get rid of the Bedouin boys."

The man made a slow gesture; his hand was very white and very long, the nails dyed red with henna. I noticed this with astonishment, for, despite his peculiarities, there was about him something too elusive for analysis, something so English it was almost laughable.

He said:

"I could not at once come to your rescue. One cannot step over thousands of years in a moment. . . . And there were thousands of years between us."

The Flapette and I stared. We began to think he might be mad. Instinctively I knew he guessed this and was not ill-pleased.

"Had you spoken to me I could not have answered," he said. "I had identified myself with that palm tree — I *was* that palm tree."

With a slow change of position his hands had fallen to his sides, his head was thrown back and he became so still it seemed he held his breath; the strange stillness that only palm trees know. It was astonishing how in the place of the man in the yellow *mandil* there was a palm tree standing. I felt angry with myself for admitting his uncanny power. The Flapette was frankly terrified; terror had got the better of her curiosity; I felt her plucking at my sleeve.

And all the time, while I wondered at the man's strangeness, I felt it was — not exactly a pose, not wholly assumed, and yet——

I knew, too, he was smiling that hidden smile, mocking and slow.

"I am in this century, but not of it," he said; and I saw the man again in place of the tree. "Before Amon-Re[6] rose I was. The blood in me was dust before time began."

He seemed muttering words to himself, yet I felt they were for us to hear, that he watched their effect.

"Oughtn't we to be getting back?" the Flapette whispered miserably like a piteous child.

"There is no getting back," this surprising man said darkly. "All my life I have wearied to Get Back. The dust of ages before Time was cries out——"

He stretched his arms, suddenly, jerkily. The gesture told, set against his other slow movements. I knew he was aware of it.

"What are you!" I asked at last, laughing a little. The wonder in my tone must have gratified him.

"That is it — what am I? What are you? What are any of us? . . . I am a man and I am a tree — I am a kite and I am a priest — I am water — and I am dust."

The words were strung together merely, with unexpected spaces. I saw them as beads strung on a wooden rosary such as Arabs use. They were just so many words which anyone might string together, and yet they had power to conjure up dim ages teeming life that lured and beckoned.

I was almost sure it was a gigantic pose — almost sure, not quite. That was where he was so disconcerting. One was very nearly sure, but not quite.

"You ask me what I am," he said, putting aside the limp red lock. "There is no answer. I know no more than you do. Were

---

[6] Amon, also spelled Amun, Amen, or Ammon, was an Egyptian deity who was revered as king of the gods. With the 11th Dynasty (c. 21st century BC), Amon rose to the position of patron deity of Thebes by replacing Montu. After the rebellion of Thebes and with the rule of Ahmose I (16th century BC), Amon acquired national importance, expressed in his fusion with the Sun god, Ra, as Amon-Re, also spelled Amun-Ra, Amon-Ra, or Amun-Re.

ch. ends p. 83

you to ask me what I do——" He paused, obviously awaiting the question.

I was not going to put it, because he expected it; but the Flapette, who had somewhat recovered from her terror, said crossly:

"Well, what do you do?"

Consuming curiosity had mastered her again, and I own I waited breathlessly for his reply; I had never met anyone quite so extraordinary.

"I write," he said "This hand writes." He raised it slowly.

"You are an author?" I asked rather impatiently.

"I am a scribe. . . . I have memories of the temples of Osiris[7] and of Set."[8]

The very order in which he placed the gods' names was studied so as to obtain a musical, sonorous sound.

"What do you write?" said the Flapette crudely. "Novels?"

I thought the smoldering eyes would blaze contempt, but the man was above all things unexpected.

I almost gasped when he answered.

"Men speak in that way of my writings. . . . I am Desmond Dulac," he added abruptly, as though he had carefully led up to the disclosure by means that should carry most effect. I was almost sure he had led up to it, but again not quite. I have had no opportunity of becoming acquainted with the names of modern authors, so the disclosure conveyed nothing to me, and I was sure it conveyed less than nothing to the Flapette. She just looked at him with her mouth open. I don't think anyone

[7] In ancient Egyptian religion, Osiris is the god of fertility, agriculture, the afterlife, the dead, resurrection, life, and vegetation, who was the brother and husband of Isis and father of Horus, and murdered by his brother Set.

[8] Set is a god of deserts, storms, disorder, violence, foreigners, and the usurper who murdered and mutilated his brother, Osiris.

else could contrive to look attractive with her mouth open. The Flapette did. She looked about three years old.

Desmond Dulac saw at once his name had failed to impress, that it conveyed nothing. I was conscious again of that slow, sardonic smile behind the mask of inscrutability, the mask I felt almost certain was assumed.

"It doesn't convey anything to you." He gave a sigh which was unnaturally prolonged but sounded genuine — the first thing I had felt to be genuine about him. "How refreshing!" he said.

The remark might have proceeded from colossal conceit or a sincere and very human relief. Again I could not be sure.

The Flapette laughed, rather tremulously, and I heard a little pent-up sigh escape her.

"I daresay we shall see you again," she said boldly; she is sometimes incorrigible.

"You may, and you may not," he said darkly. "All who meet Desmond Dulac do not meet me."

The Flapette was impatient, though I could see she was already desirous to subdue this man who was such a new type, a provoking type.

"Don't talk rot," she said, to my confusion. But the Author showed no sign of resentment.

"You are delightful," he answered, in such an impersonal way he gave the impression of speaking across the centuries, and she in her turn could not resent it. From the glimpse I caught of her face she evidently did not.

"I daresay we shall see you again," she said with a cool sparkle.

"Perhaps," the Author returned; "we see trees — we see kites — we do not know."

"That's all right," the Flapette cut in, and I expected her to tell him to stow it, if only to see whether he'd call her delightful again. She was thoroughly enjoying herself. The Author was altogether taken up with the Flapette. It was going to be her adventure, and all because she knew how to be crude charmingly.

I was astonished when the Author turned deliberately from her to me, and said with sudden earnestness,

"What do *you* think I am?"

It took my breath away.

"I think you're preposterous," I broke out.

"I think I am going to like you," said the astounding man; and with that he left us.

"Was he real? Did you see him too?" gasped the Flapette. "I can hardly believe in him——"

"I hardly believed in him at the time," I said cynically.

"I don't see why you should say that?" she retorted. I was right. She had decided to subdue him. She felt a sense of proprietorship already.

At night I went up on the roof alone. It is beautiful — the great expanse of white, shining roof and dead black shadow; murmurous sounds rising, blended yet distinct so that you are acutely conscious of each, however small. The sky is flooded still with color, glowing through the veil of dusk.

Gradually the moon's brilliance grows till it might be day, save for the indescribable mystery of an Eastern night.

It was very warm and still. We speak of breathless nights in England, but they are not really breathless; there are always leaves faintly stirring. Last night the great goldmore tree that spreads itself over the courtyard seemed caught in a mesh of stillness: not a leaf stirred, the tree itself seemed breathless as the night. There is about utter stillness something oppressive and yet alluring.

I leaned over the low white-washed parapet; the cracked plaster was warm to the touch.

Suddenly, beneath me, from the shadows into the moon's pallor a figure emerged and stood quite still.

I could not mistake that stillness, of a palm. It was the Author.

While I leaned, watching, he stretched out both hands toward those three palm trees which stand together on the border of the desert. And then the shadows took him.

I felt almost certain he knew he was watched — and yet not quite, still not quite.

His parting words disturbed me — I could not tell why — and I tried to rid myself of the feeling.

What an extraordinary man he is! . . . And the Flapette means to see more of him; her curiosity is thoroughly aroused. She has begun to think Egypt quite amusing.

Why do You look like that? You don't like Desmond Dulac. It's no good protesting. I must say I think You come to rather hasty conclusions; You know no more about him than I do. You only know what I have told You. . . . Oh, don't. You're going. Don't let me have to grope for You.

It seems the Author is "the" Desmond Dulac. There was quite a flutter in the hotel when it leaked out he had been seen at Suez. Everyone says he is an extraordinary man and that his novels are equally extraordinary; I can quite believe it. He writes about Egypt, and it is his books about Egypt which have made his name — and his money. Apparently he is collecting material in Suez. Everyone says it is just the unexpected sort of place where he would turn up; he never does anything expected.

Probably the news of his presence here will find its way into the *Egyptian Gazette*;[1] I shouldn't be surprised if that were his intention. But I don't know. Astonishing as he is, I can't be certain he is not sincere.

We are quite pleased with our adventure, especially the Flapette, who is frankly anxious to meet the man again. I don't quite know whether I want to meet him again. There's something — disturbing, I can't get nearer than that, about him. And I can't bring myself to believe in him, not altogether.

[1] An English-language Egyptian daily first published in 1880, it is the oldest English-language newspaper in the Middle East.

Miss Kershaw knew of Desmond Dulac's fame as a novelist, it seems. She has actually read his books. I asked her what they were like.

"Astonishing clever trash," she stated in her expressionless way.

"And the public likes trash?" I asked. I suppose it does. I had never thought about it before.

"The public likes to gape," she said.

She was less expansive even than usual regarding the Author. She maintained a non-committal attitude. But I somehow don't think she likes Desmond Dulac. I questioned her persuasively like a reporter forcing an interview.

"You don't believe in him?" I asked.

"Do you believe in yourself?" she answered.

The Author is going to be almost monotonously unexpected.

The Rev. Arthur arranged a launch picnic up the Canal. We were to have tea on board and land at one of the Coastguard stations.

We boarded the launch at Suez and were to touch at Port Tewfik to pick up one of the party.[2] The Flapette was frankly bored, so bored she actually turned her energies to the subjugation of the Rev. Arthur.

He was, as usual, dazzling; I saw her blinking all the way to Port Tewfik. But she was only halfhearted. The thing palled. She was wondering just how and when she would see the Author again, if at all. Egypt was going to be about the limit, or Suez was, if that exciting, inconsequent person should not turn up again.

As the launch touched the landing-stage a man, who had

---

[2] "Touch at" is a seafaring term which means to briefly visit a port.

been waiting there, stepped on board. He wore a dull gold *mandil*. It was Desmond Dulac. Everyone perceived at once who it was; a wave of excitement passed through the picnic party.

"Who had invited him? or had he not been invited?" "It was just like him to come without an invitation, to take his welcome for granted. Perhaps he didn't care one way or the other." "He was above mere conventions. He was Colossal as those huge figures of Rameses.[3] The great man had condescended to join a launch picnic!" "How surprising he was! But one would expect that from his books!" So the whispered comments went on.

Everyone hoped he would speak to him or her, and yet feared lest he should. His questions were sometimes impossible to answer.

He sat down next the Flapette, and I noted her little ripple of satisfaction.

"I seem to remember your face," he muttered. "It was not at Karnak . . . nor Luxor."[4]

"We haven't done the Nile trip," said the Flapette.

He drew in his breath sharply.

"Your face just eludes me," he murmured. "The thousands of years make it dim . . . I wonder . . . I wonder . . . "

The Flapette looked rather scared.

"What a beastly sort of idea!" she protested. She hated uncomfortable things.

Everyone was listening, trying to catch the great man's utterances above the throb of the motor. And he knew it. At least I

---

[3] The name of eleven Egyptian pharaohs during the nineteenth and twentieth dynasties of Ancient Egypt.

[4] Karnak is a village in Egypt on the eastern bank of the Nile River, now largely merged with the larger, neighboring city Luxor. Combined, it is the site of the Ancient Egyptian city of Thebes, including the great temple of Amon, and has frequently been characterized as the "world's greatest open-air museum."

thought he did; I was not absolutely sure. It was just possible he was absorbed in the Flapette, to the exclusion of the rest. One couldn't be sure.

Once I thought for an instant he looked at me in a puzzled way from behind the mask of immobility. But again I could not be sure. When I met his eyes his face had assumed its inscrutable expression — and afterward he ate anchovy patés with slow appreciation. I wanted to laugh. I always want to laugh just when it is impossible.

"Why did you come?" I heard the Flapette say.

He pressed his long fingers together, examining the nails dyed red with henna. I saw the Flapette looking at them as though they possessed a horrid fascination.

"I've been wondering why," he said.

"That's a tidy-sized brick to drop!" The Flapette was half amused, half angry.

"Bricks," he repeated thoughtfully.

He had a way of looking past you, not only past your body, but past your existence; you felt he was seeing things that lay behind the dust of countless years.

"Bricks," he said. "Bricks of clay — bricks without straw. . . . Has it not always been so?" he asked sorrowfully of no one in particular.

No one knew what he meant — I rather wondered if he did himself; but no one would admit the fact. I shrugged; should it prove just a pose, I felt it was utterly contemptible.

The entrance to the Canal is magic with distant rose-colored hills and a stretch of desert where I saw camels and here and there a brown, solitary tent. Near the bank were moored native boats, trickling and splashing color; wading waist-deep were shining Arab boys putting down nets. Soon you see nothing

ch. ends p. 90

on either side but the high banks of sand; the Canal seems impossibly narrow.

The Author pointed out to me the place where was the old pontoon that the pilgrims used to cross in past times when they took months to reach Mecca.

"Isn't a pilgrimage a curious thing?" he said. "Perhaps no one can understand its appeal as I understand it. I am a pilgrim. . . ." He lowered his voice with extraordinary effect. "But the pilgrimage on which I go cannot reveal . . . that which I seek is forever hidden."

If the man were insincere he was ridiculous; if not — he had a marvelous way of setting the imagination afire.

Suddenly he said, "Do you know what it is to seek?"

Had I known him to be sincere I felt I could have told him I was seeking Space, a thing almost too elusive to put into words. But I didn't know. So I told him nothing, at the risk of his thinking I lacked understanding. I didn't care. How absurd You are about Desmond Dulac! Just because he isn't cut-and-dried and ordinary and dull, just because he can talk — (that was hateful of me. I didn't mean it; You know I didn't). But I had thought You so big and tolerant; I can't see why You should be so prejudiced against the Author.

As the sun was setting we landed at the Second station, a house and a mud hut and the landing-stage.

Then the distant desert broke upon us — "swept" would perhaps be better, only "broke" expresses that breathless feeling — the desert broke upon us, lying in a brown and violet haze, the sky sheer gold, through which color burned and pulsed; stretches of bare pale sand, green reeds with plumed heads, making no movement in the hot, still air; beyond these mystery of dim palms and darkening hills; and just one pool among the reeds, giving back the sunset fire like molten metal; the only sound the crickets' poignant chirping.

The Author slowly took his palm-tree pose — or posture; I still don't know if it is altogether pose.

"'*When thou settest on the western horizon, the earth is in darkness, as though it were dead,*'" he murmured, quoting from what I did not know; but the words somehow conjured up dusty papyri[5] and the hot air of tombs.

". . . '*The earth is silent, He who made it resteth on his horizon.*'"[6]

The Flapette looked uncomfortable; I think she imagined he was quoting the Bible, and felt it was rather indecent of him.

"I've heard you're a sad pagan," the Rev. Arthur rebuked him with unctuous[7] indulgence — everyone looked indulgently upon this extraordinary man. He had made a name for himself.

"You will have heard many things of Desmond Dulac," the Author said, accepting genius. "You will have heard few of Me."

The Rev. Arthur was somewhat disconcerted, but he liked basking in the reflected glory the great man shed.

We came home by moonlight, Desmond Dulac and the Flapette and I right in the bows. I'd much sooner he had not been there. He would talk all the time; I admit there are advantages in being a silent person. And he would talk to me, just because he could see it annoyed me, out of sheer perverseness. Why couldn't he talk to the Flapette? I knew she would accuse me of not playing the game when we got back.

I always resent the intrusion of anyone into those hours that ought to be silent with only me and You in them. I wanted

---

[5] Plural form of papyrus; a type of paper used by ancient Egyptians, Greeks, and Romans made from the stem pith of the papyrus plant pressed flat.
[6] Hymn to Amon-Re.
[7] Excessively earnest or smug.

ch. ends next p.

to sit and feel that delicious bound a launch gives, to hear the white hiss (do sounds have colors for You, too?) of water as she dashed forward.

It was mysteriously lovely going down the Canal; the water just liquid moonlight; the high banks shutting out the night. We were nearly blinded by a vessel's searchlight, and forged ahead, as all small craft is supposed to be out of the Canal after sunset.

Coming up the Creek to Suez, my spirit, or the thing that is me, seemed free of my body, free to feel to the utmost and yet drift over a great expanse of glassy, pale water, with lights making long tremulous reflections; groups of native boats, their tall masts black against the sky; old mosques and houses dim and ghostly; wavering star-trickles.

The houses rose quite suddenly out of the water — as pale, beautiful thoughts rise unexpectedly when you are feeling commonplace.

When we stepped from the launch the Author shook hands conventionally. He knew nothing he did could be quite so surprising as the conventional — I think.

He put the red lock aside with his characteristic gesture.

"I told you I was going to . . ." he said. I hated myself because I had not forgotten.

We have had a very heavy shower. The roads are all mud, yellow, slippery mud, and pools of water; bare-footed Arabs paddling along with *galabiehs* bunched round their waists.

The sky has been black and somehow menacing. Rain in Egypt is ugly — there never ought to be rain — ugly and almost terrible.

It has changed the aspect of the place altogether — to see lights reflected in the muddy streets!

I know You think there is nothing like a soft, drifting wet day; You're positively happy in the rain, but then it is English rain. This was not like English rain; there was not even the fresh, indescribable smell after it. Why are You smiling in that exasperating way? You need not think I'm homesick. For one thing, England is not home to me any more than Egypt is home. Only, don't remind me of the fact unnecessarily today. I don't know what is the matter; perhaps it is the rain.

Rain makes Egypt — oh, desolate. You can't imagine how desolate.

Somehow today things seem so hopeless. I know I am

absurd; You needn't rub it in. Don't You ever have that what's-the-good-of-it-all feeling? I don't think I ever had in England. It never occurred to me to ask or even to wonder much; I accepted life as I accepted the turnip fields and the drear parochial[1] round, without questioning. Now I am always questioning, and it is a horribly "uncomfortable" state, as the Flapette would say.

Is it Egypt that makes me wonder — or is it You?

But then there isn't any You, and if there were——

What is the good of anything anyway?

A little child's funeral has just gone past, a man carrying the body in an open box on his head, and a few women following — one, evidently the mother, crying silently whilst the others wailed.

I can still hear the sogging of their bare feet in the slippery mud; I can still hear the distant wailing of the women.

What's the good of seeking Space?

I think Miss Kershaw suspects the Shadow. She has not said anything, of course; I mean she has not questioned me — Miss Kershaw never questions. Only, I feel sure she does, and she is worried about it. It is almost worth living with a chillsome thing like this to have anyone worry about you. It makes me feel warm secretly to know she worries. That sounds horrid of me, but You have no idea what it is like, knowing no one has ever worried on your account.

The last few days I have felt somehow desolate, and more

---

[1] It appears that both meanings of the word apply: of or relating to a church parish; having a narrow or limited outlook.

than ever I have had to grope for You, and even then it has been an effort to believe in You, instead of an effort *not* to believe in You. You seem so unapproachable; did You know how silent You're getting? You just bite your pipe stem and say nothing, and nothing I can say seems to rouse You. Is the fault in me? I have needed You badly the last few days; I have felt unaccountably alone; and yet You have seemed farther away than You have ever been — and the Shadow has crept nearer.

I think it was You who kept it from me, your big quietness between it and me. I think if ever I groped for You and failed altogether to find You, the Shadow would put out a hand — I shouldn't care much, then. Don't. What have I said to make You look like that? Is it because I've spoken of the Shadow? But You're not like that; You have your eyes on it all this time; You have not tried to forget it; You've been watching it quietly, stood between it and me. It is I who have tried to forget, though — no, I don't think I have shrunk from it. But You've watched it quietly from the first. Why do You look like that? Do You really mind — much? . . .

How alone I am! Why did I ever invent You? For I did invent You; You didn't happen. I never could have been so alone *without* You.

The wind is sifting sand about the house; the palm tree outside my window is scraping stealthily. And the Shadow has come very close.

I have never been afraid of the Shadow till now; suddenly

ch. ends p. 99

it makes me cold. It's because of You, I think — because I am losing belief in You. No, not belief; You are keeping away. Why is it? What have I done? I can't even see your physical self as clearly as I did. There is always a maddening dimness between; I know You are behind it — I only doubt at the worst moments — but I can't get at You anymore.

That is why I am afraid of the Shadow suddenly; I feel I am given over to it. And I can't stand it any longer. Why did You stop watching quietly? Why are You keeping away just when I need You most? Perhaps I shall never need You like this again.

I've got to keep the thing away as best I can alone now. I feel driven to any resource to keep it from touching me. . . .

My strength has all gone to pieces, I'm hideously weak and frightened.

I must forget somehow, keep it from me. This can't go on, I know, but as long as I can I shall struggle against it. Giving in means — to think of giving in brings so near the possibility that I may never go back; I feel I could clutch at anything to keep away the Shadow. Why did I ever invent You? I thought I could make You as I wished, but so soon You grew beyond me and now I'm alone.

The Author has given me one of his books, his latest. It is bound in a queer cover to represent papyrus with a great hanging seal. The title is in gold and turquoise and Egyptian-red — *Pagan Fires*.

It is printed upon very thick paper, and the chapters end

abruptly just when you would least expect, if you didn't know the Author.

Knowing him, you feel their unexpectedness a trifle forced. One chapter consists merely of the word "Kismet" in thick type upon a page all to itself. That seems to me a triumph of pose — if it is pose.

There appears a preponderance of unusually associated words — "Deafening colors"; "white glaring melancholy"; "bitter, dropping sun"; "the desert's blood"; "derisive pyramids" . . . ; I have just selected at random. Night is described as "aching toward the earth"; boats move "jealously"; sunrise is "a crimson madness."

Palm trees are likened to dead hands that "beckon, menacing." I have not begun to read the book yet, but I should judge Miss Kershaw was not mistaken when she summed up his work as astonishingly clever trash. He knows what is expected of him — I think.

I doubt his sincerity, and yet tonight I was nearer believing in him than before, nearer and farther; nearer believing in the man himself. Perhaps I ought to put it like that.

I wished he had given his book to the Flapette. She looked rather wistful when she saw it, but tried courageously to be "sporting" about it.

The Flapette has altered a good deal the last week. I sometimes think there must be a lot of really splendid small things done in the name of "sporting." The Flapette will read the book — not that I think it very wholesome for her; it is harmless but morbid and exotic, I should think — but it won't be the same thing. He didn't give it to her.

I don't want the book; I'd give it to her if I thought that

ch. ends p. 99

would make any difference, but it wouldn't. The fact would remain.

I don't want the book; I don't know whether I am grateful even. The Author smiled so ironically behind his mask when he gave it to me, it hardly seemed a gift.

It made me feel rather hostile, and I resented his command — it amounted to a command — that I should give him my opinion. I wonder what I shall say? It must ease the Flapette's sore disappointment that she won't have to pronounce a verdict on the book.

The Author gave me his book in the most unexpected way, the way I am learning to expect, and I think despise. I daresay the man's insincerity seems obvious to You, but it is not so obvious when you know him. Know him! — when you meet him in person. And remember You're not subtle. You put him down at once as no good. You are usually tolerant enough, aggravatingly, when I disparage people! But You have never liked the Author. Well, You must make up your mind to hear some more about him. His vagaries,[2] his extravagances interest; he piques curiosity, when he is not purely exasperating. And I have got to keep the Shadow from me somehow. I mustn't think.

The manner in which he presented the book was as follows:

I had gone to Port Tewfik with the lady of the green spectacles, who was going out to a ship to meet friends. Miss Kershaw and the Flapette were to join me on the walk back. I sat down on one of the wooden landing-stages.

There was nobody about but a sleepy native policeman.

I faced the mountains, deep violet against a saffron sky that warmed gradually — light streaming, flooding upward from

---

[2] Unexpected and unpredictable changes in someone's behavior.

behind the mountains till clear rose throbbed in the gold and color came rippling toward me in the dark, still water. A native boat, tall mast and furled sail silhouetted, was black and intense like a sudden note of sound. Turning, I saw the long line of Asiatic hills across the water, hills lying in a dream of liquid pearl and glowing rose — between them and the sea a strip of yellow sand; above, a yellow sky, faint and luminous; the water a wonderful translucent, milky blue with great emerald shadows.

The rose mountains mingled with it, green and blue growing jewel-dark near me, and in the midst a white, perfect reflection of the moon.

I couldn't look at it. I wanted to rush anywhere so that I might not see it. I think I put up my hands vaguely — and the Author touched my shoulder, timidly, not a bit as I should have expected. But then is he ever expected? Only, somehow this was different.

"You can't get away from it," he said slowly; and something in his voice made me look up swiftly. (I did not think till afterward it was strange he divined my feeling.) I looked up and almost thought there was a different expression in the red-brown eyes.

A queer, startled look slid across his face, as though I had surprised some hidden thing.

"You can't get away from it," he repeated; and this time my doubts crept back. He was looking at me from behind the mask again — if it were a mask.

Suddenly he said the most surprising thing he has said yet.

"You don't believe in me," he said.

His face told nothing. I think I must have flushed, as much because I half believed in him as because I didn't quite believe.

He waited for my answer, and when none came he laughed.

ch. ends next p.

I had never heard him laugh before. It was like everything else about him; unexpected, and it was an ugly laugh, mocking as his smile; yet I had a strange feeling that there was pain in it, or something approaching pain. It was that which made it ugly. But I couldn't be quite sure even the laugh was sincere.

He allowed a little pause after the sudden, queer laugh, and then said, "You shall read one of my books;" and I felt he was going on laughing silently, rather horribly.

I tried to stammer my thanks, wondering in what odd circumstances he would present the book. But, true to his surprising character, almost as though he had rehearsed the thing, he whipped out the volume with the hanging seal and thrust it upon me.

I must have laughed stupidly; I couldn't think of anything else to do at the moment.

He listened in silence to my laughter, and I thought it had angered him. To my surprise he smiled, the ghost of a smile that made him look rather worn and more likeable suddenly.

He watched me for a little while; he seemed puzzled.

"You mysterious woman," he said.

I know he thought it was the unexpected thing to say, in keeping with the character — the character I am almost sure he has assumed.

He did not guess it had been said before, by the Flapette and the Prawn of all people. I think I should have told him, only with one of his awkward, abrupt movements he was gone.

I couldn't help laughing because he thought the remark original; a detached part of my brain was amused — only a detached part, for I suddenly felt the loneliness intolerable. It pressed up close, this feeling of desolation, close like the still, hot darkness of an Egyptian night. In the midst of the darkness

I found myself wishing in a dull, vaguely resentful way that he had not called me mysterious "woman."

I am hopelessly small sometimes.

The Flapette has decided to grow up. She has not told me this, of course. That she has piled her hair round her head in an altogether attractive manner is only the outward and visible sign of an inward (I don't think it is spiritual) change.

Is it a change? The Flapette puzzles me. Sometimes I think she has merely a frivolous and eager desire to see what being grown-up is like and thinks childishly ridding herself of her plait[1] will attain the desired end.

And yet sometimes — I don't know; it is so hard to believe the Flapette could ever turn into a woman with a woman's weakness and strength, and capacity for suffering.

She has always been a sort of pixie-thing with no heart at all and only a problematical soul. I think I am rather sorry she has decided to grow up.

The Flapette and I went on the roof quite late with our hair loose and a soft breeze blowing through it. Miss Kershaw didn't come; I suppose she is afraid of moonlight nights. I think I shall be when I'm her age.

---

[1] Braid.

The light of the full moon seemed violet; the rose of distant hills and the turquoise, vivid strip of sea were as visible as by day, yet somehow veiled. It is far too subtle to describe.

There was a *Zikr*[2] somewhere in the town, and at regular intervals the clapping of many hands shattered the silence; it was too distant to hear anything but the handclapping, which would go on for hours.

I want to lay each night away, store it up. Each one is so different; all have some quality that is indescribable, some mystery I cannot put into words. Why do I shrink from the Possibility crouching ahead of me? Why do I care whether I go back or not? Egypt is wonderful. . . .

For some time the Flapette has been talking of nothing but a fancy-dress dance which is to be held at the English Club.

I had forgotten all about it till she mentioned it tonight.

"What are you going as?" she asked, pursuing a train of thought.

"Going as?"

"To the dance, of course."

"Oh," I said, "I hadn't thought about it yet."

I was grateful because she had given a thought to my costume, but it wasn't like the Flapette. I felt a pang, a vague foreboding.

She had always been supremely self-centered, disarmingly and frankly selfish. Somehow the complete selfishness of the child — I almost regretted it.

"But it's next week!" she burst out.

"So it is. I must get something together, I suppose."

[2] Dhikr or zikr (literally meaning remembrance, reminder, or mention) is both a ceremony and an act of Islamic meditation, associated chiefly with Sufism, in which phrases or prayers are repeatedly chanted in order to remember God.

ch. ends p. 107

"Do you mean to say you haven't any ideas?"

"I am not a person of many ideas," I said. "I have never had but one, the one which came to me in the old Church on the hill."

She looked at me rather contemptuously, rather sadly. A little while ago she would have been wholly contemptuous; I began to feel afraid, a fear I could not formulate.

"I suppose I shall have to think of something for you," she said impatiently, but it was generous; she ached to discuss her own costume.

"Supposing I went as a — as a hospital nurse?" I suggested valiantly, so that we might dismiss my costume.

"Yes, or as Summer with some daisies off your old hat!" she said scornfully. "Haven't you any originality?"

I was hurt. Everyone has a secret hankering to be original and a contradictory desire to be like other people. All our lives we are torn between them.

"I think the Author has enough and to spare for Suez," I said.

She looked as though she would flare out at me; but instead she answered with an odd little assumption of dignity that was pathetic, "I think we will leave the Author out of this. I don't see it has anything to do with him anyway. He won't be there."

The last sentence was defiant, but I felt she was hoping I should contradict her.

"How do you know he won't be there?" I said.

"Because it is the very last thing he'd do!"

"And isn't that exactly the reason for surmising he will be there?"

"What do you mean?" she asked, suddenly rather white. I thought I should meet with hostility. This changed Flapette was disconcerting.

"I meant he is always so original," I answered lamely.

"Oh!" she said and drew in a little breath.

"We haven't hit on a costume for you," she continued, obviously wishful to change the subject. I object strongly to being sidetracked, as the Flapette says, but I thought it so generous of her to go on troubling about my costume I let the matter pass.

"You ought to have something rather out of the ordinary," she said, sitting on the parapet and meditatively detaching little pieces of plaster which she dropped into the street. I thought it a pity to discuss so banal a thing — for the matter of that, to discuss anything — on such a night. Yet in a way I was glad; I don't want to think in these days; I welcome anything that keeps the Shadow away.

"Being a very ordinary person, don't you think I might look a little — tasteless in an out-of-the-way costume?" I ventured.

The Flapette laughed.

"You mean it'd 'eat tame,' as I once heard an old woman say of a banana!"

Then she sobered.

"You don't really think you're ordinary, do you?" she said. She never flatters; she was quite sincere.

"Why, of course. Painfully so," I returned.

"But it's exactly what you're *not*. Didn't I tell you there was something kind of mysterious about you?" She smiled complacently. "It was rather clever of me to discover that."

I did not remind her that the Prawn had discovered it first, nor acquaint her with the fact that Desmond Dulac had also discovered it.

"You aren't pretty," she remarked. "I don't suppose you ever have been."

I felt curiously old when she said that. My youth seemed

ch. ends p. 107

thrust into the past, a remote past. She is pitilessly young; I felt ashamed suddenly that I had got Nonsense.

I know I am not pretty; I know I have never been. But prettiness depends so largely upon knowing how to be pretty, and I didn't know how.

The Flapette has the features and the knowledge as well.

My hair doesn't curl, and I always feel my nose is an utterly contradictory and misleading feature. I ought to have had a large nose to balance the rest of my face and my idea of myself — not that I could ever have managed a large nose in the inimitable way the Flapette manages hers; so perhaps it is as well.

When I see myself in the glass I laugh at being called mysterious; I can't reconcile my nose with mystery of any kind.

"With your black hair and pale skin," said the Flapette, "you could be something quite effective if you cared. But you don't seem to care," she added incredulously.

"How old do you think I am, Flapette?" I said.

She flushed a little, and hesitated.

"About twenty-nine?"

It was nice of her to put me below thirty; I knew she believed me to be older.

"I'm thirty-four next birthday," I said, overcoming the temptation to say I was thirty-three.

She tried to show surprise, but it was not convincing.

I wonder if I look my age?

"What about your costume?" I said. "Tell me all about it."

"Not till we've settled yours," she answered firmly. I couldn't understand this new Flapette.

"I know," she shrilled, jumping up from the parapet; "you shall go as a nun!"

"Ridiculous child," I said; "I haven't the face — the nose for a nun."

"What's your nose to do with it? It's that something about you — the sort of mysterious thing."

"No," I persisted. "I haven't the face for the part, Flapette."

"The face doesn't matter so long as you've got the hair."

"A nun's hair doesn't show," I reminded her.

"I know it doesn't," she said impatiently.

"Then why——"

"For that very reason. Because you could stand having your hair hidden. I don't know how I'm so certain of it, but I am. Now I should look positively hideous without my hair," she added naively.

She was so eager I felt it was mean of me not to respond.

I didn't believe her and said I didn't. She sighed impatiently.

"How can I convince you? Come along down," dragging me toward the wooden stairs.

"What in the world——" I began.

She threw a sheet about me, drew it down over my brow, and with deft touches arranged it to her satisfaction. I began to understand how it was the Flapette wore her clothes so delightfully.

"I knew," she exclaimed, "I knew you could stand it! How odd! — when I'm pretty and you're not," she added. "Aren't you pleased?" She seemed disappointed.

"You must remember I haven't seen myself yet."

"How stupid of me! It only remains to be decided whether you go as a white or a black nun."

The thing had been taken out of my hands; I meekly submitted.

I looked in the mirror; I had that queer feeling you get when

ch. ends next p.

among a crowd you see your face in a long glass unexpectedly and don't recognize it for a moment. It seems a new aspect. This wasn't the self I was accustomed to and rather tired of: it looked like someone else.

"Well?" asked the Flapette.

"I hardly know myself," I said feebly.

"You'll persuade me you really are ordinary if you can't find anything else to say," she rejoined in a scathing tone.

"You look — you'll make people wonder about you," she said.

I don't want people to wonder about me. I did not want to go to the dance as this nun; I could not have given a reason.

"I'd rather go in something simple," I demurred foolishly.

"Something simple?" The Flapette laughed. "I don't fancy you could hit on anything much simpler than a sheet!"

I knew I should have to give in; strange, that I almost dreaded going as this nun. For an instant I debated whether I should confide in the Flapette; but how could she understand, seeing I did not understand myself?

"I'm very grateful," I said.

"You'll make everybody wonder about you," the Flapette repeated with a proprietary pride.

"I don't want people to wonder about me."

"How extraordinary you are!" she said; and then, "I'd give anything not to be obvious!"

"I ought to go as a Dresden Shepherdess," she went on, defiance tinging her voice; "but because it is the obvious thing for me to do I'm not going to!"

"What have you thought of?" I asked meekly.

"A veiled lady," she said.

"But Flapette, you're going to hide your face and your fluffy——"

Her glance withered.

"To go veiled is the only way in which I can escape being obvious," she replied with astonishing bitterness.

I can't understand the Flapette at all.

I persuaded her to compromise regarding the veil, to make it flimsy gauze that scarcely hid her Dresden China face. Her very blue eyes above the gauze were incongruous and extremely attractive.

She looked at herself for a long while in silence. Then:

"I wish I were not quite so pretty," she exclaimed. "It's still so awfully obvious——"

After a pause, as though the possibility had only just struck her:

"Should you think the Author will be there?" she said.

The dance was at Port Tewfik. As we drove down we saw a blood-red moon spilling a crimson stream over the water. There was something terrible about the beauty of it. I don't know why it filled me with forebodings, but lately I have been beset by vague, unaccustomed forebodings, the more disturbing because so formless.

I don't think the Flapette noticed my silence; she was unusually silent herself. I think she was wondering whether Desmond Dulac would be at the dance. It seemed the most unlikely thing to happen — but was he not the most unlikely of men? For myself, I hoped he would not be there: I did not feel equal to the Author. There was no strength left in me, or only just enough to fight down vague forebodings and keep the Shadow away.

The English Club has a beautiful garden — at least, it is beautiful at night, the greater part closed in by pergolas draped with bunting[1] and hung with lanterns and riotous masses of bougainvillea; in the center a round pergola with seats and a dropping, sad stone fountain.

---

[1] Flags and colorful decorations.

The Flapette's eyes shone, and clouded.

The Author was not there. . . .

A haunting waltz ended, the dance was nearly over; the dim orange light from Chinese lanterns touched here and there a figure emerging from the ballroom, bringing into sudden prominence an Arab chief's white robe or a pierrot;[2] gleaming upon the tinsel scarf of a Persian dancing-girl; glinting upon wine-glasses. In the shadow a Roman soldier with pince-nez[3] was lighting a cigarette; here and there other cigarettes shone through protecting hands, and lit faces grotesquely. There was a soft undercurrent of talk with laughter in it. Sandy paths crunched beneath many feet — and the Author came from the shadowy places into the light.

A little hush followed, and in the midst of it an hysterical laugh.

Everyone recognized the Author.

He moved with difficulty; his body was swathed in yellowish strips of linen, his arms bound to his sides, his head wrapped about so that only the face was visible, pale and set. A subtle odor, sickly, sweet, and heavy, composed of spices and perfumes, clung about him. It was somehow horrible.

He advanced a step; slowly, jerkily, leaning a little forward. There was a faint scream and a scuffling sound on the gravel as the glittering crowd swayed back. A girl was supported to a seat under the pergola. The Author stood quite calmly just beneath a dim red lantern, his eyes horribly unseeing — swaying a little. Everyone was watching. What was he going to do?

Slowly I became aware of movement.

---

[2] A French male pantomime, typically dressed in a loose white costume with a sad, whitened face.

[3] Glasses held on the face by a nose clip instead of supports that go over the ears.

With a slight shiver, an upward jerk of the shoulders, the linen bandages fell from him to the ground. He had rehearsed the thing cleverly.

He stretched his long arms above his head and left the mummy-wrappings where they lay; he was clothed in a white garment reaching his knees, bordered with blue and green, round one wrist was a serpent bracelet, on his breast an immense scarab, green and blue. His headdress was a wig of black horsehair ornamented with greenish gems that seemed to radiate rather than reflect light.

The breadth of shoulder and the narrow hips seemed accentuated. He moved with his hands stretched out before him, the fingers pressed close together.

I looked round for the Flapette, but could not distinguish her expression behind the veil. I knew the Flapette's programme was full; I had the last dance to spare and no extras booked. I wished my programme were full, simply because I didn't want to dance with the Author. There was something horrible about him; that heavy perfume made me dizzy.

I felt sure he would ask me for a dance, but of course he did not do what I expected. He said, "We will stay here, shall we?"

I tried to say no — my lips formed the word, but my strength was used up; all the evening I had been fighting forebodings and the shadow.

"Come" he said, moving slowly beneath the still, orange lanterns.

I hated myself because I obeyed, but I was too tired to do anything else. I didn't want to go. In a way impossible to explain, I, detached and aloof, saw the black nun follow the ancient Egyptian, wondering vaguely why she followed him.

Have You ever experienced that? Or are You always just yourself and conscious of your entity all the while?

Is it only women who watch themselves doing things — having no control, scarcely associating the person they watch with themselves?

We sat down on a stone bench, which gave back the sun it had absorbed during the fierce Egyptian day.

A perfect, still, moonlight night lapped us round with glamour that I can't convey. We looked up through the wooden pergola at the white stars and a slender palm tree.

Isn't it strange I should be wandering about an Eastern garden on a breathless Eastern night while You — what were You doing? I only know You kept away; I could not get at You. I wanted Your big quietness between me and this man, just as I wanted it between me and the Shadow.

Not that I feared, nor had reason to fear, the Author, but I was in the vague state of foreboding which is worse than definite apprehension.

I had identified myself with the nun again; I had ceased to watch her with a detached, impersonal interest.

"What are you thinking about me?" the Author asked abruptly.

I wanted to tell him I was not thinking about him at all; his self-conceit was astounding. But I was not sure if it were assumed. I said, "Everyone expected you'd come as something unusual; I was thinking it would have been a more subtle surprise had you just come as yourself tonight."

"As myself? Are any of us ever ourselves?"

I wondered whether it were clever. It sounded so; I wished I had been just clever enough to know.

ch. ends p. 116

"Not often, I suppose," I answered. "We seldom get the chance to be ourselves. It is safer not, or it's easier, or——"

"Or it's more profitable," he said, and there was bitterness in place of the mocking note.

"I don't think I understand what you mean," I answered, wondering whether I had begun to understand. That strange, ugly laugh shook him.

"I was afraid you didn't," he said; and then: "How much simpler things would be if we were ourselves!" he added under his breath.

But I knew I was meant to hear. I don't suppose the man ever said anything that was not meant to be heard. His quietest whispers are meant for the housetops.

And yet when he said, "How much simpler things might be!" he sighed, and I thought the sigh was genuine.

"Your little friend thinks I'm an incredible sort of person," he remarked. "Do you think I'm incredible?"

"I think you're — improbable," I said.

He was silent for a little while, moving the bracelet round upon his wrist.

"I suppose I am" he replied, and I hated the satisfied way he said it. "I'm a success, you know."

"Yes," I answered.

"It's one thing to be a success and quite another to make a success of things," he went on. "What are you?" he said suddenly.

"I'm a failure." I had never known it till then. But of course I am; I see it. I've never *done* anything; from every aspect by which a woman is judged, and rightly, I am a failure.

"Success is the worst sort of failure," he rejoined, cryptically. He said things which sounded clever — but you couldn't be sure if they would bear looking into at leisure.

I was not sure whether he was trying to say something original or whether it broke from him naturally.

It is perfectly horrible being a failure, realizing it. Why did You never tell me? You've let me go on being disgustingly content — and I've done nothing.

"You wouldn't call me a failure, I suppose?" the man demanded.

"No, how could I?"

"And yet——" He leaned forward, not looking at me, his hands clutching the stone bench, a studied attitude.

"And yet with truth you might call me the biggest failure of the century."

Music floated out to us, veiled; part of the white shimmer and dusky glow. A tom-tom throbbed; an Arab under opium's influence droned and gabbled[4] hoarsely somewhere in the night.

I think I laughed — at the man's conception of his own importance.

"Didn't you just tell me you are a success?"

"Yes, a big success, and therefore a gigantic failure." The Author owned failure. Whether it were pose or not, he was suddenly more human, more likeable.

"What do you think of this?" he said, resuming the mocking voice.

"I think it's a clever get-up."

"And you think it's rather ridiculous?"

A smile I had never seen reach his eyes glinted there. He looked away as though conscious I had surprised it.

"I think it is very ridiculous, yes."

---

[4] To speak rapidly or unintelligibly; jabber.

ch. ends p. 116

"I knew you did," he said quietly. "So do I."

"And rather horrid, somehow. The mummy-wrappings. That ghastly stillness. It's — unwholesome."

"Do you think I'm an unwholesome person?"

"No," I said slowly, but he must have heard there wasn't conviction in my voice.

"You have not read my book, then?" The ugly laugh was checked midway as though he checked it to listen. The heavy perfume came to me on the warm air; I slid a little farther along the bench.

"Yes, I have read it," I said.

He seemed surprised. For a moment he was silent, making an impress of his sandaled foot on the path.

"Why do you think I gave you my book?" he asked.

I had supposed he gave it in order to make me wonder.

"I — don't know," I said.

"The reason was not extraordinary."

"Oh," I returned, "that was extraordinary, wasn't it?"

I thought there was an odd gleam, not resentment and not altogether mirth, in his heavy-lidded eyes.

"I gave it to you because I wanted you to read it."

"Naturally."

"Do you think that follows — with me?"

"No, I don't think it does."

"I gave it to you because I wanted you to read it, and I wanted you to read it so that I might know what you thought of it."

"I supposed so," I said. I hoped he wasn't going to extract an opinion. I didn't possess any opinions tonight.

"What do you think of it?" he asked, and his eyes searched.

"I think you don't believe in it," I stated boldly, hitting at a venture. He turned swiftly.

"I — don't," he said in a queer, stumbling way with a pause between the words. "I wondered if you'd tell me. I hardly hoped you would," he ended unexpectedly. I felt in some way I did not understand my hazard thrust had gone home. I was bewildered and ashamed of myself, astonished and struck dumb.

"Thank you," said the Author simply.

I was almost certain this simplicity was not assumed. A long silence fell between us; I couldn't see past it, he seemed to use it as a cloak. There were stirrings and rustlings and a cricket's chirping in the silence — once a sharp-drawn breath.

"I wonder what you think of me?" the Author said.

I felt I ought to despise him for his continual concern as to what people thought about him. Only, somehow he made it sound as though he didn't mean "people," but just me. He wanted to know what I thought, having exposed his disbelief in his own work. Quite simply he asked it. I meant to be scathing, but I said, "I like you better because you don't believe in your book."

"But it's pretty rotten not to believe in your own stuff?" He seemed to say it in spite of himself.

"It is, absolutely," I replied; "but all the same, I like you better because you don't."

I could not see his face; I don't know whether he was gratified. He seeks notoriety, which he calls fame; he doesn't seek liking.

"I wonder . . ." he said.

"What do you wonder?" I could not help asking, though I knew he meant me to ask; he was so much more human — but I still doubted if his wonder were genuine.

"I wonder about you," he said. "I wonder a lot." And suddenly I remembered the Flapette's remark about the nun.

ch. ends next p.

Just as suddenly You came between me and him, thrust yourself between. I was angry. Angry with You. I don't know why; I can't understand. You seem harder to approach than ever now. I didn't want to go to the dance as a nun. I didn't want people to wonder about me.

Coming home, huddled in an *arrabiyeh*, the Flapette and I were very silent.

The mountains, their color almost visible, were reflected in the still green wonder of the Gulf, and one star shed a long dazzle of limpid light.

Quite suddenly the Flapette gave a little, convulsive shiver. Something was wrong. The Flapette oughtn't ever to be hurt; she might hurt others, but she ought never to be hurt. I felt indignant at once. I did not say anything; I knew she would tell me if she wished.

"It isn't that he——" she began, and my sense of foreboding grew because she had said "he." I suppose a man wouldn't have noticed?

"It isn't that he didn't speak to me or see me — you can't think I'm such a little fool, I know — but it was his awful get-up. There was something horrible about that. I can't explain. It's only a feeling — oh, I wish he hadn't!" she said passionately.

"I wish he hadn't, too." I hated the Author, but hate was an absurd effort; I was so spent with weariness.

"Oh, I wish he hadn't!" she repeated. "You don't understand. It's just — the feeling of it." She said it like a child, miserably. But a little while ago the Flapette would not have had that feeling.

The Author has been still more astonishing.

You must get rather tired of the surprising Author. I said myself his unexpectedness became monotonous after a time, didn't I? But this was different; I've made quite a startling discovery about him — at least, I didn't make it. I ought to say he made quite a startling disclosure, I suppose. I like to imagine I had suspected it all along — I told the Author I had; but then, one always likes to think so afterward. As a matter of fact, I have never been sure.

Last night the Author suddenly joined us on the Dock road. The Flapette said, "No, we're *not* wondering where you sprang from!" and made a face at him.

He smiled — past her, and I hated him. It must have hurt, more than if he hadn't smiled at all.

I have never hated anyone as I hate Desmond Dulac at times, nor been so curious about anyone. The man is extraordinary.

He said nothing, but I was glad he walked beside the Flapette and sat beside her when we all sat down on the low wall that divides the road and the sea.

I so love those walks down the Dock road with the shrouded figures shuffling past; donkey-carts on which Arabs squat with bobbing lanterns that light dusky faces and glittering eyes; the monotonous, droning songs of the tired coal coolies returning from the docks.

Occasionally one receives the greeting *"Said "*[1] or the soft-sounding *"Roh-es-salaam."*[2]

The sky was full of light streaming upward from beyond the purple mountains. Behind us lay the old town, white flat houses and a white tall mosque; great blots of shadow, glittering lights in the water's rippling calm, Eastern and strange. Then as we walked, in a sky of blue and amethyst, of peach and emerald merging to a color for which there is no name, the crescent moon appeared trembling silver, and toward us over the twilight sea crept a light which was not just light and not color, but a thousand shimmering elusive colors, so soft and bright and unearthly I hardly believed in it even while I watched. And on the water's edge a flamingo stood.

Again I had the feeling that it was almost unbearable.

Egypt is like that. It clutches, it tugs, it snatches from you. Not only the beauty of it — the sheer beauty. Queer, droning sounds in the night's warm blackness; the smell of *fessikh*; the acrid smell of burning camel-dung and palm branches, of burning corn-cobs; the reek of rice cooking and lentil soup; the dry, faint sweetness of *doura* fields; the wild Bedouin reed-pipe; the dirt and dust and odorous darkness of the streets; savage, sudden howling of pariahs; the glorious tattered squalor of Bedouin encampments — these things are not beautiful, but

---

[1] Loosely translated means: Be blessed, or be happy.
[2] "Go in Peace."

these are the things that draw and hold you, the smells and the sounds and the dirt, the infinite oldness of it all.

The things which are ugly make their appeal with those which are beautiful. Egypt is compelling.

I don't know how we came to speak of love. Perhaps the Author started the topic; perhaps I kept it going because I was curious to know what dazzling, ridiculous ideas he would expound.

I thought he would believe in — no, I don't think there is much he does believe in — I thought he would uphold soul-affinities. I was quite disappointed he didn't. He spoke of a "still, quenching flame that burned down the centuries"; love without reward or return; of the "gold glory of emptiness"; he made bitterness sound sweet — he spoke of "white suffering" and "radiant pain." He made you believe every soul contributed its hidden flame to the one vast fire. Desmond Dulac doesn't string his words into sentences. They came jerkily; he touched upon a word here, a word there, that caught the imagination. His hearers guessed at his meaning — possibly there was none — and filled the gaps between the words.

He had a way of making his sudden words seem dazzling.

"You watch for them to take form like an electric sign," the Flapette said. He merely suggested. His hearers believed their ideas were his and wondered at them.

He spoke of the relentless force of all love that has ever been . . . the limitless power accumulating through eons . . . of earth crushed by its overwhelming force . . . of death trampled by it. The words meant nothing. Looked into, they were empty and ridiculous. But it was, in fact, all he did not say which told, and the way the disconnected words, the garish colors flashed out suddenly. His book is like that.

ch. ends next p.

What there is in it of imagination is supplied by the reader. The genius lies in what he has left unsaid. His book is a mere glittering, audacious jumble of odd-sounding words.

In the same way, when he speaks his pauses are more telling than his phrases; the gaps are more effective than speech.

I saw the Flapette listening with eyes and lips; pale and rather still.

She was filling every pause in her quick child-way and wondering at the Author's power. She did not even know he paused, or that her imagination gave color to blank places. I longed to call him specious[3] humbug to his face — and make the Flapette hate me without convincing her. What would be the good?

I thought it time to turn the passionate, jerking tide of the Author's eloquence into another channel, when Miss Kershaw said, "I think this hidden white flame business is a bit far-fetched. From what you say — and still more from what you don't say," she added shrewdly — "you lead one to believe every plain, unsentimental woman like myself is contributing to this mysterious force, is keeping a white, splendid lamp — I think that's the order in which you placed the words; it makes a difference, what? — keeping a white, splendid lamp alight, adding to the great pent-up force that's going to — well, it doesn't much matter what it's going to do — something surprising. Do you possess a sense of humor, Mr. Dulac?"

He was equal to her. "As soon as one is aware of its possession it ceases to be," he answered, smiling behind the mask. "I have not discovered the thing in myself——"

---

[3] Deceptively attractive or pleasing.

"A sense of humor covers a multitude of sins," she said, "and gets you through the world comfortably."

"But I don't want to go comfortably through the world. The most desirable things are discomforts. Being in love, for instance; what could be more uncomfortable?"

"Being a woman." Miss Kershaw made that sound which wasn't quite a laugh, and the Flapette started.

"But this nonsense you talk of hidden white lamps," Miss Kershaw went on, "think of it — in connection with me, in connection with the lady of the green spectacles! Can't you imagine the precautions she'd take against fire with her hidden lamp? And she'd forget to trim it. The thing'd run up on one side and smoke."

Because I had been inclined to make fun of her myself, I said I thought her heart was in the right place, anyhow. It is always a safe thing to say, for who is to disprove it?

"It isn't often a woman has her heart in the right place, my dear. Too often it's on her sleeve, or in her mouth. . . ." I wondered where the Flapette's heart was just then?

"What rot we've been talking!" said the Flapette suddenly, in rather a small voice.

"Do you think I've been talking rot?" asked the Author.

"We've all been talking rot," she returned impatiently.

We had — only the Author had talked it consciously.

"You don't think I believe in what I said," he stated as we walked home; he had somehow dropped a few paces behind.

"I know you don't."

He smiled in an odd way, and disappeared down a side street without another word.

All I wrote last night led up to the discovery I promised to tell You about. It was this evening I made the discovery.

I had walked up toward the Sweet Water Canal alone.[1] The Flapette had decided to walk down the Dock road, "as she'd had enough Desmond Dulac to last a bit"; but I suspected she half hoped he would do that which seemed so unlikely — turn up at the same place and hour two days following. I was afraid of this, too, which was the reason I had not joined her. But of course we were both wrong.

I saw a figure sitting motionless on the bank and took it for a native. It was Desmond Dulac. He rose and joined me. I wanted to be alone with the quietness all round, and Your quietness; so I was angry when the Author joined me.

I said hotly, "I want to be alone."

"But you fear to be alone?"

I hated him because he had got so near the truth.

"Am I right?" he said.

---

[1] Ismailia Canal, formerly known as the Sweet Water Canal or the Fresh Water Canal, is a canal which was dug by thousands of Egyptian *fellahin* from 1861 to 1863 to facilitate the construction of the Suez Canal.

"I think you're abominable," I broke out.

"Desmond Dulac often is," he answered.

"Well, you're Desmond Dulac, aren't you?" I retorted.

"Do you think I am?"

"I don't think anything about it."

"That's why I like you," he said. "You're not curious——"

Was he very subtle, or quite honest? At any rate, he drew from me the truth, which I suppose he was trying to get at; I couldn't let him believe I wasn't curious, though I longed to be able to say with truth I wasn't.

"You're not curious——" he repeated.

"But I am," I confessed.

"Curious about me?"

"Yes, curious about you."

"I wonder why?"

"Well, haven't you spent your life trying to make people curious about you?"

I did not understand the swift change that came over his face.

"Making people," he said. "Yes. That's the secret of becoming a success, as differing from being successful. Making people, but not you," he laid stress on the word.

I laughed, I think a little harshly.

"You know you've tried hard to make me wonder about you."

"At first, yes," he admitted grudgingly. "It's become second nature with me, I suppose. I tried to make you wonder about me, but very soon——"

"Very soon what?"

"Very soon you had begun to make me wonder about you."

"About me?"

"Didn't I tell you so that night at the dance?"

ch. ends p. 130

"Yes."

The way I spoke made him say, and I thought I detected a shrinking movement, "You didn't believe me?"

"No," I said, "I didn't."

"Do you believe me now?'

"Yes, but——"

"You believe me, but you don't believe in me? Is that it?"

"That's it," I said shamefacedly.

He seemed all of a sudden sincere and anxious.

He laughed, a queer, glad laugh, without any pain in it. I was startled. It did not seem to belong to the man at all.

"I'm so glad," he said. "I'm so glad you don't believe in me!"

He appeared to be considering.

"I've wanted so to let you into it——" he began; "only, perhaps it was too great a risk——" He paused, and went on with difficulty: "And it has become so easy, so much a habit — to have to admit this to you——" His words were jerky and disjointed. "And yet I've wanted — almost from the beginning, to tell you — what I know you've suspected——" He bit his under lip, that was rather too red, and seemed to struggle between conflicting desires. "I know you felt pretty sure from the first," he said.

"Pretty sure, yes; but not quite," I answered, smiling, "That is just it; I've never been quite sure——"

"Sure of what?" he demanded unexpectedly.

Well, if he would have it——

"Sure it was all just a pose," I said quietly.

He seemed to make attempts at speech, but he didn't say anything. I could feel his odd, red-brown eyes searching my face, and I was rather frightened at my temerity.

I could not tell if he were angry, until he broke into another laugh and went on laughing for quite a long time, till I was as frightened by his laugh as I had been by his silence. I found we were standing still on the bank of the canal.

"You don't know the relief!" he said suddenly, stretching himself and dropping his hands heavily. "How I've hoped you'd say it!"

"What an extraordinary person you are!"

"Oh, for heaven's sake, don't!" he exclaimed, almost fiercely.

"Don't what?"

"Don't tell me I'm extraordinary or surprising."

"But you are. This is the most surprising thing you've done yet. To be glad I found you out!" I began to feel proud of my insight.

"Why do you think it surprising?"

"Because I should imagine you wouldn't care for everyone to know."

"Everyone doesn't know," he said, and I felt by the way he said it he meant he trusted me; it is always rather nice to be trusted.

"No," I answered, "everyone doesn't know," and my tone must have reassured him if he had any doubts.

He pushed back the long red lock impatiently and ran his hand over his head with a sigh that seemed to shake him. He was fumbling for a cigarette.

"I'm the most ordinary person." There was a humorous light in the red eyes, and the worn look that made his face likeable deepened the lines about his mouth. He seemed suddenly a smaller man, his shoulders drooped.

"You can't imagine what it means — when you're quite hopelessly ordinary," he went on, and a gust of laughter cut short his words.

"I'm an ordinary person myself," I said, "so perhaps I can understand."

ch. ends p. 130

"You?" he exclaimed. "You——"

Something in my face made his change. "Well, that's good," he remarked with a shade of mockery. "We're two entirely ordinary people. We ought to understand one another."

I didn't want him to understand me; for one thing, it is so satisfactory not to be understood! I did not think I particularly wanted to understand him, but I couldn't say so.

"It's good to feel you know — I mean to feel that you've said it." He threw away his cigarette with a movement which was a combined sigh and shrug. "What did you think of Desmond Dulac?" he asked, smiling a little beneath heavy lids.

"I thought he was——"

"Yes?"

"I thought he was utterly preposterous."

"Worse," he said. "Didn't you despise him?"

"I think I did rather," I admitted.

"I thought so." He laughed and was silent.

"I wonder if you think I'm being sincere with you now?" he asked. "How should you know?" His laugh was ugly; there was something like pain in it again.

"I can't tell how," I said, "but somehow I do know."

"Thanks," he answered roughly. "It's decent of you, that is." I looked round at him. Was it Desmond Dulac?

As though he had read the thought, he said, "No, it wasn't. It was myself. It's myself you're talking to now — a very ordinary person."

"You must remember I am just an ordinary person too."

I didn't know what his smile meant. It might have meant several things; and I did not want to think it meant any of them.

I said:

"It is so difficult to reconstruct my preconceived idea of you.

Hasn't Egypt really a strange attraction for you — Egypt and its awful oldness?"

"No, it hasn't. I hate dust and uncomfortable things like that——"

"Mummies?" I suggested.

"And mummies," he laughed. "I hate the desert," he said.

"'Despairful, compelling solitudes,'" I quoted mercilessly. "Do you know, I thought you liked the hot air of tombs — it would suffocate some men; I can't imagine you with the smell of burnt heather about you and rain on your face. . . ."

For some time he said nothing, but I heard him draw in his breath and let it out rather slowly. He ignored my speech when at length he broke silence.

"Yes," he repeated, "I'm a very commonplace person. I hate solitude. I like all the comfortable, unexciting sort of things." There was something almost pathetic in the confession.

"The sun is the only thing I really like about Egypt," he went on. "I abhor wet and fog. But even then it's uncomfortably hot most of the year; I'd sooner have a fire any day. . . . I had been asleep that afternoon I met you," he added with engaging candor.

"And what you said last night about — the white lamp and all the rest of it was just——?"

"It was just pose. You don't think I believe in confounded white lamps and the like? . . . I don't say my tastes are simple, but they are quite commonplace, of the solid, substantial type — mid-Victorian, I suppose," with a rueful laugh. "The ordinary humdrum thing would suit me, provided——"

"Provided you could ever disassociate yourself from Desmond Dulac. Could you give up your pose? Could you ever stop posing?"

ch. ends p. 130

A slow red darkened his face.

"I know. That's it. You see, it's almost natural by this time." He was smiling sardonically.

"It is infinitely restful to be one's self for a little while," he went on, and sighed luxuriously.

"For a little while?" I questioned.

"Yes, for a little while."

"I wonder why you have told me this?" I said.

"I wonder why . . ." he answered. "I think it must be because you're another ordinary person."

But somehow I felt that was not what he had meant to say.

"You have no desire to throw up the whole thing," I queried, "and be yourself?"

"I'm a success, remember," he reminded me, and his voice was harsh. "And I don't think I could chuck it up now," he added in a different tone. "I think you can't altogether realize what it would mean——"

"No," I said.

"It isn't a case of wanting to chuck it. I've — lived a pose so long, I doubt if it would be possible."

"So do I."

This seemed to madden him. The red eyes blazed and his words made a sudden clatter.

"You do? I suppose you would. I suppose it's natural enough. You think I'm not capable — I've just said I don't think I could chuck it . . . but——"

"But?"

"No matter," he returned in his quiet, drawling way. "I haven't words to dazzle you with like Desmond Dulac. You won't find me worth listening to, I warn you."

"I haven't said I was going to listen." I felt nettled that he took it for granted.

"I know," he replied with sudden quietness. "But you'll let me — be myself now and then with you?"

I was silent.

"I know you couldn't stand Desmond Dulac," he said.

"I own I couldn't at times."

"I've just got to throw myself on your mercy," he went on in a disarming, boyish way, but his voice sounded tired and his face looked worn.

"Yes," I said. I didn't see what else I could say.

"When we are together——" he began.

I found myself hoping it would not be often, intending it should not; I don't know why. I liked him better than I had.

"When we are together," he said, "I can be myself?"

"Yes," I repeated in order to satisfy him, because I couldn't think of anything else to say and because I wanted Your quietness.

Passionately I desired to keep him out of Never-Was.

"I believe," the Author said, "you think I'm still posing, that this is only another pose?"

I had never thought about it, but I was struck by his suggestion: it might be so. . . .

The way he spoke told me it was not.

"This hasn't been easy," he said.

"Then why did you do it?" I asked impatiently.

"Because I'm not an out-and-out——"

"Oh! Was that why?"

"Well, no. Not altogether. . . . I expect I just had to tell you."

"It is so comfortable to be able to relax now and then?" I suggested.

ch. ends next p.

"I said I liked comfort, yes. . . . You hit hard," he remarked.

"Don't ever dare to pose again for my benefit," I warned.

"Not if I can help it. . . . I hardly know when it's pose and when it isn't," he added simply.

It was so human of him. I think humanness always warms me; I can't resist its appeal, perhaps because I'm so hopelessly human myself. But I felt a sudden foreboding, one of those formless things that have come to me lately. I was in a panic; thrusting the thing from me lest I should see what it was.

He said, "Do you know why I singled you out from the first?"

I laughed because the sentence savored so of Desmond Dulac — and to give myself time to think. I don't think very quickly. You know.

"Of course," I said, "simply because the obvious thing was to single out the Flapette."

But I'd very nearly seen what the foreboding was; I only managed not by shutting my eyes.

"You oughtn't to be here alone," said the Author. He had discovered me by the Canal again. I was there alone because I thought he would not turn up at the same place a second time.

I love the Sweet Water Canal. As soon as the sunset light creeps into the sky everything takes such mystery. On the opposite bank palms stood out dark against a sky flooded with violet, rose, and gold; in the midst of the colors, where they merged, the new moon and a dazzling star hung tremulous; soft rosy clouds were part of the water; the moon and the star and the sunset glory were repeated in the Canal, winding between its tall sedges and dusky palms. Away in the distance came the sail of a native boat, so slowly it scarcely moved — a great white lotus drifting with the stream. An Arab on a white donkey passed in a cloud of rose-pink dust, the sunset throbbing through it.

This is the wonderful thing about the nights: while the sky is still flooded with color the moon rises in the very midst and the sky seems full of color after dusk has fallen — a warm, glowing dusk.

"I like being alone," I said resentfully, the more resentful because I knew I was rash to come so far by myself.

"And I don't," he replied; "I must be with people."

"People who wonder about you," I said. "You forget I don't."

"Do you think I forget? . . . I remember quite a lot of things about you. What is it that you seek?"

He evidently did remember things; I had quite forgotten he had asked me before and received no answer.

"I never told you I was seeking anything."

"I know. That is why I thought you must be."

"Ordinary people don't seek," I replied evasively.

He smiled in an exasperating way.

"Let's be sincere with one another. Won't you tell me what it is?"

I can't think now how he made me tell him — at least, I suppose he made me. I know I didn't mean to tell him. But here was someone who seemed to understand, who wanted to share my thoughts. You cannot conceive what it has been for me all these years without sympathy — I never realized it myself till now; I must admit that. Perhaps my vanity was flattered because the Author was interested by the fact that I am seeking.

I felt horrible, bitter and dried-up, last night, too, and Egypt seemed more than ever pitiless. Anyhow, I told him.

"I'm seeking — Space," I said.

If he had laughed or been silent contemptuously I should have hated him. As it was, I only hated myself; I felt somehow disloyal to myself, and to You. But he just said, "I wonder if you will find it."

The Author seemed to understand. He didn't think the notion ridiculous, as of course it is; he seemed to understand what I meant. I daresay he didn't really. Only, I felt the need for sympathy and understanding. You have given me so little lately; I suppose it is my own fault, but I can't get near You as I could, You're so unapproachable.

"Of course, I shall not find it," I broke out. "It's a delusion."

"But still you go on seeking?" he said quietly, I thought wistfully. "Isn't it a pity?" he said.

"Of course it's a pity! But do you suppose that makes any difference?"

"To a woman, no. I hope you won't find Space is——"

"Emptiness. Probably I shall. There isn't really such a thing as Space, I suppose — not in the sense I mean."

"And still you go on seeking?" he repeated, with something which might have been awe or merely incredulity.

"Yes," I said.

"You know I told you I was a pilgrim . . . that what I sought was forever hidden, or some such stuff. And you didn't believe it for a moment."

"I think I did for a moment — it was afterward I doubted."

"It was merely pose," he said. "I've long since given up seeking — anything."

"Then you did seek once?" I questioned. It was so hard to imagine Desmond Dulac before he became a success.

"Yes."

"So you can understand a little?"

"Yes," he said again.

"I wonder when you stopped?"

"I expect it was gradual . . . when I became a success."

"I wonder what you were seeking?"

"That I can't tell you."

I thought it was too bad of him, having extracted an admission from me. I said so.

ch. ends p. 136

"It doesn't do for a man who's a success to begin thinking about seeking. And anyhow — I mean I'm no hand at putting things into words——"

"Perhaps not. You're a skilled hand at putting things into pauses."

He smiled in rather an odd way. I thought he seemed hurt because I was belittling his work.

"Would you——" He hesitated. "Would you care to read another book of mine?"

"To tell you the truth, I don't think I should."

"I like the way you slap me in the face," he returned whimsically. "You didn't care for my last book, did you?"

"I've told you I didn't. I hate hot-houses. Your book was like a hot-house. I wanted to get outside all the time!"

He made a wry face, or he tried to smile; I wasn't sure which.

"I suppose it wouldn't be any good giving you another book?" he asked.

"How any good?"

"I mean you wouldn't read it?"

He was quite humble and anxious; I felt sorry for him and suddenly astonished at the way I was treating the famous man. I felt rather small and hot and ashamed.

"Of course I'd read it," I said.

"It's the book I wrote before I gave up seeking," he rejoined quietly. "It's in manuscript."

"Oh!" I said; it didn't convey anything to me.

"It was never published," he explained.

"Oh!" I said again.

He broke out savagely.

"I hawked it round for two years . . . that book. . . . Then I wrote the kind of thing you've read — and became a success," he added with a sort of dull bitterness.

I felt shaken by pity and by blind indignation against a public that could make a man give up seeking. . . . It did not occur to me Desmond Dulac had voluntarily given up seeking in order to become successful, that it had lain with himself. It all seemed piteous and unjust. I couldn't say anything of what I felt. You can't, can you? You will understand.

I just said, "Oh, please let me have it. I want to read the book you wrote before you stopped seeking."

He is going to give it to me.

"I wonder," said the Author unexpectedly — he couldn't help being unexpected — "I wonder what you are always writing?"

"How do you know I am always writing?" I retorted.

"I didn't know. It was a shot in the dark. You've told me now."

I hated him. "You needn't think I am going to tell you what it is," I said, confirming his suspicion.

"No, I didn't suppose you would tell me."

"It isn't any business of yours." I couldn't bear him even to suspect the existence of Never-Was. I was furious because I had told him I wrote. But I am always telling the Author things I hadn't meant to tell him. Desmond Dulac the Author has a genius for making people guess at things; Desmond Dulac the Man has a genius for guessing at things in other people.

"I wonder why you don't write," he mused.

"You've just told me that I do!"

"I mean Write," he said, giving it a capital. "Why don't you Write?"

It took me a long time to grasp what he meant, and when I did I thought he was mocking, till I saw his eyes, and particularly his mouth.

ch. ends next p.

"What do you mean?" I said in a bewildered, scared fashion, but with excitement leaping.

"I mean, why don't you write a book?"

"Me . . . write a book?"

"Why not?"

"But it wouldn't ever be published."

"Would that matter?"

I began to wonder if it would.

"What makes you think I could do it — possibly?" I said.

"I don't know. Your eyes, perhaps. You've got listening eyes."

Because I liked having them called listening eyes and because I didn't like his saying it, I answered impatiently, "Don't talk nonsense. You promised not to pose anymore. I knew you couldn't keep off it for long."

"You don't think I'm sincere."

I knew I had hurt him.

"You might find what you're seeking that way, perhaps," he said after a pause. He spoke in a timid, rather rough way, as though he feared I should hurt him again. I had meant to, till he spoke like that. Somehow I couldn't then. He seemed really to care whether I found what I was seeking.

I began to wonder if this were the way. The man has in an astonishing degree the power of making you wonder.

"You've got listening hands, too," he said, looking at them.

I told him hotly he was posing — because something told me he was not.

Could I write a book? I wonder! It has never seemed possible before. . . . The Author has a way of making things seem possible. I have been thinking about it ever since.

Of course, it would be a quite ridiculous book; it wouldn't ever get published. But would that matter?

The Flapette could hardly get her breath, but all the same she was trying to say things at a great rate violently.

"I'm not going to stand it. I won't stand it. That's the sort of man he is — he would be——"

"Who is? And what sort of man?" I mildly asked. I wondered if it were the Author. The Flapette has seen rather a lot of the Author lately, and she has decided she can afford to be cool to him. She has been thoroughly enjoying life again, and I've wondered whether I only imagined a change in her. I have come to the conclusion that the Author was desirous all along to cultivate the Flapette, only he can't bear to do the obvious thing. He has said no more about my writing a book; he hasn't given me the book he promised, either. I don't know why. I imagined he had turned into a reliable person all of a sudden just because he admitted the truth.

It transpired the Flapette was not referring to Desmond Dulac.

"It's that parson!" she broke out indignantly. "His beastly

searchlight humbugged me at first, but I've really known all along——"

"Well?" said Miss Kershaw dryly.

"He — he was insulting," she blazed. "He meant to be——"

"Don't you think you imagined he meant to be?" I suggested. "The parson has always been rather specially decent to you, Flapette."

"Well, what if I did?" she said unreasonably. "I keep thinking about it——"

Miss Kershaw interrupted characteristically:

"Don't think about it. Imagined insults, my dear, are like coconut chips — if you think about them you can't swallow them."

The Flapette rushed from the room and would have slammed the door, only in Egypt doors are always fixed open.

I went after her. "Tell me all about it," I said, using the time-honored formula. I sometimes think I'm a dreadfully ordinary person — I mean really; of course, I don't believe it when I tell the Author I'm ordinary. I seem always to say the things everyone else always says. I don't see how I could write a book. . . .

The Flapette's eyes were very blue and her cheeks very pink. She was shaking all over.

"The old toad said — he was monstrous — he actually had the face to say the Author" — (I thought it had something to do with the Author) — "that the Author was the biggest humbug unhung . . . that it was all claptrap — deception——" She couldn't get her breath.

A little chill crept over me, and I felt my cheeks burning. At the moment I was only concerned in not betraying the Author because he had trusted me. I couldn't find room for loathing the Rev. Arthur or for pitying the Flapette just then.

"What could he mean?" I queried feebly. I am always feeble when I want to rise to an occasion. Have you noticed it?

"Don't you understand?" The Flapette was exasperated. "He said the Author is — is a humbug. It doesn't seem very difficult to understand what he meant by that!"

"But why such indignation? How was this an insult to you? You began by saying the man had meant to insult you."

"Insult me, yes. . . . It was not imagination!"

"Well, how did he insult you?"

I had never trusted that shining face and outlook.

"I said I believed in the Author," the Flapette stated doggedly.

"Wasn't that rather unwise?"

"I don't see why."

I didn't know how to put it, so I merely repeated what she had said — the last resource of the most ordinary people in a corner.

"You said you believed in him?"

"Yes, I did."

"And the parson replied——"

"He replied there was no fool like a blind fool! He laughed when he said it," she admitted grudgingly, "but it was a beastly sort of laugh."

"The shine came off?"

"Yes. He was horrible. He pretended to talk to me as he would to a child——" She looked so like a child, flushed and disheveled, I thought possibly, after all, the parson had not pretended.

"He made out the Author is hoaxing the public, imposing on it——" She swallowed, and her breath came quickly. "He said

I should find him out in the long run — if he wasn't shown up first! It was——"

I don't know what the Flapette nearly said, but after a struggle to articulate she amended "intolerable."

I was chiefly concerned because I was not the only person who knew about the Author. Another had found him out. The parson might at any time betray him. I would not admit to myself that I was angry to find I was not the only one who knew. I was indignant because the Author had been stigmatized as humbug — when upon his own confession he had shown it to be true. It is so hard to disbelieve altogether in his pose; nearly as hard as it was to believe in it altogether.

"I think," said the Flapette, "it is jolly lowdown. Because a man isn't ordinary and obvious and uninteresting, because he shows a little originality——" I couldn't help smiling at this mild description of his vagaries; I rather think, though, that I said something of the sort myself a short time ago.

"Just because the man is not exactly like everyone else," she went on, "he's — maligned" — she seemed to like the word, anyhow she repeated it — "maligned, made out to be a rotter. People like the Rev. Arthur are just envious of his fame!"

"Or his success," I said.

"Well, isn't it the same thing?"

I didn't contradict her.

"They can't climb where he's climbed, so they must try to pull him down," she said. I wondered where the Flapette thought he had climbed, and speculated as to the advisability of smashing the pedestal myself rather than let her discover it was tottering. Then I reflected she would doubtless refuse to be convinced of his mutability with the fragments lying at her feet and the dust rising to choke her. . . .

"I've always had my back up against injustice and spite," the Flapette said. "It's so beastly and——"

"And small?"

"Yes, I suppose so. And it was rather rot being thought such a little fool I'd be taken in," she confessed honestly. The Flapette is startlingly honest at times. I began to think the secret of her indignation lay in that; she didn't like to be put down as an inexperienced little fool. I began to be convinced of it. Isn't it easy to feel convinced when you want very much to be — or are You not like that? Is it only because I'm a woman? You know I said some time ago I thought the Flapette simply had a frivolous desire to sample the grown-up state. She breaks out in such a childish way; I begin to think I have worried needlessly. And it has worried me, this which I've not formed into a thought. It has been one of the vague forebodings that flap darkly and settle again in the desert of my present outlook. (That isn't half bad, is it? Quite reminiscent of Desmond Dulac.) I'm sorry. You must be sick of Desmond Dulac, only You needn't show it so plainly every time I chance to mention him. I get just as sick of him as You do — often.

I think I shall submit the "flapping forebodings" to the Author with a view to that book of mine. I wonder if he'd recognize the familiar flavor! Sorry. I can't think why You are so prejudiced. Personally I don't dislike him nearly as much as I did before I showed him up — well, before he told me the truth. I thought You would have backed me in that. You're big and tolerant; You've a horrid way of making me feel despicably small, You know. I thought You'd be pleased. But You are so hard to understand. Are women as hard to understand if you're a man as men are if you're a woman? I've despaired of understanding You almost from the first. It was going to have been so different; I invented the Idea of You because I was so alone — and it has somehow made it worse, heaps worse. And then, lately, just when I've needed You, and the Shadow has come closer, and I've had all these forebodings, and begun to feel I couldn't cope with any of it any more — You've been ungetatable.

At first I groped desperately for You, but I can't go on. Don't You see I can't go on? What's the good? * * * Well, You never have been and never will be — but it's not a comforting thought! Yes, I'm rather bitter tonight, and unusually sane. I am adding this about ten minutes after the asterisks. You can get sane under ten minutes if you try. I've got to try these days. I believe I'm getting an unwholesome outlook or something, and it won't do if I am to face things presently — the Possibility. I feel it is growing into a probability.

You want to be exceptionally fit, your outlook wants to be fit, when you're "up against" a thing like this, as the Flapette would say.

My outlook has not been fit lately. Do You know what I mean to do? I am not going to write a word in this book for a whole day. I thought about making it a week at first, but I think a day is as much as I can manage just now. Recently I have been writing almost every day. I must talk to You, if You won't talk to me. It is rather dull and chilly being sane. . . .

I've quite decided the Flapette has not really grown up; her indignation because the parson called her a little fool proved it. I've come to the conclusion, in my present calm, horribly well-balanced state, that I have imagined all sorts of things, harbored disturbing forebodings needlessly, simply because my outlook isn't fit at present. Well, it is going to be fit; I shall see to it in future.

For a start, I won't write a word in this book all tomorrow. It is nearly tomorrow now, as a matter of fact; I thought I would write as much as I could today because I am not going to let myself write any tomorrow. I have been writing ever since dinner to make up for tomorrow! Why are You smiling like that? There is the clock. . . .

I am not so sure about the Flapette. She puzzles me. She has been thinking, and she never used to think. That she has been thinking argues to my illogical mind that she has been feeling. It isn't reasoning; I can't reason. But I can make guesses in the dark, and once in a way they turn out correct. Yes, I always feel it is going to be the once-in-a-way beforehand.[1]

The Flapette is becoming like the Author; I can never be quite sure; often I am nearly, but never quite. I've begun to wonder again.

I felt I must do something with my blank day, so I persuaded Miss Kershaw and the Flapette to take tea on the launch — just ourselves, which was much more peaceful.

The Author is such a disturbing element in a good many ways. I don't suppose the Flapette was at one with me, but, at any rate, she gave no sign and entered into things zestfully.

It was a wonderful afternoon. All afternoons are wonderful in Egypt.

I always seem to describe afternoons and evenings; that is

---

[1] Once in a way is another way of saying once in a while or occasionally.

because the mornings are still too hot to stir beyond the house, and noonday is pale and colorless: the sun seems to drain the color from things so that the sky itself is white.

I longed to go back upon the resolution I had made, when past us came a huge sailing-ship, with the glorious cross-ways sail and a prow[2] like a fairy ship, manned by scores of Arabs in vivid colors.

She was painted daring reds and greens, and the great sail made an immense dazzle of white in the jewel-green water beneath it; the very shape of the boat was a delight. She might have been sailing from Never-Was. . . .

You know I said since Marseilles, where I slept in a world of ships, they would always be Things to me afterward. Well, they are. And this was the most wonderful Thing I had ever seen.

The Flapette was in particularly boisterous spirits. It was delicious coming back just as dusk fell, tearing through the water — behind us a sea of gold, a sky of gold and salmon above the long line of hills; the waves dashing against the launch, the throb and bound of her; ahead the dark avenue with wavering lights; masts of native boats massed in the dusk rising above the trees; the red and green lights of a passing steamer; a shuddering siren.

I was feeling anything but sane and well-balanced. I was nearer finding You than I had been for a long time, when the Flapette thrust chocolates upon me and began talking about sacrifice.

It was such an astounding subject for the Flapette to open, it brought me right out of the rather pleasant state into which I had sunk, and I sat up, startled.

---

[2] The portion of a ship's bow (front end) above water.

"I've been thinking about sacrifice," the Flapette stated casually, as though it were no more surprising a subject for thought than a new hat.

The Flapette thinks a lot about new hats — unnecessarily, because you can wear any hat that was ever created if you're fluffy.

"What an extraordinary thing to think about, Flapette!" I said unsympathetically; I had so nearly got at You when she must needs thrust this discussion upon me.[3]

"I don't see why," she answered, with a rather pathetic attempt at dignity.

You can't combine being fluffy with dignity.

"I suppose you imagine I never think about anything," she said coldly, turning the contents of the chocolate box into her lap, and hunting among them with discrimination.

I believe I had imagined so, but even in my present mood I wouldn't say it.

"Well, you're wrong. I think a lot about things . . ." She was peeling silver paper slowly from a melted chocolate; I smiled.

"A lot about all sorts of things," she said. "You needn't look superior. You believe I'm still a kid, but I'm not. I've done a jolly lot of thinking."

"Since when?" I couldn't resist it.

The Flapette ignored my question, diplomatically throwing a handful of chocolates into my lap.

Feeling the Flapette desired to give her views on sacrifice, I endeavored to be amiable.

"Well, what about it?" I said.

She sighed. "It's beastly puzzling. I can't come to any

---

[3] "Must needs" is an archaic way of saying "absolutely had to."

conclusions. Look here, it's this way. It can't be sacrifice if you're not conscious you're sacrificing anything. You admit that?" She bit into a chocolate and looked at the color of the cream with a judicial air.

"Yes," I replied, "I admit it."

"Well, as I said, it can't *be* sacrifice if you're not conscious of it — (I wish I could find a ginger; that looks like a 'tombstone,' doesn't it? Beastly things. You can't swallow them when you think about them, like 'Bill's' coconut chips or insults or something) — and yet if you *know* you're sacrificing yourself it seems to miss being a sacrifice at all——" She grew confused, realizing this was an abstract subject with which she was grappling, but she went on courageously and rather defiantly, "——at any rate, in the best sense. And yet — (I do loathe the scented ones, they're just like soap) — and yet, oh, I don't know — it's all so confusing, hopelessly."

"It is, Flapette, hopelessly."

The Flapette herself is confusing; I cannot make her out. I don't like her thinking of sacrifice when she's got a box of chocolates.

And whatever put the idea of sacrifice into her head? I can't reconcile it with my conception of her. I have begun to worry again. It is quite futile for me to attempt being sane and philosophical. I can't do it. The forebodings have all come crowding back.

Keeping off writing is a failure; hasn't this proved it? I have given it a fair trial. I decided I would sit up till midnight, and as soon as twelve struck open the book and write the most outrageous nonsense . . . but sleep disposes. I fell asleep and never woke till this morning!

An Arab has just passed in gold turban and blue *galabieh*,

ch. ends p. 150

pushing a barrow filled with trailing green sugarcane, and in the midst a great golden heap of oranges. I cannot glance from my window without encountering riotous masses of color, color that would be garish save for the blinding sunlight and the dust. Now a man has stopped at the street corner selling a weird sweetmeat like Edinburgh rock[4] in a moist state. It is wound round a staff about seven feet high with a kind of rattle at the top; he keeps shaking it to attract purchasers. When he secures a purchaser he pulls off a piece of the horrid stuff in his fingers.

I can hear the metallic clatter the lemonade-seller makes with his little brass cups, the groan of a bread-seller, and the wail of a date-merchant. Goats are bleating and cocks are crowing; there is a constant soft shuffling of bare feet and feet in heelless slippers; shrill voices of women quarreling; the snarl of passing camels heavily burdened. I hear the buzzing of innumerable flies, and always all day long the rise and fall of the funeral chant — "*Lâi-lâ-ha il lâ-l-lâh.*" I have grown used to it all; I take it for granted; and yet it is always new to me, each separate sound and scent is poignant as the first day I arrived. I sit very long sometimes at this window looking out on the movement and color, the shifting, strange sights of the street.

It is so curious I never meant to come to Suez, never meant to leave the beaten track. I ought to be in Cairo now, according to my plans, or doing the Nile trip, I suppose. I don't know how long we are to stay in Suez. I don't much mind; these golden, dusty days slip by and become the past imperceptibly.

Time is of so little account in this old country, whose oldness terrifies.

---

[4] Also known as Edinburgh Castle rock; a traditional Scottish confection consisting of sugar, water, cream of tartar, colorings, and flavorings formed into sticks presenting a soft and crumbly texture.

Miss Kershaw comes to Egypt every winter for her health, it seems. I had thought Miss Kershaw was sound as a bell and tough as whipcord, but perhaps she lives with a Shadow. I shouldn't wonder; life is so unexpected every way.

She has made no suggestion about moving on, and I am glad, because I somehow feel, when we do, things will happen.

I have no foundation for thinking so — I just feel it.

The Flapette seems quite content. She has seen a good deal of the Author lately. I can't think what they find to talk about — but probably the subject of himself interests them both. When we do leave Suez I shall have to insist upon leaving these friends I have made. Good as they are, I cannot inflict my presence indefinitely. But I shall not welcome loneliness; it won't be easy. I must have people; and now I've found people, lovable people, I've got to give them up. You don't see why I should? I suppose You wouldn't; You are not a bit complex. Life must be such straight-sailing for You.

I embarked on the subject tonight, awkwardly enough. I think from the way I put it Miss Kershaw must have imagined I am sick of the present arrangement.

She screwed up her funny eyes and looked hard at me.

"What in the world for?" she demanded. "What are you driving at, my dear girl?"

I could not explain further.

"This is rank nonsense," she stated, with a kind of snort.

"You told me to stick to nonsense," I said.

ch. ends next p.

She ignored the remark.

"Do you want to be alone?" she asked.

She looked forbidding and grim and very likeable.

"No, I don't," I answered weakly.

"Then why in the name of goodness should you go?

All of a sudden her angular, uncompromising figure seemed to be standing between me and the horror of loneliness.

"You're an angel," I said with a deplorable lack of humor; I had lost it in a quick uprush of emotion.

"Hardly," she returned; "I'm too utilitarian — I'd be the sort of angel who'd use the feathers out of her wings to make quill pens. . . . That's settled, then," she added with finality.

So I suppose it is——

It is my birthday tomorrow, and no one but myself knows the fact.

But then I shall be thirty-four — so perhaps it is as well. I think when you reach thirty-four, birthdays should be allowed to slip by unnoticed. All the same — You see, I have never "kept" a birthday.

Thirty-four years, and I've not *done* anything. It is rather a depressing thought. Looking back, they seem thirty-four quite blank years.

I had not even begun to seek till I came away — till I found You and Nonsense. I don't know what You have to do with it, because I should think You have never spoken of seeking in your life, and the notion of seeking Space, such an intangible, absurd thing, must seem laughable to You. Somehow I think I began to seek from then, from that day in Notre Dame de la Garde. And I'm still seeking the thing I call Space for want of a better word. Sometimes I have a thought: that You could tell me how to set about it. Sometimes I think that You know.

I said I had never kept a birthday. Well, I am going to keep this one, very sanely and decorously; I can't forget the fact that it is my thirty-fourth. I am going to keep it all to myself, and to Yourself if You like. I'll tell You what we will do. We will keep my birthday like this. I shall get up before breakfast and go as far as I dare into the desert. I shall see the sun rise in the desert It will be rather a wonderful birthday.

You're to give me the ability to believe implicitly in You just for one day. That is how we will keep it. You and me and nonsense, plenty of it, and the desert.

I am rather sorry for the woman who is going to keep her birthday in the desert, clutching a belief that is slipping from her. It is a bit tragic. Never mind; if it's only a melancholy sort of pleasure I can get out of it, I mean to extract as much as I can.

I shall finish this book tonight. Oddly enough, I begin a new one on my birthday. I shall finish this book which I intended for a diary — for a diary! What a stale, flat, and unprofitable thing it might have been! I don't suppose I should ever have filled half the book; I should have given up after the first few tedious entries.

I hate having reached the end of my book. The diary would simply have been ruled pages of words between the black, shiny covers; instead of that. You are between the covers. The book has been the bridge over to Never-Was. I feel as though another book could not mean the same. This one has the beginning of You in it, and Notre Dame de la Garde and the little phantom ships . . . the next one — I have a feeling the next will never be filled. You may end in it; I have no power over You. So soon I found I had no power, and You have grown away from me. I expect it is my fault; I can't get at You as I once could.

I have been turning back and reading over my book tonight, a very unwise thing to do — unless one did it in the morning after eating ham-and-eggs. A diary read at night makes one disgusted or pleasantly miserable.

This book has made me miserable, not pleasantly.

It is funny to read about the voyage, the little Smiths and their Marconigram, and the Prawn. The Prawn, You will have remarked, has already faded out of this narrative. I quite forgot to mention the fact, he did it so unnoticeably. It must have been quite soon after the Flapette refused him.

It is strange, reading about these people who just touch one's life and disappear. Do they make any impression upon us and we on them, I wonder?

What is it all for? And now there is the Author. . . . I expect before I have written many pages of the next book he, too, will have faded out — or, being Desmond Dulac, disappeared with as much suddenness as he first appeared. It all seems so pointless, the lives that cross, or merely touch like mine and the people I met on the voyage. Why did I tell You about them, as though they were of any importance?

I have a feeling there is some purpose in it; that it is all leading up — perhaps, after all, I shall some day find what I seek, and realize the Prawn, and the Smiths, the baby with the plaid frock, and the woman with the green spectacles all had a hand in it.

This is the very last page of my book. A clock is striking, and the watchman at the street corner has let the butt of his rifle come to the ground with a thud.

It is my birthday already. The day I am going to keep in my own way in the desert.

I have been very dull and retrospective on this last page, but tomorrow — today I mean — I am going to begin the new book with a page of sheer nonsense. I am going to tell You all about my birthday in the desert.

My birthday turned out altogether different from what I planned.

To begin with, I slept late, and the sun had risen by the time I reached the desert — and then, I have not had to keep it alone.

Everybody appeared to know about it!

I believe I had derived quite a melancholy pleasure from the fact that no one knew; I am glad I have got a sense of humor.

I had just reached the "gardens," where *gamoos* and humped cattle were plowing on the border of the desert; I was rather hot, and a little out of temper, because I had overslept myself and was thirty-four on such a morning — when the Author overtook me. I was surprised. Lately I have seen very little of him; as a matter of fact, I have purposely avoided him. I admit I began to feel rather annoyed with the Author; he had so patently cultivated me because the obvious thing was to cultivate the Flapette, and then dropped me — tired of me, I thought.

I was surprised and resentful, but my surprise turned to astonishment when he held out a bulky package. "I thought I'd give you the book on your birthday," he said.

I took it without a word; I could not think of anything to say.

"This is your birthday, isn't it?" he asked.

"Yes."

"What are you doing out here in the desert on your birthday?" he said curiously.

"I am keeping it," I said, and began to laugh. I suddenly felt so sorry for myself and the desolate way I was keeping my birthday.

"Alone?" he asked.

"Yes," I told him, and felt disloyal to You.

"You want to be alone?" he queried, rather wistfully, I thought, and glancing at the bundle which I had taken without a word.

"No, I don't," I said; "I don't!" and then, "I mean I do — I want to be alone."

I must have spoken passionately without knowing it; he looked surprised and puzzled. Suddenly, flushing, I realized I had not thanked him for his book.

"It's very good of you," I murmured inadequately.

He seemed a little disappointed.

"I've written a birthday wish inside it," he said.

With a start I realized he was giving me this manuscript, this which evidently had meant much to him once, if not now. He was giving it to me.

"But," I stammered, "you mean me to keep it?"

"I want you to keep it."

"And you've written in it . . ."

"I've written a wish for your birthday in it," he said. He left me standing with the bundle of manuscript in my hands, looking at it stupidly.

I sat down on the sand and opened it. He wished that I might find what I was seeking. Just that. He had not signed his name.

I liked what he had written. I had seen his face when he gave me the book; he was not posing.

This man really cared whether I found Space, perhaps because he had stopped seeking himself.

I forgot all about the sunrise I had missed. It was so good to know someone had spent thought over my birthday, that I was not as desolate as I imagined. I forget even to wonder how Desmond Dulac discovered this was my birthday. That did not seem important. He knew.

Before I reached the hotel I was beginning to revert to my previous resentment; I had been done out of the pleasantly melancholy birthday I planned. I had a feeling You were quite near when I reached the desert, before the Author overtook me.

When I got back resentment grew. My lonely birthday had been turned into quite a conventional occasion with parcels on the table at my place, Miss Kershaw brusquely demonstrative, and the Flapette in a state of restless anticipation. I supposed I had unwittingly mentioned my birthday; I did not remember it. I am ashamed to confess I regretted I could no longer with reason feel sorry for myself. I gave up all idea of keeping my own birthday and let the others keep it for me.

They had planned it before I had even thought of any plan. They had, it seemed, planned a moonlight ride into the desert.

The Author was coming; the Flapette told me. I wished he were not, and felt ungrateful, for it was nice of him to give me his book — the book that was never published. I couldn't help feeling pleased he had given me the book; I think my vanity was gratified because he assumed I should appreciate such a gift. The Flapette did not know he had sought and stopped seeking.

But might he not have told her also? I didn't think he had — only, they had been so much together. The Flapette could not understand.

The Author arrived on a big, gaunt white donkey with a

blue necklace and a vicious temper. The donkey-boy uttered his hoarse "*Ha-a-ah!*" and we set out.

A few minutes took us beyond the town and a domed *Shiek's* tomb; the sudden muffling of the clattering little hooves told us we had reached the fringe of the desert.

I lost all count of time. The wonder of it — the moon a little past the full, but a dreamy softness in the atmosphere so that the vast stretches of sand seemed to melt into the moon-pale sky with its white stardust, the sky into the phantom hills. The sand looked rose in that misty radiance, rolling for miles. I felt I must ride away and away into the desert, into the heart of the night and the great brooding silence there. . . . Surely I was finding Space at last?

The Author's big white donkey pressed alongside my little black one. My foot was crushed against his stirrup. The two donkeys had dropped behind. Donkeys are exasperating creatures: they oblige you to ride with a person whether you will or not.

"I hoped you would be pleased to have the book," Desmond Dulac said, keeping his donkey close to mine.

"I was. Only — I was rather surprised!"

"Surprised? Why?"

I wouldn't tell him I had begun to think he'd forgotten about the book; that was as good as telling him I had not forgotten.

I said:

"Had you presented me with — a lotus bud, let's say, it would have been more like you——"

"More like Desmond Dulac," he corrected. The way he tried to disclaim identity with Desmond Dulac irritated me.

"It's all the same," I said.

He spoke roughly. "Can't you get that out of your head?"

"No, I can't."

"I'm sorry you can't," he replied, in such an odd tone I looked up at him. I could tell nothing from his face; it was the same mask behind which he smiled at a wondering public.

But I knew he was not smiling now; there was something sinister about his calm; only the long red lock shook with the donkey's violent action. I began to be afraid; I said anything to rouse him.

"I can breathe out here. . . . I could go on riding forever!"

I felt he turned his narrowed eyes; he seemed wondering about me, and I didn't want him to wonder.

I wished I had said something else. I wished the other donkeys would overtake us, or that mine would get ahead of his.

There was silence between us full of the clashing of silver coins on the donkeys. Then:

"You really love this desolate wilderness?" he asked.

"Haven't I told you I could ride on and on? . . ." I felt safe again.

"How splendidly surprising you are!" he said. I thought unconsciously he had assumed the pose. It was said in the Desmond Dulac manner. Because I thought he was posing I only laughed.

"There's something mysterious about you — and yet you're not quite a woman — I don't know why you are not, but you've such a desire for clear air and wide clean spaces. For desolate things. . . ."

I felt he understood dimly. In that mood, intoxicated with the sense of limitless breathing-space, I wanted to share my sensations. I welcomed his understanding.

I said, "You don't know the appeal it makes. I just want to

ch. ends p. 162

breathe it. . . . I don't want to be or know anything else, to be conscious of anything."

"I wonder if you are a woman," he answered whimsically, half to himself, "or only a desert-thing? . . . Are you human, I wonder?"

"I'm very human," I said nervously, and tried to laugh. I was urging my donkey forward.

"There's something very cold in you. I can't get beyond it. . . . I feel I've never spoken to yourself — only had glimpses of you. I want to speak to yourself," he said.

I heard the woman on the black donkey whisper, "What do you want to say?" and I wondered why she asked. While I listened for the man's reply a sudden howl tore the night's stillness across and across.

The donkeys stopped dead, pressing against one another, trembling — or was I trembling? And then I knew the Author had laid a hand on my arm.

"It's only a jackal," he was saying. "You're not afraid?"

I was not afraid of the jackal, but I was afraid of all sorts of things, terrifying, formless things; and — I've got to tell You — I was afraid of myself. I had shut my eyes so I should not see what that foreboding was; I could not shut them any longer. When I felt the Author's hand warm through my sleeve I knew — and I knew what he had wanted to tell the woman.

I don't know how to write this, but I can't keep it from You — I wanted to hear him say it. And I don't care for Desmond Dulac . . . only, I might have cared. I hate to write it — I might have cared if You had never been.

Loneliness was being taken right out of my life, I was being offered much — and I couldn't take it. Because of You I thrust it from me. I didn't care, but I know I might have cared.

You, whom I have invented, kept me from seizing the good that was coming. . . . I am not going to keep anything back; I bitterly resented You because You would not let me take — because You consigned me to loneliness. The fact of You caused me to accept loneliness when I was offered so much. . . . I wanted to hear Desmond Dulac say it, but because of You I would not let him. I urged my donkey wildly. The Author did not follow me. I found I was alone, riding away into the moonlight and the wide, sad, glorious desert.

Stillness brooded save for the jingle of coins on the donkeys, their muffled steps, and the quick breath of the Arab running behind.

Suddenly You seemed very real. I just knew that You Were. And because of it I must thrust from me all the good which was coming. . . . I had left the Author behind, but I knew sometime he would tell me this thing I desired to hear and must not hear. Sometime he would tell me; should I be able to stand out again? You were not merely keeping me from taking; You wouldn't let me give.

There was a sort of track along which my donkey dashed; it is futile to attempt to guide a donkey. I heard the others coming up behind me. They were talking; I heard the Flapette laugh at something the Author said — and I remembered her suddenly.

I allowed my donkey to keep a little ahead till I felt I had my voice under control, and then I let the others overtake me.

Presently I gave up trying to feel bitter toward You. I believed in You.

Have I not found You lately because my belief has been slipping from me? Last night I believed in You, and so You were with me in the desert.

Sometimes we galloped; I forgot the violence of the motion

ch. ends next p.

in the delight of galloping through the dust and the moonlight over those pale, endless stretches of sand, with the Arab's
hoarse, peculiar cry growing faint. Here and there were little
dips and valleys with the stark, bleached skeletons of camels
gleaming. The desert sand cried up to me. I can't convey the
beauty of it — more than beauty, something else which is in
these Eastern nights, in the desert itself, something that sinks
right down into your being. I was only conscious of the desert
and of You.

We came back a different way through fields, plowed at this
season; great clumps of palms grow there and feathery bamboo
which look unreal by night. Palm trees seem to dream in the
moonlight; there is something supremely peaceful about palms,
wonderful and very still. I have seen women with that stillness
in their faces.

The track wound between sleeping fields and dreaming
palms and over little wooden bridges where water held the stars.
And so we came home through an Arab village, queer, crumbling mud-houses, built anywhere and anyhow — some mere
huts thatched with palm branches or *doura* stalks — mostly
dark and silent. Here and there a swinging lantern shed a
yellow glow in front of a little cafe where men were playing *tric-
a-trac*[1] and smoking opium; glittering eyes stared curiously.

It was so silent, so old, utterly Eastern; we might have been
living centuries ago. We rode at a sudden gallop out of the past
and the shadows into the present — and electric light.

Belief in You slipped from me.

---

[1] Also known as tric-trac, which is a form of backgammon; a board game for
two persons in which movement of the pieces is determined by throws of dice.

I have begun writing a book — simply because I feel so restless I must have something to occupy my thoughts.

I know I could never write a book worth publishing; but, as Desmond Dulac said, does that matter? I don't think it does. Not for me.

My book is not getting on very fast. The truth is I can't keep You outside it, somehow, and it is not a book about You: it hasn't any bearing upon You at all. So when I find You thrusting Yourself quietly into it I have to tear up whole sheets and begin again. The curious thing is that I don't really believe in You; since the night when You were just a fact I could not doubt, my belief in You has been slipping from me again — and yet I can't keep You out of my book. I try to disguise You. I hook a beard over your ears or impute ulterior motives to your actions — but I recognize You all the time.

I don't believe in You. I have nothing left but the bleak knowledge of what I have sacrificed for an empty idea. Yet if I had to face the same thing again — though I am convinced

You have never been anything save an abstraction — I should keep from me with both hands the good that was coming. . . .

I don't think I shall ever meet anyone, having known You, for whom I could care, though I created You. I suppose many women cling to exaggerated ideals which prevent them from seizing reality. But You are not my ideal. You are not in the least an ideal person; that's so curious.

I have not told the Author about my book, though I never should have dreamed of writing it but for him. I felt I could not tell him about it; it seems like asking his understanding under false pretenses. I don't want to see more of him than I can help — just yet, anyhow.

Everything I had built up painfully, all the nonsense part of my life, has crumbled into dust. Dust is gilded and wonderful, but it can blind and choke. Just now I cannot see for the dust which has risen from the thing I'd built out of nonsense . . . perhaps after a time it will settle and I shall see to go on again; but it is a little dreary, that going on again. I wonder if many lives mean just "going on again?"

It is *Bairam*, and the natives are flocking to the fairground on the fringe of the desert, where roundabouts and swing-boats have been erected, and gaudy stalls. There is an air of festival abroad; *Bairam* is one of the chief Mohammedan religious festivals.

I look out all day on a street thronged with natives in brilliant *galdbieh*, gorgeous *kuftan*[1] and *cufia*,[2] making their way on foot or on donkeys to the fairground. Most of the small children are decked out in impossible European clothes, crude

---

[1] Also kaftan or caftan; a long coat-like garment or robe usually worn with a belt.

[2] A colored scarf used as a headdress, which is wrapped around the *tarbush*.

colors disagreeably contrasting with the exquisite native dyes. The little girls are hideous in cheap jewelry and tortured hair. It is a pity. To me any innovation, for better or worse, seems regrettable in this old, changeless East. Yet despite the advent of electric light and forms of modern civilization, the native remains essentially unchanged: his patient, fatalistic outlook has not altered, the outlook which is summed up in the expression "*M'alaishe.*" This is an expression I have made my own; it is so comprehensive. There could not be a word which better sums up the attitude of the East.

M'alaishe. It means infinitely more than "No matter" or "Never mind"; we cannot approach it in English. It is a gigantic shrug in a word. You hear it all day long on every side.

I am not *m'alaishe* enough; that's what is the matter with me. I am going to cultivate the condition from now onward. It is a most comfortable doctrine.

Miss Kershaw and I have been for a walk along the Dock road and have had a talk which has set me thinking. I want to tell You about it. I have got into the habit of writing things down, though belief in You has almost died. I write "almost," because even now I have an absurd suspicion that but for the dust in my eyes I should find You again.

There was a south wind blowing, and the evening was warm and rather humid. I felt oppressed; I can't bear warm dampness. But the moon was glorious. (I only tell You of the moonlight nights as a rule because they are so wonderful. Whenever there is a moon there is moonlight here; in England you miss out moons altogether.)

Across the Gulf was a broad stream of shimmering moonlight, trembling iridescent color; the mountains pulsed rose through the dusk. I can never hope to describe this; how the

ch. ends p. 172

colors are visible, how they live after dusk has fallen. In Egypt nothing seems impossible.

I was thinking of what I have been told: the longer you stay out here the less able are you to stand the climate; you don't grow used to it; it saps your strength. But is it the climate or Egypt's self?

Egypt demands so much — no, not demands, takes from you relentlessly. I have found that. To me Egypt is not as I've read, savage and passionate; it is not these, because it is so aloof, so remote — impersonal.

It seems to me passionless, but not the less pitiless; unheeding, it takes from you day by day.

Egypt is not fierce, has no pity. It is too old and vast for any human attribute. It is just relentless, the calm relentlessness which belongs to Time and Death and all the biggest things.

Thoughts were crowding upon me when Miss Kershaw, who had been unusually silent, said, "You don't know any Yorkshire people, do you?"

I could not recollect any at the moment.

"No," I replied. "And I've never been drawn to them — until I met you. Oh, and that old doctor, the ship's doctor — wasn't he Yorkshire? I liked him."

"I've heard from a Yorkshireman today," she said.

"Ah . . ." I murmured. Her tone so lacked expression I had no idea till I looked at her face that the fact was significant, that she was telling me anything of interest.

Her eyes had a disturbed look, I thought she was worried; she certainly has been worried lately, and I believed it was on my account, because she suspected the Shadow. But I begin to think this which has troubled her was in no way connected with me.

"It's an old friend of mine," Miss Kershaw went on. I was not sufficiently interested to ask his name, and later when I began to feel slightly curious Miss Kershaw's manner prevented me.

"I've known him a long time," said Miss Kershaw.

"Yes," I replied, trying to throw understanding into the word. I had not the least idea what she was trying to talk about; it seemed to have nothing to do with me in any case. Then, with one of those rare flashes of insight which come occasionally to quite ordinary people, I thought I understood. Could this be the man who had no nonsense?

That accounted for her way of referring to him. She was obviously trying to tell me something about him, something which seemed difficult.

"Tell me something about him," I said; "I am interested. I have quite a leaning toward Yorkshire folk since I met you."

"I don't know that there's much to tell," she answered, almost, I thought, suspiciously; Miss Kershaw is extremely cautious. I began to be convinced my premise was correct. Miss Kershaw wanted to talk about this man, she wanted me to question her, but she resented the questions when I put them.

"Tell me about him," I said again, trying to display just enough interest and no more.

"How — tell you about him?"

"Well, what is he like, for instance?" I was quite curious to know: I thought he would be shortish and reddish, and a judge of horse-flesh.

Miss Kershaw mistook my question.

"He's not over easy to get on with — he's that sort," she said. I had not imagined him that sort; I thought if he hadn't any nonsense he would be hearty and bluff. They had been good pals, she told me. But perhaps she meant strangers would find

ch. ends p. 172

him difficult; I suspected she was glad of this — I have felt like that about You. I don't suppose strangers would have taken to You, You know. You are not — I mean, You wouldn't have been — at all a popular person.

I said:

"You can get on with him all right, but he takes a lot of knowing?" She looked at me narrowly, with that hint of suspicion — or was it caution? — in the way she closed her lips.

"That's it," she answered. "He's apt to get misunderstood; he doesn't make many friends — acquaintances, anyway. I know him better than anyone, probably"; her voice changed, a subtle softening. We all believe that, I thought.

"But it's saying precious little," she continued. "He is very hard to know."

I felt sure by something in her voice, something which did not appear in her face, this man meant more to her than she would admit. And I wanted to think so; I began to make unlikely surmises as to why he had written. She never told me whether he married the girl with more nonsense than most. Was he writing after years of silence to say she was dead? That kind of thing did not happen outside books, I thought; but my curiosity was thoroughly aroused. More than that: I felt an inexplicable desire to hear more about this man. Had I examined my curiosity I should have found it had no connection with my affection for Miss Kershaw. I just wanted to know more: I was merely aware of the fact; I could not have supplied a reason.

"He sounds nice," I said; not because I thought so, but because I wished her to tell me more — it must surely be the man who had no nonsense?

"He's all right," Miss Kershaw returned shortly; but from her that meant much, and the way she said it meant more.

"I think I should like him," I remarked. I didn't; how could I when I knew next to nothing about him?

"I doubt if you would," she said. I thought there was a hint of defiance in her voice.

"Why shouldn't I?"

"Well, he doesn't go out of his way to make strangers like him. There's no nonsense of that kind about him."

I began to feel sure this was the man.

Yet that did not wholly account for my curiosity.

"He spares words," Miss Kershaw said.

"But I get on rather well with silent men," I rejoined, and then remembered You were the only silent man I knew, and laughed.

"Do you?" she answered, not allowing the suspicion in her eyes to tinge her voice. But I detected it.

"You said there wasn't any nonsense about him," I began; I felt certain I was right, and wanted to make her admit it if I could. To my surprise, she said, "I don't know. It's difficult to tell with a man — like that. There may and there mayn't be. I sometimes think——"

"Yes?"

"I sometimes think perhaps there is — perhaps there has been all along." Her rasping voice was wistful. She was thinking of the girl who had more nonsense than most. I felt I hated that girl.

"You haven't told me," I said, "what he is like."

"I've tried to," she answered.

"I mean his looks?"

I thought she was a little contemptuous of this question.

ch. ends p. 172

She did not seem in a hurry to answer; perhaps, after all, he was stoutish.

"Oh," she muttered, "I see." She was silent a moment. "He's big — very. And fairish." Well, big and fair might mean stout and red; it all depends how one looks at it. I resented the fact that he was a big fair man like You. How strange! — You are big and light-haired, and I am quite certain I started out with the idea of making You big and dark. But You have been so quietly independent from the first. It came to me as a surprise when Miss Kershaw said that — to find how I had pictured You unconsciously.

"Oh," I said, "I thought so; somehow,"

"Did you?" she replied. "I don't know why I spoke about having had a letter——"

"It was nice of you to tell me. I am interested——"

"Oh, as to nice, that had nothing to do with it," she retorted in her brusque manner. "You don't find me saying things for the sake of being nice, as a rule, do you? I am afraid I don't. It isn't my way. But I like you," — I knew she meant much by that grudging admission, — "I like you, and I was worried; that's about it."

"You felt you'd like to talk of it a little?"

"Well, no. I don't think I meant to; I don't quite know what made me. It's not my way to talk about the things that worry me; never was. Can't see what possible use it is. And we spare our words in Yorkshire, though we can 'talk for a terrible span' when we get going. No, I don't know what made me. I've never held with impulse. I have often told you there's no nonsense about me, haven't I? I think I've been and caught it off you — it's contagious, is nonsense."

"Yes," I said.

"I find" — there was a slight pause with an audible breath in it — "I don't know as much about him as I thought, and I was never under the delusion I knew much."

"Isn't it odd when you find that about people?"

"You've found that." It was a statement. Her eyes searched.

"Yes." I laughed again, the short laugh I suspect must be harsh. I had been thinking of You; it is extraordinary how one succumbs to habit.

"Then you know what it's like?" She checked an indrawn breath before it had time to sound a sigh. "You feel a bit at sea when you find it out, eh?"

There was a short, uncomfortable silence, the sort of silence one or other breaks by clearing the throat rather loudly. Miss Kershaw did. I don't know why, I suddenly said, "I'm so sorry — very sorry."

I rebelled fiercely against the portion fate had thrust upon Miss Kershaw. Fate was doing the same for me; perhaps that added to my indignation; I won't say it didn't.

"I don't know what you're talking about," Miss Kershaw remarked.

I thought she said this because the talk had taken an emotional shade. I was sure she knew why I was sorry.

"He was there at Tilbury when we sailed," she stated in a disconnected way. "He turned up. Never knew he was coming. It wasn't a bit like him. He just watched us leave dock. Never made a sign. Couldn't make out why he came. . . . but he's a rum sort. . . . Don't suppose you saw him?"

"No, how could I?" I said quietly. The sound of my voice deafened me, and there was a blinding light beating in my brain. It was so bright I turned dizzy. And then darkness came. When I could see Miss Kershaw again my voice was still going on saying, "No, how could I?" I had not reached the end of the sentence. Miss Kershaw was clutching my arm.

"What's the matter?" she rasped.

I had not the slightest idea anything was the matter, only I supposed the Shadow must have come a little closer. I couldn't account for it in any other way. I had been talking to Miss Kershaw about — what? She was telling me of the man who hadn't nonsense; yes, of course — and then blackness. There was no reason for it but the Shadow. I must have stood too long, I was horribly tired; that was it; the Shadow must have crept very near.

Miss Kershaw said sharply, "What is it?" I wondered vaguely if she saw.

"It's the Shadow, I expect," I answered, weary. I suppose it was. It must have been. There is no other explanation; and I have known the Shadow has drawn close. Only terror tells me that it was not the Shadow. The thing it was is just behind the darkness, so that I can almost grasp it — making me dizzy.

If it wasn't the Shadow, what was it? . . .

24

Last night I felt too shaken by what happened to write at all; I still feel shaken.

The Author had arranged a picnic up the Sweet Water Canal. It was astonishing of the Author to arrange anything. The Flapette told me she asked him — I couldn't see that explained it, but she seemed to think it did.

"He says up there his soul communes with large silences." The Flapette looked shamefaced and a little proud. I recollected what he had said about solid comforts, and smiled; evidently the Author only discards his pose with me. I felt rather gratified.

"*Mashi.*"[1] Our native boat glided into midstream, and old *Abd-es-Sadak* took his place at the tiller. It was a big unwieldy boat with the high prow that gives me the same leaping pleasure as a wave.

The boat is pulled, when there is not sufficient wind, by a donkey attached to a long rope; an Arab boy rides the donkey on the tow-path.

Nothing could be more restful than the slow gliding of the

---

[1] "She moves!"

boat, with palms and eucalyptus and sedges reflected in the water, and on either bank herds of goats and long-eared sheep browsing among the coarse tufts of *helfa* grass[2] — here and there Bedouins grouped and a blue smoke spiral rising. Men were wading knee-deep, washing vegetables in wooden crates. There passed a great *tibben*[3] boat with black Nubian women squatting amongst the straw; the reflection as distinct and vivid as the actual boat, drifting between the banks with their feathery white sedges.

The absolute peace was satisfying; the smell of "gardens" and sedges and the desert Kingfishers darted jewel-bright before us, pelicans rose slowly, and once a stork passed overhead. Sometimes a village *Sheikh* would greet us with *"Salaam alekom"*[4] or *"Allah salimah."*[5]

At the Coastguard station Desmond Dulac made fast the ferry, sublimely ignoring the likelihood of anyone wishing to cross. A *fellah*[6] in white *cufia* and blue *galabieh* appeared, leading two tired-looking oxen. He gave the customary greeting, *"Said,"* which the Author returned quietly, making no attempt to loose the ferry. I thought the old man would show anger. He merely sank down on his heels and began gnawing a piece of sugarcane, from time to time spitting out the fiber contentedly. With the infinite patience of the East he was going to wait till we should allow him to cross. The Author would have made him wait had I not protested.

---

[2] Likely meaning halfa grass, a perennial grass long known and used in human history due to its tough stems which can be woven into rope, sandals, mats, etc.
[3] Straw trodden to chaff, similar to hay.
[4] "Peace to you all."
[5] "God bless you."
[6] An Egyptian peasant.

But my protest caused no change in the man; he was not moved.

"*Katter Kherak*," he said — "May your prosperity be increased," simply the equivalent of our "Thank you." He crossed the ferry without a backward glance or sign of curiosity. He accepted the good with the ill; he belonged to the *fellaheen*.[7]

The Flapette was very silent, and Desmond Dulac silent, in a conspicuous way — a silence which makes people wonder at the thoughts behind the mask. Miss Kershaw was silent too; she is never talkative. I was glad no one spoke, because sometimes there shouldn't be speech.

The canal stretched to meet the sky; over the sky hung a great cloud neither rose nor violet — hung and was reflected in the pearly, shining water. Above this cloud the sky was maize, pale, elusive. Each side of the canal sloped sandy banks and sedges stood massed and dark, only the feathery heads catching the light, holding it; water and sky were so dream-pale they met and mingled.

Dusk was falling swiftly and silent when there came the sudden splash of a camel entering the water. A Coastguard was crossing to the station. The camel rose up on the further side, looming mysterious. A giant Sudanese sat cross-legged on the high, peaked saddle. When he cast off his khaki, and in his short white tunic stood silhouetted against the sky, his size was incredible.

"What are you thinking about it all, I wonder?" said the Author suddenly.

"I'm not thinking, I'm just feeling."

"Pale priestess . . ." he said.

---

[7] The peasant class.

I turned upon him. "I hate your pose!"

"I know," he answered.

"Then why——"

"It's difficult to remember always," he replied naively; and my sense of humor reasserted itself.

"I suppose it is," I said; I liked the man better for his candor. He did not mean to pose; he could not remember always. That was all.

"Do you like this eerie sort of stillness?" he asked curiously.

"Yes. I want to be part of it . . . don't let's talk," I pleaded.

"That chap with the smell of burnt heather or whatever it was — wouldn't he talk?"

"No," I said; and then realized I had made an admission which was misleading. But it might be just as well to mislead the Author.

"No," I repeated, "he wouldn't."

The Author was very silent, perhaps because I had accused him of talking too much. Somehow it was disturbing; I could not enjoy the silence anymore.

"Go and talk to the Flapette," I said. "She's bored. Go and be amusing."

"I don't feel amusing," he grimly returned; but to my surprise he slipped along into the stern and sat down by the Flapette among the cushions.

Going home I forgot all about the Author. I thought I was dreaming it; the boat slipping so noiselessly through moonlight and moonlit water.

When we started the sky glowed arid all the palms were warmly dark. Gradually the moon took the color from the sky; the water was a long track of silver with great curving ripples as the boat moved, ripples that just stirred hushed sedges on either side; not a sound save the bubbling frogs and the crickets, or desolate howling of pariah dogs when we glided by some Arab village — the swish and rustle and whisper of feathery reeds bending and springing up as the tow-rope passed over them. The whole sky was pale with moonlight, air and water were part of the moonlight; the great boat some dream-thing in a dream. There is a thrill in the almost breathless Eastern night; the very stillness beats, vibrating.

The delicate radiance of moonlight through still, feathery reeds is like silence made visible.

"I suppose you believe in him?" said the Author. Without a sound he had joined me, and spoke as though our talk had not been interrupted.

Painfully I brought my thoughts to bear upon his question. He repeated it: "I suppose you believe in him?"

I remembered, and suddenly I was bitter. I laughed, and my laugh sounded loud in the pale moon-stillness.

"Believe in him?" I said. "I've never believed in him!"

"I'm sorry," the Author answered, "and I'm glad too. I'm just human, you see."

"I'm human too . . ." I said helplessly; and then, "Why couldn't you let me have tonight? Why have you spoiled it?" Resentment against fate became resentment against the Author.

"Do you believe in me — not Desmond Dulac but me — more than you did?" he asked quietly.

Why did You not thrust yourself between? It was then I needed You. I could see nothing but Desmond Dulac looming darkly above me; his bulk blocked out the moonlight, he seemed gigantic as the Coastguard had done. He was waiting. I listened to the frogs bubbling, and the crickets.

ch. ends p. 181

"I think I do believe in you . . ." the woman said, crouching where the shadow fell.

Quite suddenly, from the water's edge, came long-drawn groans. I felt my face growing stiff and my body cold. The groans went on and on, unmistakably human. The donkey had stopped dead; *Abdullah* was shaking, and inarticulate.

The boat had passed them with her own weigh, and the tow-rope was hopelessly entangled. *Abd-es-Sadak* groaned at the tiller with sheer terror, turning the stem hastily into the opposite ban; he was the first to break the silence that held us all.

"It was no Son of Adam," he declared, with chattering teeth, "but some *afreet*."[8]

I was ready to believe it was a spirit, good or evil; I feared an Arab had been attacked and left for dead among the reeds. . . . The Flapette feared this too. "Will they — bring the body on board?" she whispered. The silence seemed endless, made hideous by moans and horrid pauses worse than sound.

Then the Author gave a sharp order. He was going to land.

"Oh, he mustn't, he mustn't!" the Flapette whispered; but I felt she wanted him to go. I didn't look at her eyes.

"Of course he must," I said harshly. "Help may be needed."

There was a soft hiss and rustle as the boat slid among reeds. The Author told *Abd-es-Sadak* to keep her there, and leaped ashore.

Instantly there were two figures instead of one, and they swayed on the bank. A man had sprung upon the Author as he stepped from the boat.

---

[8] Evil spirit.

"It's a mad *hasheesh*,"[9] Miss Kershaw said. "They're dangerous . . . I'm going."

We held her arms though she shook us roughly.

The groans ceased, but the man began to utter savage, horrible sounds in his throat, sounds that were not human. He seemed immense . . . his arms were locked about the Author.

The Flapette was sobbing, angry, dry sobs; she was not terrified, excitement gripped her. I don't think she knew she was sobbing.

We shouted for help; we shouted to Desmond Dulac to leap back into the boat. We could hear his long, tearing breaths, the guttural noises the Arab made; the scutter of sand and the faint splash of sand falling in the water. The horrible struggle went on and on in the white moonlight.

A part of me which was not watching distressfully wondered how I should feel had this been You and not Desmond Dulac. . . .

A bright streak passed across our strained eyes — the Flapette loosed her hold of Miss Kershaw, struggling to leap ashore, whispering broken sentences.

Then there were dark figures running swiftly; and shouts. Help was coming. The Author made a queer uncertain noise that was something like a laugh, but ended in a horrid bubbling; his arms went up and he slipped backward through the reeds. . . .

The Flapette leaned over and clutched. I leaned over and clutched. We dragged him in amongst us.

Abd-es-Sadak cowered, moaning.

---

[9] Meaning someone intoxicated by hasheesh or hashish, a purified resinous extract derived from the flowering tops of female cannabis plants, which can be smoked, chewed, or ingested to induce hallucinogenic effects.

ch. ends next p.

On the bank a crowd was overpowering the man, who leaped and gibbered. He struggled savagely.

The Author lay in the bottom of the boat, his clothes heavy with water which ran darkly over the boards. The red lock was hanging wet and limp over his eyes; his eyes were half shut, and this made him horrible. They opened suddenly.

"'The first of those who are in the West,'" he said distinctly, and I knew he quoted; I found myself suspecting him of pose — it was hateful of me. Then he swore with the same distinctness; his hand was plucking at his sodden coat. The Flapette knelt down and began to pull it from his shoulder . . . he shivered with pain. She thrust us away, using both hands. "There's blood," she said in a voice from which all the color had drained. Very old people speak like that. It was somehow piteous. I knew she could not stand the sight of blood, it sickened her. I tried to push her aside. "Not you, Flapette," I said; "you mustn't do it."

She peeled the coat away where it was black and damp; the blood was soaking through. "Flapette," I remonstrated. She shook herself free. Miss Kershaw made no attempt to interfere; she was watching with a curious expression. "She's all right. She's capable enough," she said harshly. "Leave her alone — I'll help stanch the blood." She turned to the old Arab at the tiller and gave him a sharp command, shaking his shoulders. She shouted to *Abdullah* on the bank, and the great boat began to move.

Miss Kershaw and the Flapette together stanched the blood; I could see beads of moisture standing on the Flapette's lip and brow. I sat apart; I did nothing. There seemed nothing I could do.

The dream which lapped us round was shattered, the

stillness made up of sweet, sad scents and little night sounds, full of mystery and forgetfulness. This that had happened was hideous.

The Author lay, his eyes half shut showing the whites below heavy lids. From time to time he shivered and sighed a little. The boat moved with cruel slowness.

"He'll be all right. It's only his shoulder," Miss Kershaw said once, addressing the Flapette.

As we came to the landing-place and saw our *arbaghi* waiting, the Author stirred and half raised himself.

"You do believe in me?" he asked.

I saw the Flapette lean down, and her lips were moving.

I think the Author was right when he said there was something cold in me; I was watching it all, coldly detached — I only knew I was very tired. During the struggle I had been so strung with the horror and suddenness I felt my brain would snap. But Desmond Dulac was wounded, and I was just tired.

I am sure he was right about the strain of coldness. I think I'm hard.

When he saw the Flapette leaning over him his mouth began to twitch cynically. "This will be in the papers tomorrow," he said. "It will serve to keep me in the public eye!" He tried to laugh, bitterly. I warmed a little then because I felt bitter too. He went on and on till the blood came again.

The Author's wound is not dangerous, hardly serious. He has been moved to a couch. Miss Kershaw insisted he should be brought here so she might look after him. She never liked Desmond Dulac, but since he was wounded she has changed toward him. Some women are like that: as soon as a man is rendered helpless they can't help liking him better. I should not have thought Miss Kershaw would be like that, she is so rough and brusque. But this trait has come out since the Author was damaged; because he is damaged she no longer dislikes him. It is hopelessly illogical of course — and rather lovable, don't You think? Now, I feel no different toward the Author because he has a wound in his shoulder. I can't help it; I don't. Something must have been left out. I warm to him most when he is bitter, because I am bitter too. But just now he is thoroughly enjoying the solid comforts lavished upon him, and he poses all day. He poses when I am with him, almost defiantly; his position gives scope for pose. The guise of illustrious invalid is effective. I must be cold or something to feel like this about it, mustn't I? I hate it in myself, but I cannot pretend to You. What am

I saying? I cannot pretend to this book, I mean. I've never kept anything from You — from it, that is. Do I lack something? The Author said I was different from most women; I don't like being different, but I think I am. Dust and desolate things cry out to me, things that don't appeal to other women. What is it? Why am I different? The Author felt it, but he did not mind; I suppose I should write "does not mind," only — I don't know. . . . He wanted to get beyond the coldness he found in me, but I would not let him. I cannot let him. He might have brought spaciousness into my life; at the back of the artificiality, at the back of the pose, is a man (I have read the book he wrote before he stopped seeking) — quite an ordinary man, none the worse for that.

There are so few people who really count, just three or four: the others are shadowy, sketched in as minor characters in a book; they have no meaning, they are only a background for the few people who stand out. Have You noticed it? — the parson, the lady of the green glasses, and the Prawn. But the others, the few, seem to matter so much; their significance is disproportionate. Does it mean that I lack something?

I wish I were altogether ordinary or altogether "different." It would simplify things. But you can't simplify a thing when it's a woman.

The Author knows I have begun writing a book. I did not mean him to know, but he guesses; I never mean to tell him anything. He asked me what I thought of his book, the book he gave me on my birthday. I had never mentioned it again; I did not know what to say — not because I hadn't anything to say, but because I had rather a lot. I think he was hurt, or his vanity was hurt.

As usual the question came unexpectedly, though I have

warned him I am tired of his surprising proclivities. It is habit, I suppose. "What do you think of it?" he said; "or haven't you read it?"

"I have read it . . ." I could not get any farther.

"And that's all you've got to say?" His voice was pained; pain seemed to struggle with mockery in his narrowed eyes.

"It's just hopelessly ordinary?" he said, wincing; he put a hand to his shoulder as though the physical hurt made him wince. I think that book must have meant much to him when he wrote it — and it was so ordinary; what he said was true. My eyes grew hot. I had never seen the man who was a success in a pathetic light.

"Well, isn't it?" he asked remorselessly. By my continued silence I had admitted it; there was no use in denial.

"Yes," I said; "it is quite an ordinary book."

He laughed without much mirth. "I thought you would think so." After a pause: "I hoped you'd say so. You are like that. Sometimes you answer like a blunt boy. There's——"

I checked him. "Don't say there's no nonsense about me!" I pleaded, so earnestly that I began to laugh and he laughed too; the sound had more mirth in it.

"I nearly said it," he confessed ruefully. "I don't know what I was thinking of — but you're so puzzling. There are so many of you; I suppose that's it. I don't know what I was thinking about — because it is the nonsense which makes you mysterious, I believe."

A short silence fell that seemed long.

"I put so much of myself into the book . . ." he said, "and it is so ordinary. You would not think I'd put anything into it but mere pen-driving, would you?"

He was making it easier for me now. "I think I would," I answered.

"What makes you say so?"

"What you left unsaid, not what you said . . . I think you had that same gift then."

"But the public can't read what isn't written; the public wants it all in italics. I ought to know. I'm a big success, remember."

"The public can't read what is not written; no, but——"

"You mean you——"

"I mean I think your book is rather splendid."

"Splendidly ordinary?" The tone was harsh.

"Yes," I said, "I think that just expresses what I mean."

A subtle change came over his face. "The public doesn't want splendid ordinary books," he answered. "The public wants highly colored extraordinary——"

"The public!" I retorted. "You always harp on the public——"

"You forget it's the public which has made me what I am. I've got to be grateful." His voice was grim. "I've pandered to the public, to its desire for anything dazzling, extraordinary; you've to keep the public in mind right on from the start if you mean——"

"To become a success?"

"Yes. . . ."

"Otherwise your books would never get published?"

"No."

"Does it matter? Do you remember what you once said?"

"I remember a lot of things you once said——"

"Then that's very stupid of you, because I generally talk nonsense."

"Isn't it good to talk nonsense?"

ch. ends next p.

"Yes." He made me admit it; I don't know how he makes me do things.

"Well, what was it I said?" he prompted.

"You said about — books being published; did it matter?"

"I haven't forgotten that you were going to write a book," he remarked, with a smile creeping into his eyes and making his face look worn. He has that sort of face; he looks older when he smiles because he is tired and his smile is still fresh — he has used it so little.

"How is it getting on?" he asked, before I had time to make any protest.

He startled me into another admission.

"Badly," I said, "horribly badly." And then, recovering myself, "How did you know I was writing a book?"

"I knew when you recalled that remark of mine, 'Does it matter if it isn't published?' Do you still think so?"

"I haven't got the fever of ambition, and I find it is awfully empty——"

"As empty as success. I wonder why you don't get on with your book?" How could I tell him I can't keep You out of it, and on account of You I can't put myself into it?

I said, "I lack ambition, and — I'm such an ordinary person."

"Splendidly ordinary?" His smile made it a question, but it was a statement. "May I see your book?" he said.

"No, you may not." I felt my cheeks flare angrily. I hated him. "No," I repeated, "you may not."

Then a sense of humor came to the rescue, as it often does, rather tardily.

I laughed a little. I was angry with Desmond Dulac, the Author, for asking tentatively to read my book; I had refused him in a way which amounted to rudeness. Indignation left me. I was suddenly overcome.

"It's so difficult to remember you're Desmond Dulac," I stammered.

His eyes darkened, the red in them flared and dimmed.

"I suppose it means nothing to you to say that," he said very quietly. "To me it means rather a lot, you know."

We have been to see the *Mahmal* procession, the Sacred Carpet[1] returning from Mecca.[2]

All the afternoon the Flapette was very silent; I put it down to the fact that the Author was not with us. He will not be able to get about for some days. I thought she was bored.

We took up our position at a picturesque point of the route, in an old and narrow street. We were rather late, and missed the fanatical *Sheikhs* at the head of the procession.

The natives were wildly excited, surging forward to touch the Canopy or kiss the sacred camel; children were passed over the crowd to touch it. People were pouring holy water or incense from upper windows upon the procession. The Flapette, armed with a Brownie camera,[3] stood on the box of the *arrabiyeh*

[1] The holy carpet of kiswa is used to cover the most sacred shrine of Islam: the Kaaba. Every year the best Egyptian masters wove and embroidered a holy carpet that was placed into a special reliquary called *mahmal*, then transported from Cairo to Mecca — a pilgrimage considered a sacred duty in Islam.

[2] A city in western Saudi Arabia and the birthplace of the prophet Muhammad in 570 AD, where he taught before his emigration to Medina in 622 AD. On his return to Mecca in 630, it became the center of the new Muslim faith, and is now considered by Muslims to be the holiest city of Islam.

[3] First released in 1900, the Brownie was a series of cameras made by Eastman Kodak which introduced the "snapshot" to the masses.

clutching the *arbaghi*, and endeavored to obtain a snapshot, but was hauled down in time. We explained she had stood a good chance of being stoned by the Faithful.

It was very impressive. The narrow street thronged with shifting colors and shouting natives; through the crowd the procession winding its slow way, the glorious *Mahmal* glittering as shafts of dusty sunlight fell upon it between tall buildings that leaned inward — the Canopy swaying with the earners movements.

There came an ancient priest, wound about in what appeared to be carpets. He was held upon his camel by men walking either side. He must have been very aged. In this old, old country death seems to have passed some of the aged by, forgotten them.

Behind him, on another camel, was the *Sheikh* who appears every year; he looked comatose, borne along, motionless save for the slow rocking of his body to the camel's stride. There followed men in white, with green turbans, *Hadjis* who have made the pilgrimage more than once,[4] some carrying banners. There were Sudanese Coastguards and troops in khaki; the Governor with a great deal of gold lace and complaisance. The Carpet is known as *Kisweh*.[5] There are eight pieces which are stitched together in the Husaneyn Mosque at Cairo;[6] it is then taken to Mecca and placed on the Prophet's tomb, the Carpet that had rested there a year being brought back to Cairo, where it is cut

[4] Also haji or hajji; a Muslim who has been to Mecca as a pilgrim.
[5] Also kiswa or kiswah.
[6] Also known as the al-Hussein or al-Husayn Mosque, Mosque of al-Imam al-Husayn, and the Mosque of Sayyidna al-Husayn; a mosque and mausoleum of Husayn ibn Ali (626–680), a grandson of the Islamic prophet Muhammad, originally built in 1154 and considered one of the holiest Islamic sites in Egypt. Some Shia Muslims believe that Husayn's head is buried where the mausoleum is located today.

ch. ends p. 194

up and sold. The money goes to mosque charities. The Carpet arrives here by train; the carriage containing it is painted bright yellow and decorated with flags and gilt. We saw it arrive from the hotel windows; while the train rushed through the station, Arabs, in a frenzy of religious excitement, were running along the carriage roofs, leaping from coach to coach.

I was full of the procession, its suggestiveness, the fanatical atmosphere, when we returned; but the Flapette was curiously unresponsive.

"Egypt is wasted on you," I said. "You might as well be in England. I don't believe you cared a bit for the procession, and it was such a chance to see it; in a few years, they say, it may die out altogether. I don't believe you cared for it."

"Well, I didn't!" she replied defiantly. "If you must know."

"How was that?" I asked, softened. I could tell something was wrong.

"Look here," she said, standing up and struggling not to look fluffy, "I'm going to put an end to this — it's a beastly shame."

"What is, Flapette?"

"All this they're saying about the Author. That loathly parson's at the bottom of it. He's been spreading his rotten suspicions about. It was bad enough when he kept them to himself, or only favored me with them——"

"Who has been talking nonsense, Flapette?" I asked sharply. I felt I must try to keep the Author's secret because he had trusted me.

"Nonsense! — it's worse than nonsense! Oh, I'm just fed with the whole thing. I'm going to put a stop to it. The Rev. Arthur has been poisoning Miss Simpson — she seemed quite pleased to think the Author wasn't what he pretended to be. She talked as though she'd found him out herself. She said he ought to be shown up publicly, that his books were rubbishy things when the gilt came off — that there was nothing in them. Up till now she's read every one as it came out, you bet! He's taken no notice of her, that's the secret. She actually said his books were not nice, unwholesome——"

"His books are harmless enough. They're just rather extraordinary. They dazzle."

"They're brilliant, of course," she said, mistaking my meaning.

I wondered what she would think of that pitifully ordinary book the Author wrote when he was seeking. It was only rather a splendid book for what it left unsaid.

Suddenly the Flapette turned to me, with a sickening fear in her eyes and a wistful appeal in her voice.

"You believe in him?" she asked.

I gripped the back of a chair.

"Yes," I said, "I believe in him, Flapette." I believed in the man, though I couldn't believe in the writer.

She drew a long breath, and the fearful look left her eyes.

"I knew you did," she answered. "But this sort of thing can't go on——"

"What are you going to do?"

"I'm going to ask the Author to deny it!" she said, with anticipated conviction in her voice.

I knew I must stop this at any cost; the Flapette must not ask him. If she should find out — she must be spared this cruel blow to her childish faith. She had made an idol of his fame, which was only success. The idol should not be shattered. But supposing the Author should shatter it recklessly? I knew no one else could shatter it. The Flapette must be spared; fluffy people must always be spared.

"Flapette, you couldn't do that, you mustn't do that. It is quite

ch. ends p. 194

impossible," I said. I had no argument to advance, no tangible reason, and she saw I had not.

"Why is it impossible?" she demanded.

"Well, it simply is — can't you see that?"

"No, I can't," said the Flapette bluntly.

"Anyhow, you won't do it?"

She vouchsafed[7] no answer, and I knew she was not convinced.

We were sitting on the balcony overhanging the courtyard. It was a close, hot night, and the Author's long chair had been carried out. A *soffraghi*[8] was attending noiselessly to his many wants; he had a cup of Turkish coffee on the chair arm and a cigar in his mouth. He looked comfortable. Miss Kershaw was just inside the open window, playing Patience with the maiden ladies; we had the balcony to ourselves. It was lit by electric bulbs, but beyond the white light was blue darkness, warm and full of subtle fragrance, jasmine, rosemary, and musk.

The Flapette had been playing ragtime till the wooden veranda shook. She had come out rather breathless, and was sitting on the balustrade,[9] with her little high heels wedged in the woodwork; she was smoking a cigarette, and talking nonsense at great speed. She was making a lot of noise quite attractively. I don't know how she does it; perhaps you have to be fluffy. I supposed she had thought better of her threat or forgotten it. I ought to have had more insight; the rather noisy nonsense she was talking and the rather nervous way she was laughing should have warned me. I have felt like that myself.

She threw away her cigarette and watched the red spark

[7] Revealed.
[8] Waiter.
[9] An ornamental railing at the side of a staircase, balcony, or terrace.

amongst the ghostly, pale flowers beneath the balcony; then she slid from the balustrade and came and stood near the Author. I knew then that it was coming, but it was not possible for me to slip past them. The Flapette mustn't do this thing. I appealed with my eyes; she did not or would not understand.

"Well?" said the Author, a little startled; she was so grave.

"I want you to deny a — a beastly rumor that's got afloat," the Flapette replied, pausing dramatically; I think the pause was quite unconscious and was filled with quivering appeal.

The Author's red-brown eyes took a humorous gleam. "That sounds very serious, Miss Leigh." I knew he had no inkling of what was to come.

"It is serious," said the Flapette, hurt because he was treating the matter lightly. "It is time it was stopped."

"What is this — rumor, little girl?"

The Flapette flushed; her fingers were tightly locked. "They say it's all a pose——" Her voice shook. "They say you don't believe in your books, and *they* — don't believe in you!"

A dark red spread to the Author's temples, leaving him pallid as before, because I was there, listening, I somehow knew. Then he laughed, the ugly laugh I had come to know, which touched me.

"You believe in me, Flapette," he said, using her name, "don't you?"

"I believe in you, yes," she answered simply.

"I am afraid——" He hesitated; it was a hard thing to do.

"You deny it, of course," she said; but I saw fear looking from her eyes, which were very wide. "It is untrue, absolutely — say it is untrue."

The Author laughed, and his laughter made her shrink. She knew then.

ch. ends next p.

"Don't say it!" she exclaimed. "Don't say it!" She put up a hand to ward it off.

"It's true," said the Author.

"I wanted to know — the truth," she answered with a white-lipped smile, courageously.

As soon as she and I were alone I expected she would lose her control; it must have been a bitter blow for the Author himself to shatter her faith in him.

I wondered whether she would be most bitter, astounded, or grieved.

Her eyes shone, but not tearfully; her mouth was glad. I waited for the outburst.

"I don't suppose you'd understand," she said, "especially after the way I've talked and stuck up for him, but I'm — I'm so glad this has happened. I'm so glad he's admitted it."

I could say nothing.

The Flapette went on. "I hated them all for saying what they did. How I hated them! . . . but I somehow like him more than before because he says it's true. . . . I can't make it out," she added, a wondering smile breaking in her puzzled eyes. "I can't make it out; can you?"

I didn't want to make it out.

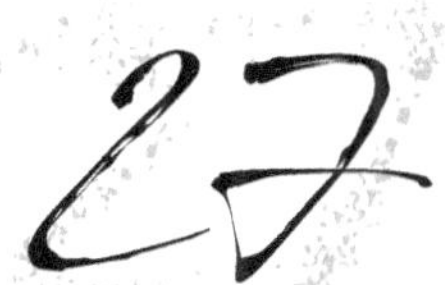

I told Miss Kershaw I was going to Cairo. "Then we're coming with you. You can't shake us off like that!" she said in her brusquest, which is also her most demonstrative manner.

I can never stand out against Miss Kershaw. We are all going together.

I have just said goodbye to the Author. We had about three minutes alone; for at least two and a half he posed most shamelessly till I remarked, "I did not come to say goodbye to Desmond Dulac."

Suddenly he dropped the pose. He had kept it up in rather a self-defensive way.

"And you didn't come to say goodbye to me, either," he drawled, with an odd smile creeping into his voice rather than his eyes. "At least, I am not going to say goodbye to you," he said.

"But why not?"

"Because I shall very probably see you in Cairo. I have a way of turning up unexpectedly, you may remember! When I can get a move on again I daresay I shall honor Cairo with my successful self. I go to Cairo sometimes, you know."

"You can obtain solid comforts in Cairo, I suppose?"

"Yes, particularly at Shepheard's. I often stay at Shepheard's.[1] It's got up in the Eastern style, decorated like a mosque and all that, but there's a distinct Victorian flavor about it; the cuisine's of the good substantial order. It's comfortable. . . . I like Cairo," he said.

"It must be wonderful," I whispered, realizing how soon I was to see it.

"I suppose it is," he returned, shrugging. "It's comfortable. That's what appeals to me. And you needn't have too much ancient Egypt unless you want it. Better still, in Cairo you can get away from the desert; it isn't thrust on you, but kept in the background as it were."

I could not help laughing, recollecting the man who made the public wonder. I laughed out loud.

"You'd be impossible inside a book," I told him. "The critics would declare you were not convincing!"

"Why don't you put me in your book and see?" he said audaciously.

I was turning to go. I thought he would be smiling, his mocking smile. It was somehow rather hurtful to find he wasn't. . . . What is it all for? What is the good of anything, I wonder?

Last night we arrived in Cairo, I must tell You all about the

[1] Shepheard's Hotel, established in 1841 and renowned for its opulent stained glass, Persian carpets, gardens, and terraces was the leading hotel in Cairo and one of the most celebrated hotels in the world until its destruction in 1952 during the Cairo Fire.

journey; I felt too bewildered and too weary to write last night, and there is so much to tell.

The first part of the journey lies through the desert. I have conceived a mad desire which I will impart to You, but not yet. I saw the scene of our moonlight donkey-ride, and started wondering about the Author, whether he really will turn up; I hoped he would not, he is so disturbing. And I am so tired of it all. It is easier to keep it from me when I don't see the Author; not that I could ever care for him. It is as well for the Flapette, perhaps, though already I begin to think her desire to grow up was merely actuated by a wish to experiment. The way she took the blow might mean she was no longer a child, or it might mean just the opposite; I begin to incline to my previous conviction. On the journey she was full of wild spirits and laughter, certainly genuine laughter. Several times I caught Miss Kershaw's dog-eyes fixed upon her in a tender, humorous fashion; I wondered if she had come to the same conclusion.

The day was very brilliant, but there were great, still white clouds whose shadows lay blue and deep on the desert; everywhere, as far as the eye could see, rolling miles of sand, orange and tawny, pale and almost gray, nothing but sand.

There is something so wide about the desert; the sea gives that same sense of boundless space. I felt the desert.

On one side sand stretched away with only gray desert scrub; each dry bush had its intense blot of shadow. On the other were palm trees and an occasional Bedouin encampment; here and there pools of water, surrounded by tough, spiked rushes and a white, glittering crust of salt.

For miles the desert had stretched arid and bare, when I became aware of water that quivered, flowed like quicksilver, and vanished. I saw a great calm lake in which hills were

ch. ends p. 202

reflected and low-growing bushes, and while I gazed, breathless, the lake melted, flowed, and mingled with the hot trembling atmosphere, and was gone.

At Faïd[2] we passed the salt lakes; I thought I could not imagine a more glorious solitude. The Canal opens out into a series of lakes — so wide, the far shore is dim and pearly-pink.

Faïd is a place of delicate colors, faint in the sun's white furnace-heat.

Palms and soft dusky tamarisk and oleander grow beside the lake. The water was still as a mirror, and a wonderful, shining blue — so pale, it was almost white toward the horizon, a blue I cannot describe, one of the subtle dream-colors of Egypt. . . . And the golden desert sand sweeps down to meet the blue, sleeping lake.

At Ismailia we had a long wait, which we spent drinking syrupy Turkish coffee (I have acquired a taste for it) among a motley crowd of natives and Frenchmen, Greeks, Italians, Maltese, and buzzing flies. We wandered into the town. It is a French colony, and quite a French town, entirely different from Suez; handsome white houses amid glorious trees, houses smothered in bougainvillea, stephanotis,[3] and great orange and crimson blooms.

The roads are shaded by splendid avenues of acacia trees.

I think it appealed to the Flapette; it had an atmosphere of well-being and comfort. It would have appealed to the Author, I suppose. I regretted the tumbledown[4] mud-houses and half-finished ramshackle buildings, the waste places of Suez

---

[2] Fayed is located halfway along the Suez Canal, about 12 miles south of Ismailia on the western shore of the Great Bitter Lake.

[3] A Madagascan and Malayan climbing plant of the milkweed family with leathery leaves, cultivated for its fragrant waxy white flowers.

[4] Dilapidated; run down.

— and the dust. But then I am in some way different. The town was so French the Flapette began recollecting Marseilles and comparing the two, greatly to the disparagement of Marseilles.

"That was a jolly day, though," she said; I think she felt my unspoken hostility. "Do you remember, there were exciting cakes at that rum little shop we discovered — exciting all through, not just on the outside like English ones," she laughed, gaily reminiscent; "and I bought an exciting hat."

I wish I had bought an exciting hat; I wonder why I didn't — I had just got Nonsense in Notre Dame de la Garde.

"I remember, Flapette, I remember," I said hastily, because I wanted to forget. What is the good of remembering?

A long string of camels, some hundreds of them, tied head and tail, passed down the avenue — come from the desert or going to the desert. That in me which the Author found and I cannot understand went with them. . . .

After Ismailia you see nothing but sand, pale in the heat — sand, and the blue, pale sky with shining cloud masses; nothing but that — sand and sky and a white glare of sun, sun draining the color from the earth, drinking it up. And then a camel with a swaying Bedouin, and the desert seems wider, more utterly desert for that one dark figure in the waste.

A longing like no longing I had ever felt took me; I know I shall always feel it now when I see camels in the desert. The desert was mysterious, vast, inscrutable as Egypt's self. Its nearness made me glad and a little terrified.

At Zag-a-Zig (the name suggests its tortuous, narrow streets and twisting ways) the Flapette bought pistachio nuts from an old Arab with kohl-smeared eyes[5] and a wide, toothless smile.

[5] Kohl is a black powder, usually antimony sulfide or lead sulfide, used as an eyeliner or eyeshadow, used especially in the Middle East.

ch. ends p. 202

After Zag-a-Zig the country becomes more cultivated. I thought I heard a little sigh of relief from the Flapette, nibbling her nuts; the desert dreariness made her feel uncomfortable. The desert is left behind, palm groves and plantations of trees appear, and everywhere fields of *berseem*, vivid, live green; bean fields; fields of *doura*, yellow and rustling; purple-stemmed sugarcane standing in water; cotton fields with immense sacks piled up, thousands on thousands. Always Arab villages of crumbling brown mud which glows a wonderful warm color when the sun is low; groups of sycamore and acacia trees, and under each the creaking *sakiyeh*[6] with blindfold oxen walking round, drawing water from the little *khalig*[7] that follows the rail, and in which are reflected brilliantly white donkeys passing amidst clouds of dust; blue *galabiehs*; slow-moving women with the two-handled *balass*[8] carried sideways on their heads; strings of camels burdened with great blocks of granite or bales of cotton; flocks of goats and long-eared pie-bald sheep grouped near the water, guarded by tiny girls in black. Sometimes a white Arab horse with streaming tail gallops past, stirring a cloud of dust which hangs in the sun-drenched atmosphere.

There are fields, rich and black, being plowed by oxen with heavy wooden yokes; oxen, or more rarely a camel and a donkey. There are fields of tomatoes where natives in blue and green and white pile the scarlet fruit into heaps. There are long vistas under vine trellises that cast cool, grateful shade — a green dusk like twilight beneath the sea — where white turbans move to and fro; mostly the fields are fields of *doura* or sugarcane.

[6] A Middle Eastern water wheel.
[7] Canal.
[8] A two-handled water pot.

Now and again an Arab cemetery appears; the dome of a *marabout's*[9] tomb, a few whitewashed graves, often not enclosed by any fence; a group of dark trees near it. The richness of this irrigated land about the Nile is wonderful: every inch of it seems cultivated; groves of trees rise everywhere among glorious fields and gardens. The natives passing through the fields, the natives working in them, all are part of the glowing, prodigal color.

I saw brown figures working the graceful age-old *shadoof*,[10] water splashing over their shining limbs.

Long before we reached Cairo we saw the Pyramids, gigantic in a misty haze of heat. I could not share the feeling that at last I was looking on the Pyramids; Miss Kershaw would not have understood, nor the Flapette (who likes comfortable things). I felt suddenly more alone than ever, and smaller than ever. Would You have understood in your silent way, had I not lost belief, I wonder? The Author would not.

I think You could never look at the Pyramids unmoved however well — I was going to say, however well you came to know them, but that is just it: You never would come to know them; they are so utterly remote.

We are at the Semiramis,[11] close to the Kasir-el-Nil bridge,[12] overlooking the Nile and distant Pyramids. Our rooms are high up and have French windows and little balconies from which I can watch the wide, shining, slow Nile with *dahabeahs*,[13]

---

[9] A Muslim holy man, saint, or hermit.

[10] A mechanism for raising water, especially for irrigation, consisting of a long suspended pole with a bucket at one end and a weight at the other.

[11] The original Semiramis Hotel, opened in 1907 and demolished in 1976, was a premier luxury hotel located near the British Embassy on the east bank of the Nile in the Garden City district of Cairo.

[12] The first modern bridge to span the Nile.

[13] Houseboats on the Nile.

ch. ends next p.

feluccas,[14] and *giassas*[15] and flat barges drifting down as they drifted ages ago; the distant bank clothed with palms, gleaming white buildings, and delicate minarets. Beyond the palms loom the Pyramids, huge, remote, somehow watching, where the desert lies dimly mauve.

I can hardly tear myself from that balcony. I told You, passing through those desert wastes of dust and beating sun, a sudden desire gripped me. I think perhaps I am going to find Space in the desert. . . .

---

[14] Small open boats used for ferrying or pleasure purposes.
[15] Cargo boats.

Miss Kershaw as sightseer is tireless, the last thing I should have expected. She goes at it in a dogged way, without showing enthusiasm, merely imparting it. She insists we shall miss nothing. Perhaps it is for the Flapette's sake, the Flapette who grows piteously bored and rather cross toward the middle of the day when the heat is worst. Yet even she imbibes some of Miss Kershaw's hidden enthusiasm by fits and starts.

Miss Kershaw is a relentless guide; she maps out our days and insists on adhering to her plans, though in this way we are allowed only a glimpse of some things — and everything here is wonderful. Our remonstrances have not the slightest effect; I think Miss Kershaw is the most independent-minded woman I ever met, and yet there was the man who hadn't nonsense. . . .

For my part, I would be content at present with the life of the streets: wide glaring streets and handsome glaring houses and flats; banyan[1] and acacia trees growing in little pits; the incongruous clang of trams; motors and polo ponies going to

[1] An East Indian fig tree.

Gazireh;[2] smug *Effendis*, fat Pashas in *arrabiyehs*, Copts, Maltese, Italians, Greeks, and Turks; harem carriages with ladies in clinging black satin and filmy gauze veil.

Or the older streets, odorous and dim, where are water-carriers bent double under their dripping goatskins; the *Khodari*[3] with his donkey and wide panniers; a blind *Mobakharati* burning incense;[4] the *Hallaq*[5] squatting at the street corner shaving a *Baia Ballassi*[6] who has laid aside his heavy burden of water-jars strung together; boys driving turkeys, glimpses of interiors, a reeking public kitchen, or potter's shop with white and reddish earthenware. . . . But Miss Kershaw will not let me tarry.[7]

She decided we must see the Coptic churches the first day. The Flapette was appalled at the prospect; she thought she would be bored to death, so she protested: "But aren't they dirty?"

"Dirty?" snapped Miss Kershaw. "Matter in the wrong place, my dear!"

"Dirt means gruesomes,[8] and we don't want those in the wrong place," said the irrepressible Flapette. Miss Kershaw snorted, and we know her snort is final.

The churches are situated in Old Cairo, or Old Babylon as it is called. Over many houses is written "*B'ism'llah, ma'sha' llah.*"[9] That part of Cairo is entrancing, so very old, such narrow, twisting streets and high old buildings, leaning against

---

[2] Gazireh, or Cizre, is a city in Turkey near the borders of Syria and Iraq.
[3] Vegetable seller.
[4] A *mobakharati* is one who burns incense.
[5] Barber.
[6] Water-jar seller.
[7] In this context: delay.
[8] Refer to footnote p. 69
[9] "In the name of God, may God keep evil from it."

one another for support, all built on different levels; and glorious hanging windows of *mushrabiyeh*.[10] These windows and balconies look as though they would crumble into dust. There are old stone archways with half-effaced carving, and heavy wooden doors studded with iron nails. Always the shifting crowd, giving place now and then to silence, a silence full of dreams and the dust of dreams.

Sometimes the streets were so narrow our *arrabiyeh* could hardly pass. The dragoman, a dried-up unexpansive soul, with a tweed coat and flowing robe, rode on the box; otherwise we were unaccompanied.

We came to *Abu Sirga*,[11] supposed to be built upon the spot where the Holy Family rested during the flight into Egypt. We went through a massive wooden door studded and clamped with iron and fastened by an immense wooden bolt. To reach the church we went down a steep flight of steps, a fat, swarthy woman leading the way, carrying a candle. The church is small, dark, and oppressive, giving the feeling of vast age — and giving me personally an unpleasant sense of imprisonment. The ancient paintings meant nothing to the Flapette and me; but the crypt impressed even the Flapette, I think: a tiny stone chamber with very low roof and a little hollow scooped in the wall where St. Joseph is said to have rested.

On coming out the Flapette was terrified by a paralytic who crawled in from the street making inarticulate sounds. He was horrible, but he was only requesting *baksheesh*. Crowds of dusty children, their faces black with flies, pestered us whenever we alighted from the *arrabiyeh*, and often followed it.

---

[10] Ornate wooden screens enclosing balcony windows in Arabic structures.
[11] Saints Sergius and Bacchus Church, also known as *Abu Serga*, is one of the oldest Coptic churches in Egypt, dating to the 4th century.

Under dim archways where we must pass to these old buildings beggars ravaged by ophthalmia,[12] maimed and scarcely human, shuffled after us, making strange noises, holding out their pitiful withered limbs.

Moallaka[13] is a much bigger church, and the wonderful rich inlaid ivory and brilliant painting, which age had softened, appealed strongly to the Flapette. She had a fit of enthusiasm at *Moallaka*, but it had spent itself before we reached the Mosque of *Amr*.[14] Miss Kershaw derived much satisfaction from the discovery that we could see this mosque at the same time as the Coptic churches. It is built in a square round a vast, open courtyard with a *meydaah* or tank in the center covered by a dome; the water was supposed to have its source in the Holy Well at Mecca. There are cloisters all round, rows of massive stone pillars, each pillar of a different type. There is a very high, beautifully carved wooden *mimbar*[15] with a stairway.

Once a year the mosque is still used for worship, when the Khedive attends and some thirty thousand Moslems, each performing his ablutions at the *meydaah*.

Our dragoman showed us a white streak across a marble pillar which was railed round, explaining that Mahommed whipped it and the pillar flew from Mecca. "Most people do not believe till they look in their guidebook and find it written there!" he said ingenuously. At the opposite side of the mosque were the two famous pillars about which has grown a legend.

Any good man, whatever his size, can pass between them

---

[12] Inflammation of the eye, especially conjunctivitis.

[13] Saint Virgin Mary's Coptic Orthodox Church, also known as the Hanging Church (*al-Kanisa al-Mu'allaqa*), is one of the oldest churches in Egypt, dating to the 3rd century.

[14] The original Mosque of Amr ibn al-As was the first mosque ever built in Egypt and the whole of Africa.

[15] Pulpit.

and is assured of entering heaven. The Flapette was very nearly kept out of heaven by her Marseilles hat.

We drove down endless narrow streets to the river; the shining expanse broke upon us with tall masts, and beyond were the distant Pyramids.

A man with a goatskin tried to make the Flapette take a photograph; she shook her head: his goatskin was limp and empty; nothing daunted, he put his lips to it and blew it up. We crossed in a ferry to the Island of Roda,[16] which is supposed to be the site of the discovery of Moses. The Flapette refused to be comforted because there were no bulrushes,[17] but I think she wanted her lunch.

The island has an old Sultan's palace built upon it; he has long since left the place to tourists.

There are pergolas and trellises covered with vines and bougainvillea, with plumbago and orange blossom and jasmine. The terrace rises from the Nile; it stretched a wide, turbid stream, opaque and tawny-brown, shining in the distance till its silver was lost where the heat-haze rippled. I thought of Cleopatra drifting down, which proves I am, after all, a particularly ordinary person.

Our dragoman showed us an ancient water-meter for measuring the rise and fall of the Nile; these meters are supposed to have been made by Joseph.[18] The Flapette lost interest at once. "I never could stand Joseph," she said; "he was such a swank. Are we to starve today?" she whispered. "This is going to be worse than any old famine!"

Miss Kershaw consented that we should take tea on

---

[16] An island located on the Nile in central Cairo.
[17] Cattails.
[18] In the Bible, Joseph, son of Jacob and Rachel, is an important figure in the Book of Genesis.

Shepheard's Terrace. She looked hot and tired, but dogged still; her efforts were rather pathetic; they were so wasted upon her weary niece. For me it was a sheer delight to see so much — I have seen so little; but all the time the desert thrust its wideness between me and what I saw.

We sat on the famous Terrace, celebrated in countless books. It is only a few feet above the street, and you can watch all the life of Cairo, which is the life of the world, go by as you sit there.

Crowds of fat dragomans in sumptuous robes lean against the railing. Men selling "antiques" and beads, the inevitable *minsha* and *kurbash*[19] men selling camels made of fiber, men selling loofas and picture postcards and tinsel scarfs, thrust them at you through the railings importunately.

Jugglers come on to the Terrace, squat down, and perform their tricks among the tables, or a *koradati* with a sad-faced monkey.[20]

The Terrace was crowded. I looked round — and saw Desmond Dulac.

"You are too ridiculous!" I exclaimed. I laughed rather uncertainly.

"I told you I sometimes honor Shepheard's with my presence," he calmly said. "You'll like those squashy-looking little chocolate things," indicating them. "Groppi's," he explained. "I must take you to tea at Groppi's one day[21] — why shouldn't it be tomorrow?"

I noticed he was wearing his right arm in a yellow silk sling.

"Is the shoulder worse?" the Flapette asked.

"There's nothing whatever the matter with it now," he replied.

---

[19] Whip of hippo hide.

[20] A *koradati* is a boy with a monkey, or "monkey boy."

[21] One of the first and most famous ice cream shops in Cairo, located in Talaat Harb Square and founded in 1909 by the Swiss Groppi family.

"Then is there any need for that?"

"Not the slightest."

People on the Terrace were pointing him out to one another, watching him. He seemed gratified. "That's Desmond Dulac," they whispered.

But I knew they were wrong; it was just an ordinary man who liked solid comforts, and little cakes, and had written a quite ordinary book which none of them would ever read. I experienced a warm sense of pride because I possessed that ordinary book which no one else would ever read.

The Author has turned dragoman; he is still consistently unexpected: I really think he cannot help it. I feel grateful to him, for he knows Cairo and just what to see.

When we protested feebly his answer was characteristic. "You don't want to do me out of a boom like this? Everyone will be talking about it — Desmond Dulac going around the mosques like a tourist. I couldn't do anything that would surprise them more!" He laughed, and, as always when he laughs, I felt drawn to him a little.

He took us to the Blue Mosque with its glorious tiles.[1] "I may as well show you the lot, go the whole hog," he remarked. "Tomorrow the Gazette will have headlines: 'Desmond Dulac visits the Blue Mosque,' 'The Author as Tourist.' Perhaps it will enlarge: 'Having recently recovered from an alarming adventure in the desert' (I needn't say it happened in the desert), 'Desmond Dulac has appeared in our midst with characteristic

---

[1] The Aqsunqur Mosque or the Mosque of Ibrahim Agha is located in the Tabbana Quarter of Cairo and is one of several "blue mosques" in the world. Originally built in 1347, it was renovated in the 1650s by emir Ibrahim Agha al-Mustahfizan who had the mosque decorated with blue and green Iznik-style tiles, hence its unofficial name "Blue Mosque."

suddenness, seeking to regain strength.' *Ad lib.*[2] They'll think I've come here to regain strength."

"Well, haven't you?" the Flapette asked.

"No, I haven't," he said quietly.

We drove through a bewildering labyrinth of dirty, weird-smelling streets that teemed with natives, camels, donkeys; with goats and hens and ducks, with cats and pariah dogs.

After the Blue Mosque we came to *Ibn Tulun*, disused and almost ruined.[3]

"I have brought you to see this mosque," the Author said in a low voice; "this is your mosque — mystic, puzzling woman."

"Don't pose," I said; it seemed uncanny he should know so much about me, and so little. His voice made me fearful.

Ibn Tulun is just a great courtyard with cloisters all round and in the center a dome like the mosque of *Amr*, and two minarets. It is built of a curious sandstone which takes all sorts of soft shades; the great dusty space is entirely shut away from the city by high walls and massive pillars. It is all soft, sad fawns and reds and grays; its absolute austerity impresses.

The air of desolation which hangs over *Ibn Tulun* breathes of the East and its oldness, and overhead circle great brown kites whose whistling note is the only sound that penetrates the vast deserted place where men have prayed.

Suddenly I knew You would have understood, if You had been. I stood very desolate in the dusty, desolate court. The Author was watching me.

"I knew this would be your mosque," he said. "I can't

---

[2] Short for *ad libitum*, a Latin phrase meaning to spontaneously improvise all or part of a speech, piece of music, etc.

[3] The Mosque of Ibn Tulun, completed in 879, is the largest mosque in Cairo in terms of land area and one of the oldest mosques in Egypt as well as the whole of Africa surviving in its full original form. Its most recent restoration occurred in 2004.

ch. ends p. 217

Mosque of Ibn Tulun as seen from the top of its minaret c. 1900

understand what appeals to you in these forsaken places. I can't understand you. You are not like other women . . . but I knew you'd think this mosque beautiful."

"Yes," I whispered.

He looked at me curiously. "That chap who likes — rain, wasn't it? — would he have understood?"

"I think he would," I said.

We climbed the minaret and looked down on the great open court and the pearly soft colors of the distant Citadel.

We could see the whole of Cairo beneath us — white buildings, minarets and cupolas, a city where countless thousands bowed themselves at the *muezzin's* cry. I heard the whisper of it at this dizzy height though the sun had not set — the echo of a voice which had been silent for a hundred years.

"I don't like this place," said the Author uneasily. "It's melancholy. It sets you thinking of might-have-beens——"

I made no reply.

"The many might-have-beens. They're rather pitiful, aren't they?" There was no bitterness in his voice, it was just tired. "They're rather pitiful," he repeated.

"Not so pitiful," I said, "as the endless never-could-have-beens."

We were both very silent after that.

Infinitely far beneath us, close to the mosque were rookeries, ancient Arab dwellings, the roofs crowded with turkeys and cats; women smoking, women washing clothes or cooking lentil soup and *riz-bi-leban*.[4] It was squalid and odorous, but possessed the inexplicable fascination of the East.

---

[4] Rice with milk.

I found the sheer unbroken height of the *Sultan Hassan* mosque somehow satisfying to the eye.[5]

The carving and inlaid work and beaten brass did not appeal so forcibly to me; but there were long chains hanging from the roof, chains which once supported hundreds of lamps, and these stirred my imagination. I pictured the dim vastness pricked by the swinging lights. . . . "All those 'white, splendid lamps' must have taken a deal of trimming," Miss Kershaw remarked dryly.

We drove up the steep hill to the Citadel and the great mosque of *Mahommet Ali*, whose pale domes and delicate minarets rise above the city, trembling pearl.[6]

"This is our mosque, Miss Leigh," said the Author, smiling at the Flapette from beneath heavy lids. Her eyes shone.

When I saw the interior of the mosque I knew what he meant.

Before we entered we were obliged to put on enormous native slippers; Arabs tied them insecurely round our ankles. The Flapette could not keep her small feet in hers. She lost one in the mosque and hobbled back in a single slipper, walking on the heel of the other foot in order to touch holy ground as little as need be; she was rather horrified at what had happened, and limp with laughter. The man at the entrance was not perturbed, merely remarking *"M'alaishe O Sitt"* as he dusted her feet.[7]

---

[5] The Mosque-Madrasa of Sultan Hasan, built between 1356 and 1363, is a monumental mosque and madrasa (Islamic college) located in Salah al-Din Square in Cairo. Considered remarkable for its massive size and innovative architectural components, it is still considered one of the most impressive historic monuments in Cairo today.

[6] The Great Mosque of Muhammad Ali Pasha or Alabaster Mosque, commissioned by Muhammad Ali Pasha between 1830 and 1848 and situated on the summit of the Citadel in Cairo, is the most visible mosque in Cairo and the largest to be built in the first half of the 19th century.

[7] "No matter, miss (or lady)." Also refer to explanation of phrase on p.165.

Stout tourists off Lance Thackeray[8] postcards shuffled along in these huge yellow slippers and flapped up the steps, endeavoring to look dignified. As Desmond Dulac flapped after them in his immaculate attire, silk sling and slippers, they whispered, "That'll be Desmond Dulac, the Author. What a surprising place to see him! One always associated him with tombs and the desert and all that."

We left the vast court with its running water and entered the mosque; it is like a sumptuous banqueting-hall rather than a place of worship. The enormous floor space is entirely carpeted with crimson Persian carpets, and from the roof hang crystal chandeliers.

The guide drew back a curtain and disclosed a *mimbar* which I thought terrible. The place was tawdry; there was too much gilt. I knew what the Author had meant; this mosque was in use, it was sumptuous, richly carpeted, comfortable. Desolate things and dust were shut outside.

Suddenly a thought struck me: how these two, the child and the Author, shared their dislike for discomfort, how oddly in sympathy they were.

We came out from the mosque into the sunset splendor, the vast white city with its palms stretching beneath us veiled in mist through which color trembled; everywhere minarets rising out of it, not white but dark against its paleness; far away the desert and distant Sakkarah pyramids, faintly mauve, wrapped in soft color and mystery;[9] the great shining, burnished river; and, dominating all, immense, remote in a glory of light, the

---

[8] Lot "Lance" Thackeray (1867–1916) was an English illustrator.

[9] Located approximately 30 km or 19 miles from Cairo, Saqqara (also spelled Sakkara or Saccara) is an Egyptian village that contains ancient burial grounds of Egyptian royalty, serving as the necropolis for the ancient Egyptian capital, Memphis.

pyramids of Gizeh.[10] Behind them one fierce flame of color, spreading over the whole sky, burning through purple cloud masses, turning the west to fire and blood.

Out there lay the desert, and the desert cried up to me.

"What is it?" said the Author wistfully.

"I think I'm going to find Space," I answered.

He laughed quietly, very tired laughter.

[10] Giza, on the western bank of the Nile River, is Egypt's third-largest city after Cairo and the site of the Pyramids and the Great Sphinx.

I feel as though life no longer held any good thing; we have been round the *Moski*.[1] Nothing could be more fascinating, nor more tiring, than a morning in the *Moski*. The Flapette went with the expressed intention of having "a real, wicked old spend." It is a wonder even I at sane-and-thirty returned with a piastre[2] to my name.

The bazaars are so dusky, and the massed glowing colors, the heavy scents, the brassware piled in the streets, everything combines to intoxicate till you grow reckless, unless you keep a very tight hand over yourself and your purse. After a time I was quite bewildered by the sumptuous stuffs, the old brass and silver and copper, the Persian rugs, the gems, heaped up and piled and hanging to tempt the tourist.

Natives dash out like pale fat spiders and try to lure you inside; they nearly all knew Desmond Dulac and respected his power of striking bargains. The mystic and dreamer among

[1] El Mosky or Al-Mosky is an important and crowded market district of Cairo and has been described as "a place where you can find anything."
[2] A monetary unit of several Middle Eastern countries, equal to one hundredth of the primary unit. Similar to a penny.

tombs appeared to derive satisfaction in beating down plausible, obsequious persons in the *Moski*.

The Flapette said she did not know what she had bought till we got back and she opened the parcels. She remarked that the Arab Johnnies[3] could afford to throw in free Turkish delight and glasses of Persian tea.

I wanted to devote a day to the Museum, but the Flapette thought my desire to see a lot of pickled corpses was beastly. I think she knew the Author would agree with her in feeling mummies were uncomfortable things, but he announced he should take me to the Museum. The Flapette seemed surprised.

We were of course rushed. How is it you always feel rushed in a museum? You have that sickly feeling you get hanging pictures, too.

I am telling You about it because of its bearing upon my relations with the Author. What struck me most was the extraordinary life in almost all the sculptured faces: they are wonderfully, mysteriously alive. Modern sculpture, any I have seen, does not possess this amazing life which is in these terribly ancient things. I could understand how so many legends have grown around them.

"Aren't they marvelous?" I asked, awed.

"They're horrible," said the Author uncomfortably. "I hate the place."

"Whatever made you come, then?"

"I thought I should like to watch you here," he answered unexpectedly.

"I don't think you'll find that very interesting."

"I'm finding it extremely interesting," he returned calmly.

[3] A "johnny" is British slang for an unknown man, often implying that he is unimportant or insignificant.

ch. ends p. 228

"I do hate you sometimes," I said.

"And other times?"

"There won't be any other times if you don't take care."

He laughed, still watching. "You're the most extraordinary thing in the museum."

"I hate you when you pose," I said.

"I know. But I'd rather you hated me than——"

"Than ignored you altogether. That is typical of Desmond Dulac. Can you never rid yourself of pose?"

"I don't seem able, do I?" he said, suddenly humble. I always feel so small and ashamed when the Author is humble.

We stood before the statue of the Goddess Hathor, the cow-goddess with the King's figure between her feet in front of a splendid painted tomb. It is not just a cow; you feel the divinity in it. I can't explain. Does it seem impossible to feel divinity in a cow? It is there. I told the Author what I felt. "I can understand how people could pray to Hathor," I said.[4]

He looked shocked. At heart the Author is irredeemably conventional. It was so uncomfortable of me to say such a thing and rather scandalous to feel it. He smiled and coughed. The cough was sincere; the smile wasn't. People always cough and smile when you shock their susceptibilities.

"I think anything which makes you feel — like that must be good," I said, trying to follow out a train of thought. He agreed hastily without conviction.

"That cow makes you uncomfortable; it makes me wonder," I mused. "Isn't it good to wonder?"

[4] Hathor — often depicted as a cow, although her most common form was a woman wearing a headdress of cow horns and a sun disk — was a major goddess in ancient Egyptian religion. As a sky deity, she was the mother or consort of the sky god Horus and the sun god Ra, and the symbolic mother of their earthly representatives, the pharaohs. She was also one of several goddesses who acted as the Eye of Ra, Ra's feminine counterpart.

"It's good to wonder about you," he said.

"You make me feel tired. Why didn't you take the Flapette to Groppi's?"

He winced.

"I thought I'd rather watch you looking at ancient Egypt," he answered lightly. "When you've indulged your passion for mummies to the full, we'll go to Groppi's if you like——"

"And indulge your passion for little cakes. Very well, that's only fair." But my heart was heavy because the Author could not understand. You might have understood.

These very old things spoke to something in me, stirred strange longings, questionings. Am I rather a mystic? The Author sometimes says so. A mystic sprung from among turnip fields; it does not seem very likely. And yet I wonder so — since You began. I wish I were just like other women. Perhaps I am; I am simply a woman seeking. There must be many women seeking.

I had looked a long time at the cow which expressed divinity; I think I had forgotten the Author.

He said: "Which is yourself — the mystic or the cold woman who talks like a boy and loves desolate things? Which is yourself?"

"They are both me, I suppose."

"But which is most of you?"

"I don't know. Why?"

"I want to get at that. I want to know which it is——"

"Why?"

"I want to get at yourself. I have never come near yourself yet."

"No, you haven't."

"Aren't you going to let me?"

"No, I can't. . . . You won't ever find——"

ch. ends p. 228

"What prevents me?" he said roughly and rather loudly.

I could not tell him You prevented him. There would have been a certain grim satisfaction about it. I searched wildly for some way of changing the trend the talk had taken, but I knew evasion was futile.

"I am tired," I said; it was childish of me. "I get tired rather soon in these days."

I thought there was a taut look about his red mouth; his eyes softened.

"I'm tired too. It is tiring being a success." The weary sound in his voice moved me.

"Well, having decided we're neither of us so young as we were, suppose we agree museums are uncomfortable places——"

"And go and have tea at Groppi's?"

He smiled; the young smile which made him look old. I knew he was not to be trifled with; one day this thing would come, I should not be able to ward it off. I am afraid of myself. Afraid some time I shall let him — just say it.

How shall I tell You about it? It will be difficult, though I have ceased to believe in You. The Flapette was in raptures at the thought of a Semiramis dance; we had a party for it. At dinner the Author sat opposite me; I could not see him for smilax[5] and roses, but I felt he was watching me, watching the abstract me, if You understand. The knowledge that he watched weakened me curiously. He possessed, I thought,

[5] A genus of over 300 species of climbing flowering plants native throughout the tropical and subtropical regions of the world.

determination for which I had not given him credit, and his determination took from mine. The extremely young men on either side of me made fruitless and impatient efforts at conversation. Their interest was centered in the Flapette, and she knew it and seemed enjoying it to the full in her old, heedless way. Her slang dominated the table, and she was childishly and fascinatingly frank over her passion for marron glacés.[6] She was triumphantly fluffy. The Author was talking to her, but he never ceased watching me. The idea, when once it had a hold, gained like hypnotic suggestion; and I should have to dance with him presently, I supposed. I felt tired; the thought of dancing exhausted me, and, realizing I was tired, I felt bleakly old.

Save Miss Kershaw, I supposed I was the only one at the table who was not impatient for dinner to end, unless perhaps the Author, who was enjoying this substantial form of comfort.

Denisty's orchestra was tuning up.[7] The Flapette's eyes were brilliant beneath dark brows: anticipation made her cheeks glow.

We began booking dances in the lounge. The Author secured my program, and wrote his initials three times before I could protest. The newly fledged subalterns[8] merely gave me a duty dance, and returned to flutter round the Flapette; I felt somehow grateful to Desmond Dulac, and rather ashamed of being grateful.

The ballroom is rose and white and gold, with glass doors opening on the garden, and many palms, the sumptuous setting of musical comedy (I once saw a second-rate touring company

---

[6] Chestnuts preserved in and coated with sugar.
[7] The Gaston Denisty Orchestra was a short-lived but popular orchestra in Egypt before WWI.
[8] Officers in the British army below the rank of captain.

ch. ends p. 228

in *The Merry Widow*).[9] The scarlet uniforms enhanced this effect; there was even a man with a patch over his eye who had been in a skirmish up-country. I expected the chorus to form into a semicircle and an Odol smile about the chief comedian.[10]

I supposed the Author must enjoy it all. The remote, vast pyramids and terrible desert were shut out; in this place of light and gilding and music he must feel so safe.

When the Author claimed his dance, "I think I'm tired," I said. "I think I shan't dance."

"That's all right," he coolly replied, "because I don't dance, you know."

"You don't? What do you mean by booking dances, then?" I began to feel angry.

"I mean," he answered imperturbably, "I want to talk to you." His quiet audacity disarmed me.

"Let's sit out on the terrace," he said, drawing my arm within his; I hated him for touching me.

I tried to dissuade him. "Wouldn't you rather stay here in the lounge with the divans and Persian rugs? Out there we shall be able to hear the Nile and feel the desert. . . ."

"I want to talk to you," he said. "It wouldn't be yourself in here."

"And it won't be me out there," I retorted. "Haven't I told you that you will never——"

"Yes, you've told me quite a lot of times. . . . I think this door leads on to the terrace." He held it open, and I watched myself pass through. From the time he opened the door, I felt that

[9] An operetta, premiered in 1905, by the Austro-Hungarian composer Franz Lehár (1870–1948).

[10] Odol Original Concentrated Mouthwash, a blend of antiseptic with essential oils and identified as the world's first mouthwash, was created in 1892 by renowned German chemist Bruno Richard Seifert (1861–1919).

strange sense of detachment I have described. I simply watched the woman, wondering in what way she would act. I was listening to the slow lapping of the Nile beyond the warm darkness.

The woman was listening to the Author — at least she seemed to be; she leaned back in her wicker chair, and he leaned forward in his.

I dwell on this disassociation of myself with her so You may better understand what took place.

"Don't look out into the darkness — the desert is there," the Author said, almost jealously.

"I'm not seeing the desert," said the woman.

"What are you seeing?"

"I'm seeing my life, I think . . ." she answered quietly still, but rather bitterly.

He leaned forward a little. "And your life has been?"

I could see him moisten his lips; I thought the woman saw this and was afraid. I wondered what she feared.

"It has been a meager, very empty thing," she whispered grudgingly, as though his eyes made her say it.

His words came stumbling, with short pauses, which were not for effect; they signified sharp breaths drawn. "But — must it — always be that?" he said.

She looked with wide eyes at the darkness hiding the desert.

"Yes, it must," she answered.

"It must not——" He pulled the wicker chair forward, and it grated; I thought of that night at sea and the Prawn, and I thought how conventional the Author was to choose this terrace with its chairs and palms——

The woman laughed.

"What makes you laugh like that?" he asked wondering.

She said tonelessly, "Because I am a fool." I knew she was

thinking how she clung to emptiness for the sake of something which had never existed.

"My name is Naomi," she stated suddenly. I thought it was ridiculously theatrical.

"But not Marah——" he answered.

She laughed.

"You have always puzzled me," the Author said. "From the first you made me wonder. I can't understand you now. Only, your life must be not that——"

"It must," said the woman drearily.

"It must not," he repeated.

I watched her grow limp and quiet in her deep chair, as though she no longer struggled.

"I think it must," she said.

"Why should it?" he asked impatiently.

"I can't tell you." Her eyes were pitiful.

He burst out, "I suppose——" then checked himself.

There was silence for a time, and he looked round desperately as though he expected an invasion of the terrace.

"It needn't be. Don't you know it needn't?" he said. His face was very lined and white in the white glare; his lips had no color; his eyes had a strained, waiting look.

The woman sat very still. Looked round wildly. Then was still again.

"Don't you know it needn't be?" he repeated, watching her.

"I know it needn't be," she answered in a low tone, slowly.

"Then if it needn't——" He leaned forward, his hand gripped her chair, and I, watching, marked his nails stained red.

The woman suddenly shook, as with cold. "Don't," she was whispering; "don't try——" She broke off, crouching back in the chair and the shadow. I believed she was yielding, and I wondered; I had not thought she would yield. . . .

Then I knew it was not Desmond Dulac who leaned forward in the other chair; he loomed much larger. It was not a chair on which he sat, but a stone, and gray rain drifted. About his feet I saw blackened heather, and the stone was black. His head was bare. I looked at him with no astonishment; the woman saw him too as gradually he became distinct. The wet was white like hoar-frost on his brows; he rubbed a piece of bracken[11] absently between his palms; in his mouth was an empty pipe, and the eyes of the man were watching. There was no reproach in them. They just watched. . . .

I found myself where the woman had sat; the Author's chair was very close to mine.

I sprang up, trembling.

"Shall we go inside?" I said. "It — is cold out here."

"Cold? . . ." he returned, in a helpless, dazed fashion.

I laughed. "You never would believe I was ordinary and commonplace; but you see I can actually think about feeling cold, out here with the Nile, and — and I am sure you would rather be inside where it's comfortable." I said anything for the sake of saying something. I think I hurt him. He said slowly, "I'm sorry — you're cold." He put a hand up vaguely to his glistening forehead. "I ought to have thought — about your being cold," he muttered. He was fumbling for his cigarette case; I don't think he knew. His hand shook a little, and when I saw that — I cannot explain why — I grew very calm; I had complete control over my voice. I sat down again.

"We may as well stay here till this dance is over," I said easily.

---

[11] A genus of large, coarse ferns.

ch. ends next p.

"Thank you," he answered, and began to light matches which flared and went out.

Silence fell, and the wicker chairs creaked loudly.

Had there been reproach or doubt in the eyes of the man sitting on the blackened stone — I thought for an instant's space I was going to yield . . . but his eyes were just watching eyes. He never doubted.

A burst of music floated out to the terrace; the band was playing "Dixie." The Nile, beyond the warm darkness, lapped old and cool and stealthy. I knew that You had sat on the blackened stone, watching.

We are going to Mena today to see the Pyramids. The Flapette wanted to ask Desmond Dulac, but he has disappeared. We inquired at Shepheard's; he left this morning.

"Just like the Author." I tried to speak casually. The Flapette's eyes searched my face.

"I believe you know why he has gone," she said in rather a small voice, accusingly.

"I don't know. How should I, Flapette?" I certainly had not expected it.

"I think the Author cares rather a lot about you," she remarked, with a quietness which was unchildlike, unlike herself.

"Do you think he cares much about anybody but Desmond Dulac?" I retorted; I was sore and weary of it all.

"I don't think you mean that," she answered. Her strange quietness frightened me. "I believe he does care rather a lot about you"; she steadied her lip with her teeth. "And you're so — sort of cold and weird. Don't" — a half-pleading, half-fierce note crept into her voice — "don't make him care too much."

I knew she was not thinking of herself. I honored her and lied.

"My dear child, the Author doesn't care, there's nothing in it. How should there be?" I wished I could make him hate me; I almost hated him.

We motored to Mena. My heart sank to see trams in the beautiful avenue of *lebbek* trees. There is quite a steep hill up to the Pyramids. I never imagined this, somehow; did You? I think I have always pictured them in a vague waste of sand; the surroundings did not matter.

Close by are excavations on a vast scale. Arabs swarm like flies over the mounds of earth.

We lunched at Mena House, and I could hardly restrain my impatience when Miss Kershaw insisted upon examining the old *mushrabiyeh* and Persian tiles.

I was wondering with a sinking feeling if the Pyramids would prove a gigantic disappointment, seen at close quarters.

And then we approached.

There is something infinitely old and remote about them, but to my mind in no way terrible. So much has been written, but You want my impressions. At least, for so long I have pretended that You did.

The Pyramids are so vast you can hardly take them in at first, they are too big to grasp. They rise sheer and austere out of the sand; their shape seems awful and inspiring, and the glorious color of them against throbbing blue; they woke so many emotions I cannot put into words.

Like all the biggest things, concrete or abstract, they won't go into words; you feel them. What I felt I cannot speak nor write. I can only go on wondering.

The Flapette was very quiet.

"How beastly to spend your life making your grave!" she said. "Always to be thinking about — death." She did not much like speaking the word. She looked uncomfortable, and I knew the Author would have understood this feeling.

"Oh!" said the Flapette, disappointed, "is *that* the Sphinx?"

I shared her disappointment till we drew nearer.

The Sphinx is much smaller than I had pictured, in proportion to the Pyramids. But the great battered face is mysterious, inscrutable as I had imagined always. Hewn out of the natural rock, the crumbling stone takes warm, delicate colors. Calm and unmoved through ages, the Sphinx gazes out over the great plain, faintly smiling, smiling secretly. I am glad there is no temple in the head; the mysterious riddle is still unsolved.

Miss Kershaw was moved to say, a little ashamed, "It was a big thing to do, wasn't it? A big thing to conceive?"

All that one reads is in the face, and much more. The Arabs call it The Father of Fear, but to me there is nothing fearful about the Sphinx. Like Egypt, it is beyond and outside human attributes. Always it smiles faintly, gazing across the plain.

The austere simplicity of the Temple of the Sphinx impressed me, and perhaps the fact that it is open to the sky. The size of the vast granite blocks made me speechless; the tomb of the priest has a roof hewn from a single block. The silence within the granite walls almost restored to me my belief in You for a little space. The Flapette thought it dreary, but the tomb of Rameses' daughter she liked; the floor and walls are alabaster and dark red granite.

We saw a typical stout tourist lowered down the Great Pyramid with the assistance of three Arabs, and a cord round his waist. He had lost all pretense at dignity: his one thought was to reach the bottom in safety. I felt no desire from the first to

ch. ends p. 234

climb the Pyramids; I felt it would take away some of their remote mystery.

As we came back Sphinx and Pyramids were steeped in the sunset glow against a sky of still, rose-pink clouds; the desert steeped in a great cool silence.

Leaving Mena, the Pyramids rose black, clear-cut, sheer into the starlight. It is a sore disappointment that there is no moon at present; but we are not restricted by time. I had looked on the desert stretching very far, and I wearied for it.

We entered the lounge at the Semiramis, and Desmond Dulac came forward to greet us. He met my eyes. I could not meet his.

"I am going to take you all to Sakkarah tomorrow," he said. "I have arranged everything."

I found no words with which to protest; I saw gladness in the Flapette's face, though her mouth was grave.

"At what unearthly hour must we start?" asked Miss Kershaw, with tolerance and amused, impatient eyes.

I could not trust myself to write last night. Today I am calmer, and am beginning before breakfast because that is such a sane, unemotional hour. I am still very weary, body and mind, but mostly mind, I think.

At Mena we found camels and a sand-cart waiting; camel-drivers, donkeys and donkey-boys, and a dragoman. He seemed a plausible old knave with an oily tongue and smile. Back view on his little white donkey he looked like Sancho

Panza.[1] It was an imposing cavalcade, or caravan? Each of us had our attendant boy. Miss Kershaw was to ride in the sand-cart with the lunch; she took it in good part, but I thought the eyes looking from the rough-featured face were wistful. I wished I could have driven with her, then; but the Author had provided camels for the Flapette and me. He himself rode a gaunt, sad-eyed mule.

A camel has a peculiar way of rising, four distinct jerks; the boys warned us to lean well back. When a camel lies down the jerks are still more violent, and it grunts and growls in a lovable, impatient way. Though all my bones ache it will always tug at my heart to see a camel in the desert after this.

The *hagin* or running camel is a beautiful creature. The walk is a long swing, to which you must let your body go, relaxing every muscle, a delicious sensation; when the camel breaks into a half-trot the discomfort begins. I understood then why the Author had chosen a humble mule.

At the end of fifteen or sixteen miles I was aware of muscles which I didn't know I possessed, achingly aware; but few things could be so good as riding over those miles of burning sand beneath a cloudless, deep sky.

The dragoman advised us to ride astride and rise as though the camel were a horse. The Flapette was enjoying herself enormously; I almost forgot the quiet, unchildlike things she had said the day before.

I could have ridden twice as far if the camels had kept up this rapid motion all the time, but the poor boys have to run through the thick sand: it is distressful to hear their labored breathing; breathless though they are, they talk, every sentence leading

---

[1] Don Quixote's squire in the 1605 novel *Don Quixote* by Spanish author Don Miguel de Cervantes Saavedra (1547–1616).

ch. ends next p.

inevitably to *baksheesh*. My boy kept saying "You like it?" and "Thank *you*," at intervals between panting breaths; "You happy? Then I happy too!" They may well desire *baksheesh*.

It was only the fringe of the desert, but I cannot describe what I felt — nothing but sand and sky, and the camel beneath me. I could feel the heat of the camel against my ankle beyond the saddle-cloth. It was a splendid beast. The Flapette chose hers because it had such a sweet face; it lagged in the rear. The way a camel stretches out its long neck, snarls, and dashes into the burning sandy wastes . . . but I must tell You all that happened.

We dismounted to see the Temple of *Abou'sir*,[2] a few crumbling, small pyramids and any number of huge stone and alabaster basins with little holes which the dragoman said were used for candles. He told us most of the basins were baths, and they had lit candles all round. The guidebooks incline to the theory that they were used for sacrifice. There was a vast altar made entirely of alabaster and wonderfully preserved. *Abou'sir* bored the Flapette — the sun made her head ache. It was very desolate and dusty. I loved *Abou'sir*.

We rode along the fringe of the desert to Mariette's House;[3] we rode in a beating, savage glare of sun so that sky and sand seemed molten, burning, and the dust blew up in burning clouds about us.

I was possessed as I rode by an unreasoning joy. And always, riding alone, a little ahead, I *listened* to the dust.

---

[2] Abusir or the House or Temple of Osiris is an ancient Egyptian archaeological pyramid complex comprising the ruins of 14 pyramids dating to the Old Kingdom period, and is part of the Pyramid Fields of the Memphis and its Necropolis.

[3] The headquarters of French scholar, archaeologist, and Egyptologist August Mariette (1821–1881) and his staff while conducting excavations in the Necropolis of Saqqara.

I had to break off before I had reached the happening which
has made me miserable; but I have a little while to myself —
I am supposed to be taking my siesta.

We dismounted at Mariette's House. The camel-boys squatted in the sand and fell asleep while we shared our lunch with
some timid pariah dogs. When we raised our veils the color and
blinding glare of noonday seemed doubly vivid, hardly bearable.
A breeze came across the desert, cool and clean and limpid; we
took great breaths of it.

Now I have to tell You of that which I knew must come,
though I have tried to keep it from me.

We entered the *Serapis*, the tomb of the Sacred Bulls.[1] We
went down a steep incline, and guides went before with candles
and magnesium wire.[2] I was glad it was not lit by electric light.

We traversed dim, vast galleries of hewn granite, the air

---

[1] The Serapeum of Saqqara was the ancient Egyptian burial place for sacred
bulls of the Apis cult at Memphis. It was believed that the bulls were incarna-
tions of the god Ptah, which would become immortal after death as Osiris-Apis,
a name which evolved to Serapis in the Hellenistic period.

[2] Burning magnesium wire, similar to how a candle wick burns, gained
wide use in the late 19th century as a form of lighting for photography due to
its incredible brightness.

growing hotter and more stifling as we penetrated deeper. I looked round rather wildly; I began to wonder if I could endure it.

All along the main passage are alcoves and enormous granite sarcophagi in which the bulls were found. The incredible proportions of these sarcophagi took my breath away. They are all beautifully hewn and polished. The largest is at the end of the main passage; we had to climb up to examine it. The air was so close I felt a horrid pressure against my temples.

The Flapette whispered her hands were ice-cold and clammy; she thought some gruesome spell had been cast upon her because she had mocked at mummies. I found myself listening without comprehension to the guide explaining how the kings had to wash the bulls before they were buried . . . how they were all piebald[3] bulls . . . I wanted to get out; a dull foreboding oppressed me, a premonition of what was to come.

Our guide showed the last sarcophagus, and the pallid flare of the magnesium wire died out. For a moment I thought we were in darkness; I was suffocating; but the guide and the dragoman and the Author carried candles that gave a faltering yellow gleam, making darkness visible. Slowly we made our way along the hot, silent galleries. The Flapette and Miss Kershaw were in front with the guide and dragoman. They stopped while he expounded something, gesticulating, his gigantic shadow leaping up the polished wall. We stopped also. The others went on, but we did not follow; I knew there was no escape. I stood, waiting.

"I didn't plan this," the Author said; and I could hear his breathing in the silent place: "I didn't mean it to be here. I think you know that."

---

[3] Having irregular patches of two colors, typically black and white.

I was faintly amused because he had chosen this hot, airless tomb; it was characteristic of Desmond Dulac, so unlike the man himself.

"It had got to be," said the Author.

"Yes," I returned wearily, "I know."

"It had got to be, and it might as well be here and now. I seldom see you alone." His voice trailed off and softened. "I've as good as asked you several times to marry me, and you know it. You knew what I meant that night on the terrace?"

"Oh yes, I knew what you were trying to say. I'm not a child." My voice sounded tired.

"Then why," he said roughly, "did you stop me?"

"I cannot tell you that."

"You didn't wish to hear me out——"

"I would not hear you out," I said.

He looked at me curiously, the candle flame making flickering red points in his red-brown eyes. I noticed vaguely that the granite walls were red.

"You've got to hear me out this time," he said quietly. Had he said it in any other way it must have sounded aggressive.

"I know," I answered just as quietly.

Candle grease was dripping on the back of his hand and between his fingers. He did not seem to know.

"I want you to let me fill your life for you," he said, and his tone robbed the words of self-assertion.

"That you can never do."

"Why?"

"Because I cannot let you."

"And you cannot let me——?" His fingers absently were molding the wax which guttered down the candle.

"I cannot tell you why."

ch. ends p. 240

His eyes, smoldering, suddenly flamed. When he spoke his tone was sardonic. "Many women," he said, "have tried to make Desmond Dulac care——" I was repelled, but underwent a revulsion of feeling when he added wistfully, "But you are different. You never believed in Desmond Dulac or set store by his success. Do you know, for you I'd throw it all over? Perhaps you hardly realize what it would mean, after all these years." I thought I did.

"Don't," I said. "You must not give up anything because of me. I have tried to stop this, haven't I? You know I have."

"Yes," he admitted, "but it was no good. I'd got to have it out. I mean to have it out."

"Is there anything more to say?" I asked, watching the candle drip on the sandy floor. I thought his lips tightened and his eyes grew dark.

"What is it," he said, "what is it keeps you from me, and me from you?"

I could not tell him. I dreaded at some future time through sheer weariness I might give in. Instinctively I felt he divined there was between us nothing tangible.

He said:

"I'm a success, but I've never grasped one of the things I've tried to grasp. . . ."

There was silence, a horrid silence which pressed close and hot in that dim place.

"Since I knew you, I've begun to regret things," he said, fingering the candle wax. "It's too late now to begin seeking again. . . ."

I said nothing; I was trying to gain time. Somehow, I must prevent this ever happening again, for his sake as well as my own. And I was afraid of myself.

I watched his shadow, grotesque and distorted, leap up the granite wall, and as I watched I thought of the Shadow that has come very close.

I longed to tell him of the Shadow, to let him believe there was no hope — but I could not tell him; I did not know how.

We stood in the silent gallery. The silence which lurks underground is absolute.

Suddenly I broke out:

"Why should you care for me? Why should you? The Flapette believed in you. . . ."

He was smiling, his eyes were smiling.

"Yes, I know. But you didn't believe in me!" Life is like that, I suppose.

"We've got to come to an understanding," the Author said.

"Haven't we come to an understanding?"

"No."

"I wonder what more you desire? I have told you it cannot be."

"Is that all?"

"Only this" — suddenly I did not care what I said: "if you went on and on I might give in. There, you know now. . . . But you won't."

"I won't," he answered.

"I can trust you." I had no need to make it a question.

"Yes."

At moments like that the hampering barriers of convention, of civilization, fall away; we were just two humans stripped of all pretense.

"Then I think I can tell you — had circumstances been otherwise, I might have cared. I suppose women don't say these things. You've told me I'm different; perhaps I am. I feel I must say this, I feel I owe it to you——"

ch. ends next p.

He leaned his forehead against the granite wall, and his hands fell limp and heavy to his sides; the slanted candle shot up black smoke, burning away the wax. He did not heed it. For a dreadful moment I suspected him of pose, and then shame flared in me. A long shiver went through him; he had shivered like that with the pain in his shoulder. The smoking candle dropped from his slack grasp suddenly. I felt as though the light had gone out for me too; I had put it out.

In the hot muffling darkness I heard his voice, rather quiet, "You can trust me. We've said all there is to say. . . . Now we must go on," he added dully, moving forward.

"Yes, now we must go on again," I repeated drearily. My heart seemed dead in me. There is so much of this going on again. . . .

We came up into blazing daylight; it struck chill after the stifling furnace-heat underground.

The wind felt bleak. It numbed my body and brain. I had cut myself adrift.

Desmond Dulac put aside the red lock with his familiar gesture, smiling painfully.

"It was like you to be frank with me," he said; there was that in his voice which told me what I had sacrificed.

"I think I've come nearer to yourself," he said; "I'm going to keep the thought of you — saying that . . ." He might have been posing, he might have been sincere. I believe now he was at that moment splendidly sincere if never before.

Miserably I kept silence.

I have given up much — because of You. Is to give up a form of giving?

It was of You I was thinking. Surely it is hardest of all to lose what one has never had?

We had to go on. No one but our two selves would ever know what transpired in that short space we were alone underground. We had to go on.

The Author rode behind with the Flapette, whose camel lagged. I heard her low, gurgling laughter.

We came to the Temple of Ti[1] and the Step Pyramid.[2] Our dragoman showed steps leading to the black hole where Ti hid his body — I mean, caused his body to be hidden — hoping it would never be discovered. I felt ashamed because I had looked on it in a glass case at the Museum. The temple is all of stone, built in an austere style, with narrow passageways and wonderful wall-pictures. They are so old, it is impossible to grasp their age; it conveys nothing. They are not the familiar stiff figures of the bas-relief, with which I have always associated Desmond Dulac, but exquisitely conceived and painted,

[1] Ti was a high-status official in the era of the last king of the Fifth Egyptian Dynasty, and the Mastaba or Tomb of Ti was discovered at the northern edge of the Saqqara necropolis by Auguste Mariette in 1865.

[2] The Pyramid of Djoser, sometimes called the Step Pyramid of Djoser (also Djeser or Zoser, the first or second king of the 3rd Dynasty), is a 6-tier pyramid and the earliest colossal stone building in Egypt.

showing not only a marvelous knowledge of the decorative, but of nature; animals and birds are vital, the startling life which is in so many of these very ancient things. The pictures teem with interest; they represent the building of boats, cutting flax, catching and salting fish, scribes with papyrus and cases of reed pens, courts of justice, the sacrificial bulls. The sacred was no less sacred because the secular was interwoven.

"The Egyptians treated religion almost humorously," I remarked.

"No one without humor should be allowed to write about religion," Miss Kershaw answered succinctly. "It's usually parsons or schoolmasters who make the attempt — or the two combined, resulting in the most humorless thing on earth."

The dragoman told us a delightful story to explain some of the pictures. It was about a "picnic" given by Ti and "Madame Ti."

"Madame Ti" invited to the picnic a man whom Ti disliked, so Ti ran away in a huff to Palestine. She went after him, laid wait in the dark, and caught him by the foot; she is depicted thus frequently. She then gave another "picnic" for those who had aided her, and sent the rest to prison.

I was delighted in this tale, it seemed so human; but I fear the unctuous old knave invented it from a desire to please.

As we rode on, I found myself listening to the dust that whispered up to me. . . . The happening in the tomb seemed remote, I regretted it with an effort. For, as I rode through the burning dust, I had almost grasped what Space is; I had come nearer to it than I ever was. It only just eluded me.

It was evening when we reached the plain and rode through fields of tall *doura*, faintly sweet and rustling, to Memphis, with its palm groves. The low sun behind us made a golden haze of the dust, filtering through gray and gilded palm fronds; dust and sun were caught among the still groves, hung there like a glittering web.

The sun turned fields of *berseem* to a green so vivid the heart leaped to it, as though color were sound. We were riding over the site of old Memphis; our camels padded softly beneath dusky palms, the low sun burning through, gilding the dry, dust-laden atmosphere. A sweet cool smell rose after the heat; frogs rippled and crickets shrilled.

We passed the colossal statues of Rameses the Great, both lying prone, impressive, as are all these giant figures. We rode through a village of huts made of palm branches, and mud-huts roofed with *doura* stalks, where were evil-smelling, stagnant pools, and square, whitening heaps of empty corn-cobs. We came to Bedrachien[3] in the warm, sad dark of a moonless night.

"Hasn't it been topping?" the Flapette whispered. "I shall never forget today . . . and he has been most awfully decent. We seemed to get on so well this afternoon. He was killing. I feel I know him better——" Her voice was eager; her eyes, with tired rings, shone.

Fate has a hideously humorous twist.

---

[3] Badrashin is a city in the Giza Governorate, approximately 18 miles southwest of Cairo on the west bank of the Nile river, and home to the oldest Egyptian monuments.

34

I am writing to You in the desert, sitting at the doorway of my tent, with sand drifting between the pages. My hope has been realized; we are wandering in the desert.

All day I can listen to the whispering dust; at night the doorway of my tent is crammed with stars. Bitterness has slipped from me; the desert and desert silences are large. I draw nearer discovering what Space means — already there have been moments brimming silence when almost I grasped the meaning. . . .

I never thought Miss Kershaw would give her consent to this desert life. Perhaps I rather forced her hand. I told her my desire, my determination. I could not go alone, though I was mad enough even for that, having listened to the dust; so Miss Kershaw consented.

The Flapette declared it top-hole, if it did not mean sleeping on the ground and tinned-meat sandwiches with grit between. The Flapette was suspicious of discomfort, but I overruled her.

We have been in the desert two nights and two days — I think; Time ceases to be in the desert, and the flowing wideness sweeps away regret, blots out and muffles what has been as the sand, wind-driven, covers foot-marks silently.

I look into this wideness as I write, and everywhere is sand, tawny and fierce orange, peach and dun and gray, with purple sudden streaks. The sun is low, and all the desert colors live. Soon a swift darkness will swamp color and the desert lie wan and whitening under remote, white stars.

One of the Arab boys is beating a tom-tom where they squat smoking their pipes of *keef*; a hoarse, monotonous voice is chanting.

In a little while they will bow themselves, facing toward Mecca, at that solemn hour when from countless mosques the voice they cannot hear cries out, "There is no God but God."

Mahommet, the dragoman, is bullying the cook, as he prepares our evening meal of beans and Arab bread, *mish-mish* and *yusef-effendis*.[1] In a moment they too will prostrate themselves.

Yesterday a sandstorm overtook us. The dust no longer whispered, it cried out . . . it choked and blinded, parched and scorched. A glad frenzy entered me so that I could not feel cracked lips and smarting eyes; the dust caught me up, whirled me where it would. I think I shouted things which had no meaning, as we pressed forward seeking shelter. The air darkened, the darkness took a lurid purple, blotting out sky and desert — this purple, moving darkness, hot and blistering,

[1] Mandarin oranges.

wrapped us; swirled past us ceaselessly. Movement without sound is awful.

We pressed on, eyes bloodshot and straining. A feverish excitement burned in me; I exulted.

There were shouts somewhere in the drifting dark. Our boys halted; I heard the complaining snarls of the baggage-camels, heavily laden.

Quite suddenly the fierce wind sank, the dimness paled, ragged dun spirals like rain-clouds were detached and hung suspended. . . . Before us stood several tall white figures, muffled to the eyes. They were Bedouins. One of these men came forward and our dragoman touched his hand, placing his own on heart, lips, and forehead.

"*Ana huashtini ya akhuya*,"[2] he said, greeting him in the extravagant manner of the East.

Our boys squatted patiently, faces haggard, eyes and lips swollen.

I commiserated. I could never deal with natives. "*Ma'alaishe ya Sitt di min Rubbani*,"[3] their spokesman answered, displaying the Arab's amazing resignation.

The Bedouins wished to offer us hospitality, our dragoman explained.

Eagerly we accepted. The tall man who had met us led the way to his tent, outside which several Bedouins were kindling a fire of camel-dung.

"*Mahubbah!*"[4] he said as we entered, cramped and dazed with fatigue. The women-folk, with shy, kohl-darkened eyes, set before us figs and bread, dried dates, cumis (which is curdled

---

[2] "I have longed for you, O my brother."
[3] "No matter, O lady, our Lord sends it."
[4] "Welcome!"

mare's-milk), and water from a large seer in the tent corner. They retired, and the men watched us eat, speaking little, maintaining the curious aloofness which lends dignity to the Bedouin, yet subtly making us welcome. We crouched in the dusky goat's-hair tent, too weary to talk, very grateful for the silent hospitality of these desert men.

Acrid smoke from the fire drifted into the tent. Outside all was very still. After a sandstorm the desert stillness is almost terrible. It held the thin, sweet note of a Bedouin reed pipe, plaintive, insistent.

When we rose to leave, "*Roh-es-salaam*" our host said gravely. We answered, "*Ma salaami.*"[5] We went out into the dazzling light and brooding stillness to mount our camels. The thin sound of the reed pipe followed us. . . .

---

[5] "With my blessing."

Miss Kershaw has been talking again of the man who hadn't nonsense. When she speaks of him her voice rasps and I see the woman who crouches behind the wall of reserve; her eyes are tender and puzzled. She does not understand him, and yet she believes she knows him better than anyone else. Women deceive themselves like that.

"I don't know why," Miss Kershaw said, "I get thinking about him out here in the desert. He spends his life amongst grime and bricks, and mortar." I suddenly felt sorry for him; I had spent my life amongst grime and turnip fields. And there are wide spaces, sand shimmering liquid in the stark noon glare, stretching white under stars. . . .

"He belongs to Leeds; he's in wool." Her voice rasped like a file against her closed teeth; she sounded grim and regretful. "But whenever he can, which isn't often, he goes tramping over the moors, always by himself. He never tells anyone about these tramps, he doesn't tell me. You don't know the Yorkshire moors, of course? Like as not you'd think them ugly; the heather and rocks are mostly blackened. Soot from the towns. They're bleak, too. The wind whistles through the stone walls. Unless you're Yorkshire——" She broke off, defiant because she had shown emotion and was ashamed.

"The rain drifts over the moors. It's more often wet than not, that's my experience, wet and gray; the walls are gray, and the sheep . . . he's a rum sort," she added irrelevantly. "Never could make him out. What does he tramp the moors for? I always imagined he was pretty matter-of-fact, rather hardheaded, that he was——"

"That he had no nonsense about him?" I suggested sadly. Miss Kershaw rubbed her hand over her mouth and chin, a gesture I've come to know. She grimaced a little with wistful eyes.

"Yes," she said, "no nonsense."

As before, I was eager to hear more about this man. He piqued my curiosity. I liked hearing about him, I liked listening. I wonder if I am beginning to have a wider interest in humanity?

I found I was quite interested in Miss Kershaw's disjointed talk concerning this Yorkshireman. She was certainly fond of him.

"I think somehow I should like Yorkshire," I said musingly. "You say it's ugly——"

"I didn't," she snapped; "I said you might think it was."

"I don't think I should. There must be — you must get near Space up on those big, bleak moors. . . ." I was running sand through my fingers. I could feel the warm drift of it across my palm, but I could not see the glitter; I could see drenched heather, blackened and with a smell of burning, I have never seen heather in my life.

Miss Kershaw looked at me curiously, then at the hand

through which the sand was running; I looked down at it too without knowing why. All the sand had gone, as in an hourglass. My hand was arrested; I remembered vaguely the Author had called it a listening hand. How long it seemed since that day in the *Serapis!* . . .

"What odd things you say!" Miss Kershaw remarked.

"Do I?"

"Yes; d'you know, when I first set eyes on you I mistook you altogether. I thought you were quite an ordinary woman who'd never questioned much, rather taken things for granted, didn't possess an uncomfortable imagination——"

I smiled at her:

"Your insight wasn't at fault. I was all that."

She screwed up her eyes. "You mean you're not now?" she said.

"Yes."

"You've discovered you didn't know yourself, eh?"

"I've discovered I knew no more about myself than I knew about other people. People have only touched my life, I haven't known them from within. It's been the same with myself, I think."

"You never realized you were not just like other women?"

"But I was just like other women——"

"Until?"

"Until I suddenly got nonsense." I laughed evasively.

"I see," said Miss Kershaw, in the tone which makes you feel she sees a great deal more than you want her to see.

"This subject isn't the least bit interesting," I remarked impatiently. "Let's drop it."

"Very well. But you are different somehow, you know."

"Oh, I do hate being told I'm different! It gives me, as the Flapette would say, such an uncomfortable feeling."

"You must be prepared for discomfort if you cultivate the — visionary, isn't it called?"

"I've never cultivated it," I said indignantly.

"I don't think you have," she admitted. "But you get through life much more satisfactorily——"

"If you're 'nice and sensible.' Do you think so?"

"No, I don't," she said with blunt emphasis. "An entirely satisfactory method of getting through life has yet to be discovered, my dear."

"Do let's leave this subject alone," I pleaded. "I think far too much about myself as it is; even — my friends sometimes tell me so." I meant You. "I'm introspective in these days."

Miss Kershaw said, "When you begin tracking down and dissecting emotions it's like a jig-saw puzzle; you're forever finding one that doesn't seem to belong to the puzzle at all — or the very one you're looking for is missing; maybe it's only under the carpet, but it worries you and you begin all over again. There's no end to the game when you start; you spend your spare time and a lot you can't spare upon introspection. It fascinates after a while. . . . I used to have a weakness for jig-saws," she confessed whimsically.

"I think you're right," I said. "But when you are always alone you get like that."

"Are you always alone?"

"In a way, yes. Sometimes I think I always shall be. Sometimes I think I must lack——"

"My dear girl, you don't. On the contrary, your head——"

"Oh, as to my head——"

"Your head's overcrowded; that's about it."

ch. ends p. 255

"Overcrowded?" I laughed. "Not with brains. I've never *done* anything." I thought of the book I tried to write — the only thing I have ever tried to do, even.

"You haven't done anything yet," said Miss Kershaw. She likes to qualify statements, her own as well as other people's. "You've thought a lot," she added.

"What's the good of thinking? And my thoughts are so absurd."

"Absurd thoughts. Hmmm. I never let myself think absurd thoughts. . . . Stick to nonsense," she said tersely. She watched me a minute. "What are you thinking about now?" she demanded.

"I'm thinking about — the Yorkshireman. At least, not exactly thinking; wondering, perhaps. Do go on talking of him. I like to hear."

"Oh! Well, what do you want to hear about him?" Miss Kershaw has this disconcerting way when she is at all suspicious.

"Anything. I don't know. You had begun to tell me things——"

For some time I had endeavored subtly to bring the conversation round to the subject, but Miss Kershaw is like that about this man; it makes me think he is more to her than she cares to admit. She begins talking of him suddenly, rather disconnectedly, then she drops the subject, and it is difficult to induce her to begin again.

"Why should he interest you?" she demanded.

"I don't know," I said honestly. "I suppose because he is a friend of yours."

"As much a friend of mine as anybody's." She spoke rather wistfully. "He's so hard to get at — Northern, very, and I expect I'm not the right sort to try; I've built up a kind of a wall myself, I daresay."

"I've seen behind it once or twice," I said fondly and injudiciously. A harsh, difficult flush deepened the rough red face; I had never seen her flush before. It was painful. She thought it almost indecent that I should catch glimpses of the crouching woman, whose eyes were tragic.

"I never imagined Yorkshire people so likeable," I said. I daren't say "lovable."

"As what?" she asked.

"As you."

"I think you mean that," she replied with a kind of softened rasping.

I wanted her to go on talking of this man she could not understand. The subject roused my curiosity. No, I don't think it was curiosity quite. I just wanted to listen. That was all. I felt in some ridiculous manner disloyal to You because I liked listening. And yet I have lost belief in You; I had to cultivate it, and that sort of belief is really doubt from the beginning.

"You might have seen him at Tilbury when we sailed." Miss Kershaw became expansive. "I've told you he turned up? He didn't come on board, though. He never saw me; it would have been the last thing he'd do, to come and see me off. I could only suppose he had some friend sailing on the '————.' He'd never mentioned it; but then, he's so silent, reserved and all. I could only suppose he had some friend on board, yet I never saw him speak to a soul. I hadn't known he was in London, even. He just watched the ship leave dock."

I could not remember a man standing alone, conspicuously alone, but there are so many people standing alone at Tilbury you don't know they are alone. That is the worst kind of loneliness. I can't conceive a place where you could be more desolately alone than Tilbury.

ch. ends next p.

The man who hadn't nonsense, if this were he, evidently did not marry the girl, I mused. But he came to Tilbury to see someone off; I felt a warm uprush of pity for Miss Kershaw. A long time I sat thinking, or rather my thoughts drifted through my brain as the sand drifted through my fingers. I could not overcome senseless curiosity.

"What is his name?" I asked at last.

Miss Kershaw looked startled, suspicious; then a light seemed to break in her eyes, to flicker there. I wondered what it meant. She reflected or hesitated; I thought she was debating if she should tell me.

She came to one of her abrupt decisions.

"David Olroyd," she said, a shade defiantly.

Again my thoughts were running on like the sand. I groped. I was trying to seize some memory which eluded me. For a long time I must have been silent. Suddenly, searching among vague, meaningless recollections, I remembered. That was the name. David Olroyd. It must have been three years ago, quite. . . . Odd I should have remembered, for the man had only just crossed my life, touched it and passed out of it, leaving nothing behind but the name. There had been a period when I should have liked his friendship, I think, looking back; I suppose I did not realize it then. Somewhere about the time my uncle died and I was given freedom, he drifted out of my life again, as people had always done, making no impression upon it. The name recalled these facts. The name, too, I had forgotten till now. Probably it had remained somewhere in a vacant corner of my mind because it was peculiar.

I had met a man of that name; I tried to fit it to a personality, but I could not; I had forgotten what the man was like, forgotten completely. Yet at one time, I think now, I should have valued his friendship. Perhaps I might have remembered what he was like if You had not come persistently between, almost reproachfully. I could not recollect the man for seeing You; You haven't been so real since — I began to lose belief, I suppose. I tried hard to picture him, but You would not let me; every time You got between. At last I gave it up.

I knew there had been no mistake about the name; I remembered that: it had an odd sound. How strange I should have met this friend of Miss Kershaw's, this man who hadn't nonsense; and all the time I never knew it! He was difficult to get on with, silent. . . . I remember that, in a dim, very dim, sort of way. It must have been the same man. I have seen him; it exasperates me that I cannot remember him. Why will You thrust yourself between? You are an exacting friend. Can You be prejudiced against him too? You were like that about the Author.

I thought I had better not tell Miss Kershaw I remembered the name, knew the man once. I don't think she would want me to have known him, somehow, even though my knowledge was less than nothing. I think I understand how she feels; I might have felt the same, if You had been.

We are wandering toward the Libyan desert, I suppose. To me it is only the desert, simply that; and just now the desert is all-sufficing.

We have no destination. We move slowly through the sun and the hot dust of days which are not marked by time. Just as the track of our caravan is swallowed in the desert, so the days dwindle and become the past. We move slowly. *"El agela minin esh Shaitan,"* [1] the Arabs say.

Sometimes the day is marked by a flock of flamingo, like a rose-streak in the blue; once, looking down upon a shallow wady,[2] I saw a vulture, with its naked neck and ghastly hopping; it made a dark, loathsome blot against the paleness of the sand. Often I see the little timid jerboa[3] at some distance from the camp. We see no jackals; only at night their dismal wailing tears the silence suddenly. There are these little things in the

---

[1] "Haste is from the devil."

[2] Also wadi; a valley, ravine, gully, or streambed that remains dry except during the rainy season.

[3] A nocturnal desert-dwelling, mouse-like rodent with large ears, very long hind legs, and a long tufted tail.

days, trivial things that seem happenings. For the rest, there is sun and dust, a profound silence, such as might be under the ocean; it drowns sound from the outer world, filling day to the brim. The throb of the *tabla*,[4] Arabs' harsh voices, and camels' snarling are lost in this silent void. I lie in my tent and let the silence lap me round . . . the dust whispers through the silence. I lie and listen.

Today I was watching night steal swiftly across the desert; it was that moment when the horizon takes a dun-gold,[5] dim above the darkening sand, and the sky is maize, and pulses faintly with the afterglow. There is always this moment of dun-gold before night falls. I wait for it.

The Flapette sat beside me, with one foot under her and the light pale round her head. She has been rather quiet of late. If she grows bored, she will persuade Miss Kershaw to go back. Out here I never feel shut in; the thought of going back to Cairo stifles me, gives me a prisoned feeling.

I laughed and spoke.

"The Author would liken such a night to a grief-stricken woman with copper hair, or a brown kite stretching wounded wings over the earth — wouldn't he?" I merely mentioned the Author because the Flapette never mentioned him now, and I could not quite understand her attitude; we might have had a tacit agreement not to touch upon the subject. I was able to speak of him in an altogether impersonal way; he had become so remote, a part of all that was, or seemed to be, before the desert swamped the past.

The Flapette watched a beetle in the sand, a beetle, like the

---

[4] A pair of drums, differing in size and tone, attached together.
[5] "Dun" denotes a dull grayish-brown color.

ch. ends p 262

scarabs, buried in countless *mastabas*;[6] it was crawling, little grains giving way beneath it; moving its legs without visible advance. I knew by the Flapette's face that though she watched she did not see. I expected she would turn upon me indignantly when I spoke of the Author, but she did not.

"It seems — all wrong for the Author not to be here, doesn't it?" she said jerkily.

"Wouldn't it be all wrong if he were?" I ventured. "He would hate the discomfort of it."

"Oh, it's not so bad. Just that sandstorm was rotten. And the possibility of finding a scorpion in your bed. And the flies. It's roughing it, of course, but——"

"I mean the discomfort of the desert's self, the way it stretches on and on . . . the Author hates the desert," I said.

The Flapette looked at me wistfully. "He told you a lot about himself, didn't he?"

"He always tells everyone a lot about himself, Flapette."

Her insight is quite unchildlike. "Oh, no," she answered sagely; "he only tells everyone about Desmond Dulac."

"He annoyed me by the way he over-emphasized that; disassociated himself from Desmond Dulac."

"And yet he wasn't — isn't Desmond Dulac."

"I wonder."

"I don't. He didn't tell me as much as he told you, but I somehow feel I know more about him, all the same."

"I think," I said, recollecting the ways in which they were alike, "I think you do."

The Flapette sighed.

"I am hopelessly obvious and all that, of course. Now, he's

---

[6] Ancient rectangular, mud-brick Egyptian tombs with sloping sides and flat roofs.

entirely opposite, and you are too," grudgingly; "I've always said there's something kind of mysterious about you. 'Bill' once said you were doing your best to combine a sensible, sane outlook with that of a — visionary, I think it was, and she thought the what-you-may-call-it, the visionary, didn't give the other much of a look in; something like that. You and the Author must have had quite a lot in common."

"Nothing, Flapette. He has much more in common with you, as a matter of fact."

"Perhaps"; she was unconvinced. "But you see he believes he's more in common with you — and, after all, that's what matters, isn't it?"

"You're wise in your generation, but you're wrong this time."

"Aren't you anything to the Author?" she demanded.

I was glad she put it like that.

"Nothing," I said; "nor ever could be."

She knew I was sincere. Her eyes were wide and puzzled.

She began, "I always imagined——"

"Don't imagine. You can't think how disturbing an imagination becomes, Flapette. It's just a bad habit."

"I wish I had more. The Author has so much."

"Have you forgotten he does not believe in his books, what he writes——"

"He must have had imagination to invent the pose, in the first place," remarked the Flapette profoundly. A fluffy girl when profound is nearly as piteous as a practical girl when flippant. In both cases it means she isn't happy.

The Flapette was looking at the beetle and the moving sand-grains; the tilt of her head was despondent. I wondered whether she knew that most bleak feeling——

I moved nearer. "What is it?" I asked, trite as usual: I'm only "different" regarding my feelings, the part of me I have shown You in this book; the rest of me is ordinary, quite.

"It's some sort of an animal or other," the Flapette said, wilfully mistaking my meaning. "One of those things they buried with mummies, I think. It's a grues."

I mean, what's the matter?"

"How the matter? I don't understand you." She resorted to the pitiful dignity of that well-worn phrase. I have resorted to it untold times myself.

"Are you sorry the Author isn't here?" I asked.

"Yes. A bit. Well, naturally. Of course. Aren't you?"

"No, I can't say I am."

"You're so odd," she said; and then, smiling wanly, "I suppose that was why he — liked you so much."

"He liked you, Flapette."

"Oh, yes, he liked me," she said; and then, with quiet bitterness, "But I know just the sort of way he liked me!"

I was silent. I felt responsible for this; it hurt. I had dismissed the child lightly, feeling convinced, because I desired to be convinced, that she was only a child still. I began to realize I had been blinding myself, and willfully.

"Of course, it was not your fault he liked you," she went on. "It was up to you to make him — but you didn't. It wasn't your fault. I know that. It was just — I was so rottenly young and — obvious, I suppose. If I weren't pretty it might have been different."

Sometimes I wonder whether anything might have been different, whatever we did or were; I think I am imbibing fatalism.

"He was ripping to me often. That Sakkarah day——" she drew a breath — "lots of times. But of course I knew. A woman does. . . . Oh, it's absolutely the green limit being a woman!"

It was a child's wail against that which it could not understand, but I knew as she uttered it the Flapette ceased to be a child.

She dug both hands into the sand and scattered it, drawing little quick breaths.

"I suppose I shall never see him again," she said. "Well — what does it matter?" She flung that at Fate, she was hurling defiance. Then she sank back on her heels, whispering rather brokenly. "You may as well know. You must have guessed long since. I don't mind if you have. . . . I'm not ashamed," she broke out, and defiance flared in her cheeks. "Dash it all, you can't help things like this. I care, d'you see——"

I knew she would not wish me to touch her. I groped for something adequate to say; I grieved over her, and I too felt bitter against Fate, and against the Author. Why could he not have cared for her, when so many men cared? Things would have been simple. . . .

"It's pretty ghastly — caring," the Flapette broke out; "isn't it?"

"I don't know, Flapette. I think — I mean I've never cared."

"Why couldn't you care for him?" she demanded unreasonably, fiercely. I understood; it was rather splendid of the Flapette. "Why couldn't you?"

"I shouldn't have made him happy," I said.

She took off a ring and rubbed the sand from her finger.

"I don't think you would," she answered reflectively. "Somehow . . . What's the good of it? What's the good? He won't ever know. And I won't ever be able to do anything for him——"

What is the good? The pity of it; the waste!

"Oh, do you know——" She paused, locking her fingers, and the words broke, vibrant with emotion: "I wouldn't mind

ch. ends next p.

what I did for him. I'd — I'd mend his socks when they came back from the wash with sand in them! I wouldn't mind how uncomfortable anything was so long as I did it for him."

The Flapette could not have said more than that.

"Perhaps," I murmured, trying to believe my words, "perhaps some day the Author will show you how to give." I had no hope of it, and she knew I had none; she had none herself.

We sat staring into the cool darkness, which robbed the sky of color and swept up, shrouding our tents.

I felt very weary. Life, even quite an ordinary sort of life like mine, seemed so hopelessly involved; where was the good of trying to disentangle threads? They were just part of a monstrous web of circumstance in which we struggled. I was very weary. A strange thought came: that it would be sweet to feel the sand sift over you, touching your lips, weighting eyelids softly, taking your breath — pale and glittering. . . .

How such a thought would horrify the Author! — a morbid, almost an indecent thought. He doubtless wished, when the end came — only, one did not think about uncomfortable things — it might come in a suitably darkened room, with suitably assembled relatives. I laughed aloud, mirthlessly.

The sand would drift upward so palely cool, weighting heavy lids. . . .

What is to be after this?

Just as the desert has blotted out the past, so dust wraps the future. I feel there couldn't be anything beyond this; sometimes I don't want anything more.

To give up wandering, to face that meaningless "going on again," seems unthinkable. And I have lost the Author's friendship, a sincere, desirable thing; most dreary thought of all, I have lost that which I have never had. I haven't You any longer — my belief in You, I mean.

"Do you know, Flapette," I said, "I get such a funny feeling; I can't conceive of any future existing beyond this desert-time. What lies ahead is blank, a blank void, so much so I sometimes think perhaps there isn't going to be anything more — after this."

The Flapette looked startled and uncomfortable.

"What a beastly sort of idea! And — kind of morbid, you know. Unwholesome, and all that. I wish you weren't so odd. How could there be nothing after this?" Her tone implied it would be pretty rotten if we were never to eat bread-and-butter again without an admixture of sand.

"I don't know," I said; "I can't explain; I have these feelings. I can't shake it off."

"Oh, hang it! You give way to that sort of thing," she answered impatiently. She seemed to accuse me of making mountains out of molehills, while she was keeping her own volcano well in hand.

"It's all right having moods, but you can carry the thing too far." She was speaking very gravely from newly attained experience.

Then she laughed, as though she would place conversation upon a more wholesome plane.

"There's no harm in indulging moods now and then, I daresay. Perhaps I wouldn't be so obvious if I had moods more often. They're a safety-valve too, and all that, you know. I occasionally feel downright 'maungy,' for instance——"

"Whatever's 'maungy,' Flapette?"

"Oh, when you chuck ragtime and play something sloppy — and feel pleasantly sad and reminiscent over all the nice little friends whose names you can't remember for the life of you! I get — at least, I mean I used to get attacks now and then. Generally when I'm fed up with someone or about something. I know when it's coming on."

"The symptoms?"

"Oh, a general all-overishness chiefly. You know."

"Yes, I know the feeling, but I can't rid my system of it so effectually."

"You don't play. That's a pity, of course. Suppressed in your case. Result: complications. What?"

The Flapette ran on loquaciously, but I could see her mind was absent; her great blue eyes were wistful in her freckled pink face. I am almost as dark as an Arab after these desert weeks, but the Flapette told me she has been within measurable distance of doing me a mischief during sleep because I burn and she only freckles. "When you have to use cold cream," she said pathetically, "the flies settle on your nose; it draws attention to my worst feature!"

I watched the Flapette looking distant and aloof; she was only near, and pink, in a bodily sense.

"Well?" I said, though I can't bear anyone saying it to me.

"You remember——" she hesitated, embarrassed — "what you said about — about wanting to give? Well, I think I rather begin to see what you meant — sort of." She paused, as though pondering. "Is giving up a kind of giving?" she asked suddenly.

I started. She is sometimes astonishing; she even advances ideas I had thought were my own. Perhaps I am not really so different from other women after all.

"I've wondered myself, Flapette," I said. She looked at me curiously; she seemed to see me in a new light.

"Have you had to give up anything?" she asked in an awed way, and almost resentfully.

She slipped her arm through mine, a thing she seldom did. "Have you?"

"Yes."

"Was it — was it something big?"

"It was the only thing I've ever had the chance of giving up," I said. "And, Flapette, I didn't want to, I didn't want to give up."

"I wonder why you did it?" she replied; her eyes were veiled and questioning.

"So do I — very often."

When I said it I seemed to see You as I saw You that night on the terrace, and Your watching, quiet eyes hurt; I shrank from the pain of it. I realized with a sick pang that You believed still

ch. ends p. 269

in me, though I had lost my belief in You. I suppose I am writing nonsense. It is a pitiful sort of nonsense. I wonder if a Catholic who has lost belief feels as I felt, on looking at a crucifix? An idea like that would shock the Flapette or the Author, I suppose.

I think something of pain was in my eyes, for I saw the Flapette glance at me compassionately, full of a vague wonder.

Then I laughed. The grievous thing was nothing real, nothing tangible. Why should I suffer because of it? It was habit merely; You have become a bad habit, that is all. But You have been my friend. And more; I could not help it — You have been something more. Is it only habit that keeps Romance going in the world? The thought is dreary.

The Flapette spoke with simple earnestness. "I am so sorry. You see, I can understand."

I felt a warm sense of communion and companionship. Though she could not know nor guess what I had given up, she understood in the blind, instinctive way women do understand. A woman does not need to be told the facts before she can understand.

"Little Flapette," I said, venturing to become demonstrative. We were drawn suddenly so near; she had bridged the gulf her youth kept wide.

We walked on through the thick sand, near one another, in a satisfying silence.

But youth is pitiless.

"It's rather rot having to give up," the Flapette said. "I — I have my doubts whether it's worth it, you know. . . . Do you remember what it felt like, having to give up?"

I was suddenly conscious of the sand in my shoes. The mutual silence drawing us was rudely shattered. I had deluded myself, believing we had drawn very close. We had not. There was a great gulf between. The Flapette allowed me a remote past, but a present was out of the question; I did not possess a present. That was true enough now, I reflected. And a future? What was the meaning of my inability to conceive anything beyond the desert?

We had wandered a long way from the camp. Our tents and the white skull-caps and blue *galabiehs* came in sight; a smell of lentil soup and burning camel-dung drifted up to us; I swayed a little.

"I am not well," I murmured; "I think I'm tired. We've been rather far."

From a great distance a voice answered me; I could not grasp the words — I tried stupidly to grasp them with my hands: my brain would not work.

Then there were more voices, and I recognized Miss Kershaw's rasping tone. The words were distinguishable; I could see again clearly, horribly clearly, as though I had always seen before through a film. Things were so distinct they made my eyes tired.

"Oh, I'm all right," I said. "It is nothing. We went rather far, that's all. I'll just lie down a while——"

"I hope it isn't sun," Miss Kershaw rasped anxiously.

I laughed, and they were reassured. I laughed because the Shadow had crept very close; it was waiting for me just inside the tent, and I didn't care.

*　＊　*

The water, carried in earthen pots slung in nets on the baggage camels, has begun to run short.

ch. ends next p.

I am responsible for this shortage; I insisted upon lingering at our last camping-place. It was backed by a great wall of stone that glowed orange and crimson with curious streaks, and ledges pale with drifted sand; rising flame-like into the white-hot sky, where great brown kites hung poised, glinting copper in the sun's relentless glare. The huge rock mass thrust itself, splendidly sheer, out of the desert sand. The place held me, its splendor of savage color and vast, unattainable height.

The Shadow still waited, is still waiting. I had no wish to go farther; the spirit which spurred me on was exhausted; bodily, too, I was exhausted; my limbs were heavy, effort oppressed me. But the water was running low, and Mahommet insisted we should press on to an oasis lying within a half-day's camel ride.

I am sitting under palm trees; the drifted sand clings to their stems; the gray rustling of their fronds is above me, against a blue, changeless sky. There is a *marabout's* tomb where are two cypresses, somber amidst a dazzle of sun-drenched green; there are *mish-mish* trees and oleanders, a garden of cucumbers neglected and rampant, and a garden where bright tropical blooms hang in a languorous sweetness. Hoopoes[1] flit through the green, and doves. In the midst is an old stone well, where the women of the little oasis come with their water-pots, and where green lizards dart with glittering suddenness. A splash and gurgle of water is in the air, which is heavy with the scent of rosemary and musk. At sunset a cool dampness rises.

The Flapette is frankly delighted to see something other than sand, but already I am chafing to be away again with

---

[1] Any of several Eurasian and African birds with pinkish-brown plumage, long down-curved bills, black and white wings and tail, and notable for their distinctive "crown" of feathers.

nothing save the red and gray and gold and pitiless blue; the sand and the sky.

I have come so near knowing, finding, what Space is, in a little while I think I shall know. I am wearying to leave this green place, to be where the dust is and such wideness.

Would You have understood, I wonder? I like to think You would. The Author hates the desert; the Flapette tires of it; and Miss Kershaw — Miss Kershaw has no nonsense.

Were You more than just a part of Never-Was, we might have been here together in the desert, and listened to the dust; earth-dust and stardust in our eyes; so near there were no need even to touch each other; we should be silent mostly, and when we talked, we'd talk splendid Nonsense. The desert silence would have taken us. . . . Am I giving way to sentiment? I know You can't endure that; only, You see this book is my thoughts, and sometimes I can't help them growing foolish. What is the good of imagining? It is not even a might-have-been. The aching desire to be moving gives me no rest; I think You, too, would chafe to leave this cool riot of green behind and be away in the trackless waste that stretches always, seeming to have no end and no beginning.

Three whole weeks have gone since I last wrote in the green oasis.

I am writing now in Cairo with difficulty and a pencil. They have let me write because I was fretting; I expect they wonder what I write; they must know I never receive any but business letters.

It seems strange to turn back and find what I had written on the last page about my unbelief in You. I have lived a lifetime since then.

I must tell You all that has happened; so much has happened. I have got back my belief in You. . . .

That first night in the oasis I lay wide-eyed, feeling the sweet murmurous greenery pressing close through the dark; branches stirred and lifted between me and the stars which had filled my tent-door. The hot hours dragged, and as I lay I heard the ageless dust whispering up to me, the desert dust. I strained feverishly to listen, because the plash of water came between, as the branches came between me and the stars.

Just before dawn I rose and crept out noiselessly. All my

faculties were clear with the intense clearness that comes from lack of sleep; sight and hearing, every sense was abnormally acute. The whispering dust seemed loud. I peered cautiously into the night. We had one *Gaffir*[1] in this oasis; in the desert we had two, armed.

I could see a muffled figure, head sunk between his knees, motionless, his rifle propped against a palm tree. He was drugged by whisky or by opium; I knew he slept.

It was not possible to go into the desert on foot; a strange weakness had seized me so that my limbs trembled as I stood. I must secure one of the camels. Dimly, I could make out the shadowy group, with necks stretched along the ground. I slipped toward them; my camel *Hamidieh* knew me, and in her surly way would only make pretense at resistance. She would snarl and grunt when she rose up, but I must risk that.

I touched the soft wool tassels on the bridle; the little white shells were cold. I unloosed *Hamidieh*, and then came a blank. These blanks ensued in the midst of vivid, painfully vivid consciousness.

The sun had leaped suddenly over the desert's rim; I heard the buzzing of flies following the camel. Looking back, I saw a little group of palms and no pursuing figures. I think I laughed. I know I urged *Hamidieh* forward, and stretching her neck and baring her yellow teeth, she broke into a swift run. I urged her, letting my body relax to her long, jerking stride, and the dust swirled about me as I rode; I listened to it.

Hamidieh was tearing — I could not have stopped her — tearing into the blinding glare which ran molten over the sand, tearing into the sun. . . . The desert seemed to fall away beneath

---

[1] Watchman.

ch. ends next p.

her stride, to flow backward; but always the sand rolled up ahead, stretching endlessly. There came a blank, and the sun was high above the horizon; I was still riding; *Hamidieh* had slipped into an ambling trot I urged her, snarling, into her long stride.

Heat made the sky pale and colorless, the sun had drawn all color from the earth; the sky had a veiled look — ahead, the desert rippled in white waves of heat, rippled and flowed, and became vast lakes where palms rose tremulous and gray. Everywhere were scattered iron-red stones, half buried in the drifting, pallid sand; and gray-green *mit-minan* bushes,[2] each with its sharp-defined blue blot of shadow; the wind had driven the sand into ridges, as on a seashore; here and there were the little purple flower and spiky stem of *helga* that blossoms in these wastes. . . . Nothing escaped me; I even realized calmly this was madness, riding alone into the desert. But I did not care. Within the silent void, where was only shimmering gray heat, I could listen to the dust, and it whispered loudly up to me. The blood seemed fire in my veins, my body was a part of the furnace through which I rode — I was riding into the desert to find Space. Surely in the desert I must find Space? Wildly I urged *Hamidieh*. . . . We crossed a broad track made by innumerable prints of human feet and camels' feet, a caravan road to the great Sahara. Pools of blue shadow lay in the deeper imprints. *Hamidieh* glanced this way and that, turning her small head rapidly upon her long neck, snuffing the wind and making little guttural sounds, lifting a sneering lip. A blank followed, and I was still riding; I rocked to *Hamidieh's* slow walk. My eyes were hot and bloodshot, sand gritted between

---

[2] Sage-like shrubs often growing to a height of six or seven feet, and in clumps of as much as forty feet in circumference.

my teeth; my tongue was parched, and my skin, but still I urged her, feebly now. With the straight rush of an arrow she sped, her neck thrust forward. The desire to find Space clamored in me, spurred me on. . . .

There came a blank, and then I turned, despairing, for I thought I heard the quick, muffled padding of another camel. I must not be overtaken. The camel came alongside, and *Hamidieh* gave no sign. I did not turn, but suddenly I knew beyond any doubting, knew for all time that You were and are; I believed in You, and could never lose belief again. A sense of restfulness stole from the desert silence, wrapping me. When at last I looked back, there was only a single track, hidden where the sand dipped into hollows, stretching till it was lost in the gray, flowing heat waves. There was only the track *Hamidieh* had made. But still I believed; I could never doubt anymore that You were. I do not know why I believed; I simply could not and cannot doubt again.

After a time I was no longer conscious of *Hamidieh* beneath me, only the swaying motion; I seemed to sway not merely forward but from side to side, and the heat-shimmer made a haze which danced dizzily before my eyes. . . .

Suddenly came a crash that filled the desert with hideous sound, a stupendous thunder and rocking. I staggered to my feet, and groped helplessly; I could not see. I could not see through the red darkness. I tried to rush from the horror of it, yet somehow I knew, anguished, it was Your sight that had been destroyed, not my own.

39

Miss Kershaw found me. Only an hour after I left the oasis the camel was discovered missing; Miss Kershaw and the dragoman followed the track in the sand. I had taken the swiftest camel, and had been gone hours before they found me. I cannot bear to think what that ride was for Miss Kershaw, but I knew nothing when I rode out seeking Space; I was not responsible for what I did. They found me lying in the sand, with sand drifting over me, and *Hamidieh* not far away. That is all Miss Kershaw will say; I think perhaps she had seen birds hovering somewhere near. I remember how I saw one once, a dark blot on the desert paleness.

They brought me back to the oasis and to Cairo; I have no recollection of it. After the horror of blindness. Your blindness, struck me down, my mind became blank, and remained blank till the period when I lay partially delirious, conscious enough to know I was raving and to remember afterward vaguely what I raved about. I was told I had had a nervous breakdown; a serious touch of sun; that my heart was affected; that the ride into the desert had been madly rash. Miss Kershaw had never suspected anything serious, though, morbidly brooding, I imagined she suspected the Shadow. They thought one day I would die, and I think I should have died had I not regained belief in You. It seemed something to which I could cling amidst the vague, dark waters where I struggled; I clutched at it, and saved myself from sinking. I saw this belief in You as a tangible thing which hung above the bed — I would clutch at it with my hands as it swam toward me; sometime it wrote itself upon the darkness, and I spelled the letters out laboriously.

Belief in You was always there, whatever fevered, grotesque form it took. It was always there to clutch at. The desire to return to England kept me, too, from slipping into the darkness; what had been a dread of not returning amounted to an absolute and crying need to return. There was no reason for it, but all along there had been no reason. Monotonously, I repeated over and over again, "I must go back, I must go back." I knew I said it, and it was difficult to say, to drag the words together while they eluded me all about the room, but I kept saying it over and over, "I must go back."

At last light came, and sense, and a great languor. I asked for the Flapette.

"You'd hardly have recognized the Flapette — as 'nice, sensible girl,'" Miss Kershaw said, rasping tenderly. "She's thought of nothing but your comfort."

The Flapette would; she understands comfort. Dear Flapette! Illness is such an uncomfortable thing. Before she came I had lost desire to see her through sheer weakness. I lay inert for days, hearing the Nile lapping in the night I was told I must lie still, and I had no wish to move; I had no restless longing for the desert now, the desert had satisfied; the desert did not give what I sought; but it had given me, somehow, understanding,

ch. ends p. 280

and understanding brings peace. I knew I could never find Space in that way. You cannot come up with Space or grasp it, but I think I am learning the meaning of it — what Space is.

I don't know why I am going, why I must leave the desert that I love, and Egypt which is so old and pitiless and so alluring.

In the desert I found You again, You and Nonsense; I can't ever lose my belief in either, but something stronger even than the desert draws me, something nameless. I cannot tell what it is. . . .

The Flapette has had letters from Desmond Dulac. She does not show them to me, but she smiles in a secret, brooding way. Can it be possible the Author begins dimly to realize she understands him, that there is a bond between them?

I wonder if, after all, the Author will show her the way to give? Giving up may be giving, but I don't want the little Flapette to give like that. . . .

Does the Author realize I should have been uncomfortable to live with? I don't feel to mind any of it anymore; once I might have felt bitter, but not now. The desert silences lifted that from me. I shall never be terrified by being alone; something calm has sunk right down into me since I was in the desert, and found You again.

But I must go back. It irks me to have to wait till I recover my strength. Parting with Miss Kershaw and the Flapette hangs over me, but not that nor anything shall stop me from returning.

I have been sitting staring at this book dully, too numb to

write or think — though it happened yesterday. I think I must have sat here ever since; I feel I have sat here all my life and known all my life. But it only happened yesterday.

When the mail arrived, Miss Kershaw stood very still, passing her hand over her mouth and chin, then pushing her grizzled hair that grew far back on her brow.

"No bad news?" I said.

She answered simply, "Very bad. Couldn't be much worse. Happened quite a month since. He wasn't able to write before. He's written" — her mouth twisted — "at least he's dictated this——"

"What — kind of an accident?" asked the Flapette. Accidents were horrible; there was blood.

I remember each word of it, dropping abruptly and heavily, like stones dropping into deep water; the silence was deep.

"It's not David Olroyd?" I said, though I knew it was. I had not forgotten the name.

"I've always wanted to look after him, mother him, tried to," Miss Kershaw said in a dreadful dull way that was broken. Her lip was a network of fine, quivering lines.

Was David Olroyd not the man who hadn't nonsense? I felt bewildered, and a sickening coldness stole over me.

What did it mean? There could be no connection; how could there be any connection?

"It's a bad job, a bad smash-up — is this," Miss Kershaw said. "He'll be lame always" — her voice was almost brutally harsh — "lame and——" She did not seem able to go on; her lips were drawn back from her teeth stiffly.

I wondered why she tried to say it. For I knew. . . . Yet how could there be any connection?

ch. ends p. 280

"He's lost his sight," Miss Kershaw explained at last, tonelessly. "It may be permanent. He's blind," she said.

I thought she shouted, because I was losing consciousness. . . .

Afterward I asked helplessly,

"Isn't David Olroyd the man who hadn't nonsense, the man you——"

"Good Lord, no, child! The man you mean, he was married years ago. Didn't I tell you?"

"I have met David Olroyd," I said. . . .

Miss Kershaw has gone. She sailed at once. She must go back to look after him; he was helpless. She has been very brusque, almost brutal in her manner since the news came, but her eyes show suffering like a dog's. They hurt like a dog's. Now she has gone.

Oh, it is unbearable to think of this coming to You — Your watching, quiet eyes. That You are all battered . . . broken. . . . Why are these things let to happen? What's the purpose of it all? Is the scheme of things outside and beyond pain? Something bigger than we can conceive?

There seems no mercy in the scheme of things. My mind must be numbed with pain — for I can write. I think this is too big to feel at first. . . . You may never see again. They've told You that, they've pushed You down and are keeping You there. And I can do nothing. I must not write like this. I have always written with restraint, even in my book, because You so hate emotion. You don't need words, and don't like them; You understand without. And I do. . . . But that this should come to You — I feel savage, terrible. There is no resignation in me. Not to your suffering. Your eyes. Surely it might have been anything but that? It is unthinkable. I am all broken too — because

I could not keep this from You. . . . What have I written? What have I said? My brain feels so numb. I've been writing as though this thing had come to You. It has — I know now. I can't put it from me any longer.

I thought I would never be able to write anymore in my book when I knew. I thought I must burn it. But I faced this out, and I am not going to burn the book; it is all of You I shall ever have. I can't give it up.

I am coming to You. You won't ever know because — You can't know now. I must come. It may be a strange thing to do, but I must come. Such a little while ago, I did not understand the appeal of a man's helplessness. I must do something. Miss Kershaw must let me do something. You won't know.

The dust of crumbled ages whispers, the dust of all women that have ever been, urging us to give. It was not just desert dust crying to me, it was the clamorous dust of dead ages. I can do nothing, save this, and this is nothing. Only if I could do some little thing — You are battered, sightless. O God, why should it have come to You? . . .

I thought I was different; I thought I wanted all sorts of things; to find myself, to express myself, to understand myself.

ch. ends next p.

But I am not different; I am only a woman, just a woman like any other woman that has ever been.

A long roar of waves against the ship; they sound as though they were breaking on shore calmly. A gray soft rain lashing the gray, glittering sea; white crests gleam through the iridescent vapor floating. We are coming to Marseilles. I watch for the golden figure above Notre Dame de la Garde. I know now what Space means; I think I knew when I heard You had been battered, blinded. I knew suddenly. I can't tell why I knew then. God is Space.

We are in port among the many ships. . . .

Is it possible You need me?

You say so little, almost roughly. But it is enough; I feel You do, though You feared to let me know — were too big. You are not hard; You are big and rather tender. You have a large tenderness in little things that big men have. What has kept us from each other? You say so little, yet I would not have You say more. And You have written it with Your own hand, in the dark. You need me; it seems such wonderful nonsense. I see now how I have blinded myself willfully all along.

I am coming to You. This is wideness, to be needed by You.

These letters, all I have written, are yours; they were written to You; You shall have them. They shall be the first thing I give to You. I don't think I could read them to You, so they must wait till — if You see again. We have got to face it — the possibility. I am not strong enough yet to put it quietly in words as You can. Perhaps we will keep them to read in the desert where Space is, and dust. . . .

I suppose what has happened to me has happened to many women. I thought I was different, that I needed to express, to find myself. I thought to find Space, and found God; I thought to find myself, and found You.

I am going up to the old Church on the hill, because in the vague dusk I first got Nonsense. I want to know if my laugh is still there among the prayer-echoes and the little ships. . . .

To you with
the Author's love.

It is strange, reading about these people who just touch one's life and disappear. Do they make any impression upon us and we on them, I wonder?